Divided by Magic

by Rebecca Danese

For Daniele,

who is waiting for the movie version.

CHAPTER 1

The first punch breaks his nose. I can hear it from across the road and it makes me feel ill. The blows land on his face and ribs making crunching noises that I can hear even from here. I fight with my feet, urging myself to move and do something, anything at all, but all I can do is watch them beat him until he falls.

"STOP!" I shout from across the road. Finally I manage to make my body move in the direction of the fight.

"Get lost, Augur lover," one of them says, shoving me away roughly. I scramble up just as I hear one of the boy's ribs crack under the weight of a boot.

"You're going to kill him!" I shout, trying to pull one of them off of him. The punch to the eye I get in return sends me spinning. The street lamps flicker, sparks fly from the boy's body and his assailants fall to the floor one by one, pinned down by something that I

3

can't see. I recover only just in time to scramble away, the sound of sirens coming closer finally pushing me into action. I run.

The memory hits me at the strangest time, although the bruise has already faded. I stare at my gaunt face in the bathroom mirror and sigh, thoughts of the Augur boy being crowded out by the realisation that I have to get ready for work.

The smell of bacon is wafting up the stairs and through the crack under the bathroom door, which is the signal I'm looking for to get myself moving. It being a Saturday means I get to spend the whole day with *her*. Ella. The girl of my dreams, as far as I'm concerned anyway. The fact that she hasn't realised it yet doesn't perturb me.

I wash, dress and grab the printed-out concert tickets from next to my computer. These are what I spent most of the night in a bidding war over against *@foolsfan69* and are, I hope, the key to getting Ella's attention. *The lack of sleep better be worth it*, I think to myself. They were three times the face value by the time I'd finished, and I gulp at the thought of my bank balance. I slip them into my back pocket for safety and come downstairs to find a typical Saturday scene.

Dad reads the newspaper that he got up early to collect from the newsagents. Mum is standing at the kitchen sink, which is pretty much her permanent location I find. She's usually either in the kitchen or at work, and rarely anywhere else during her waking hours.

I grunt at Dad and he grunts back. That's about the limit to our morning conversation on the best day. I kiss mum on the cheek, who in turn smiles at me and waves a rubber-gloved hand at the grill where my breakfast is keeping warm.

"Thanks, Mum. You didn't have to," I say, and shovel a forkful of scrambled eggs into my mouth while still standing.

"I did too," she replies, not even putting down the scrubbing brush that she is attacking the frying pan with. "Can't have you going to work on an empty stomach," she says as a stubborn piece of blackened fat flies up and hits her in the face.

I wait tables. Probably not the career I'd originally considered, but it keeps me out of my parents' way and earns me cash for ridiculously expensive concert tickets.

Plus, there's Ella. If nothing else she's the reason I work every evening and all weekend, even if she doesn't know it.

"Will you be able to get lunch at the restaurant, love, or would you like me to pack you one?" Mum is a typical Northern mother with a heavy dose of West Indian in her, always making sure that I've got food in my stomach and I'm looked after.

"Ah, don't worry, Mum, I'm sure I'll manage something," I reply, knowing Ella usually steps in at lunch time and makes sure I've eaten.

"Don't coddle him, Mar," Dad says gruffly.

"Don't be silly, Pete. Honestly, Curtis, don't listen to your father. I'm more than happy to make you food and you don't worry your head about it," she says, finally finishing the washing up and setting about wiping the kitchen table.

Mum's family lives in Yorkshire but originally come from the West Indies. It makes for a homely combination of caring and comfort as well as never letting much bother her. Perhaps it's the fact that she's a nurse and is used to looking after people, or maybe it's that she has to make up for Dad's permanently disgruntled attitude, but she always puts others first. I've never understood how two people so opposite to one another have been married for so long.

I finish inhaling my breakfast and go to make myself a coffee, but realise that she's already beaten me to it, strategically removing the empty plate from my hands and replacing it with a freshly made cup.

Dad, who always reads the paper back to front, has now evidently taken his fill of the sports, travel and property pages. He's finally getting to what can loosely be described as 'news'. The sound of tuts, just loud enough to be heard, tell me he must be outraged by something that he has just read.

I plonk myself in a chair opposite and read the glaring headline on the front:

AUGURS TERRORISE BONFIRE NIGHT

No doubt Dad is reading the article associated with it, and although I know I shouldn't really goad him I can't help myself. It's like pissing off a bee. You know that swatting at it will only annoy it more, but instinct makes you do it anyway.

"Something the matter, Dad?" I say, feigning interest and slurping my coffee loudly.

Dad usually blocks out the sound of my voice, but the question must register somewhere with him. He clears his throat loudly and then says, "Bloody terrorists again. Attacked a town on bonfire night and terrified the locals. They should be bloody hanged, the lot of them. It's not natural, you know!" Dad, known to his friends and everyone else as Peter Mayes, is a total Augurist (although in my head I've re-dubbed him as an Augurphobe, which sounds worse). That is, he completely hates anyone with enhanced abilities. For as long as I have been alive there has always been discrimination of one kind or another against Augurs —people who can manipulate energy in a sense that might loosely be called 'magic'. But with a small group of idiots calling themselves The Magic Circle, they've gotten the country in an uproar. I reckon they're probably a group of kids just pranking and giving Augurs a bad name, but all the same the media is going bonkers about it at the moment. My mind flashes back to the incident I witnessed just a few weeks ago. Witnessed, but didn't do anything about. Suddenly the coffee tastes bitter in my mouth and I put down the mug in distaste.

Dad has always been offended by the thought of Augurs. The fact that someone can do something that isn't per his definition of normal offends his sensibilities or something. But now with The Magic Circle appearing in every paper and on every half-hour news update, Dad is at an all-new level of hatred for Augur kind. The practice of 'magic' is illegal in all major cities around the world, the Augurs tending to be pushed out and hidden away in little villages outside where they can live their lives in peace. But there's no denying that there's discord between us, the 'Normals' as we often get called, and them.

I've never personally had a problem with them. I'd had a slight fascination with the whole thing when I was a kid, but I never found out where they really came from. Popular theory is that they're some form of human evolution, becoming more and more prevalent now that artificial energy is being bandied around left, right and centre. I'd read somewhere that they were another race all together that mingled with humans thousands of years ago. When I was a bit younger I used to wish I had abilities too so that I could turn my Dad into a frog, but an Augur kid at my school told me that it didn't really work like that. Shame.

Thanks to The Magic Circle, Dad is now mentioning his hatred for all Augurs everywhere on a daily basis. I feel grateful that my schedule is so weird that I barely have to speak to him, let alone listen to him rant every day.

"Says here that seven people were left in shock after The Magic Circle tampered with a local firework display somewhere in the countryside. The field exploded, and the flames could be seen for miles. Hooligans!" he finishes with slap of his fist on the kitchen table.

"Was anyone hurt?" I ask, almost not wanting to know.

"No, but someone driving by was severely distracted and crashed their car into a tree, and it says here that several residents were traumatised. Traumatised!" he says just as emphatically. It rubs me up the wrong way. If Dad had been there at the time I'm sure he would have kicked that Augur kid along with the rest of them.

"Believe everything you read in the papers, do you, Dad?" I snark. I've crossed a line and I know it, so I hastily throw on my jacket before he can retaliate. There's a sudden thickness in the air which is a sure sign for me to leave.

"Going to sort your life out and get a proper job one of these days, lad? Rather than scrounging off your parents?" It's a cheap shot, I know, but it pushes my button. I attempt to shrug and smile nonchalantly but fail as I open the front door.

"Can't wait for the day, Dad," is my only parting shot, leaving before I can get into a real argument.

I shake my head angrily as I walk the twenty minutes to work, to help me clear my head. It's twenty minutes through the quiet back streets and onto the high street which is plenty of time to concoct all the smart answers I could have given but didn't.

Almost every weekend we have a similar conversation. When am I going to get a proper job? When am I going to figure out what I'm doing with my life? When am I going to leave home? Every time I tell myself I won't get annoyed, but he has the ability to sound disapproving even when wishing me 'Happy birthday' or saying 'job well done'. It's like his own grumpy-old-git power.

The morning is colder than I expected, and I turn my collar up against the chill. I can see my breath hang in the air, and there's a sparkling layer of frost on the lawns and the last few remaining leaves. Most of the trees that line the streets are bare though, and on the high street some poor sod has had to get up early to grit the pavements. I crunch along, realising that my polished black shoes will probably be ruined by the time I get to work.

It's the usual quiet Saturday morning. Very few people in their cars yet, unlike the weekdays where the roads are jammed with vehicles. There's the odd person taking their kids to football or swimming and the occasional jogger, but otherwise it's deathly quiet. Two doors down from my house a man stands on his doorstep in his dressing gown and slippers, a cigarette in his mouth. The smoke remains suspended a few inches in front of his face with every puff. He glances at me for barely a moment as I walk past, and I intend to give him a nod and smile but he's already averting his eyes. Eye contact isn't really a done thing in London if it can be helped.

On the main road I pass a series of shop windows, boarded up and graffitied. A series of crude-looking stickers have been plastered along it with the familiar picture of a circle with a large red 'M' in the middle of it. This is the Magic Circle logo. Over the top of it someone has spray-painted *Death to Augurs.*

I don't know who I dislike more, the Magic Circle pot-stirrers or the Normals that hate them. The discord between them is just barely being held in check by people desperately trying to appear social and civilised towards each other. What happens when that pot boils over?

I remember a kid from school that I used to be friends with, before it was completely illegal to practise magic in London and the Augurs all went into semi-hiding.

He'd been blamed for causing electricity surges during a class experiment and suspended, whether it was a fair accusation or not. It could've been a problem with the National Grid for all they knew, but the Augur was blamed and that was the end of it.

What was his name? Evan? Ewan?

Before I have a chance to dwell on it any more I realise I'm nearly at work. Time to prepare for one of the scariest things I've had to do in a long time: ask a girl out.

Cutting down a narrow alleyway, I take the kitchen entrance at the back of the building. Federico, the chef, is standing at the griddle, heating it up in preparation for the first customers that will probably roll in within the next half hour.

"Good morning, Fred," I say chirpily. Perhaps it's because the staunch Italian hates the name 'Fred' or possibly because he just hates me, but he never replies.

I drop my jacket in the cloak room and don a serving apron before getting a wet cloth and bucket from the kitchen. Through the swinging double doors I can see the dining room, and as I enter I catch a glimpse of Ella behind the bar polishing glasses.

A small butterfly tries to leap out of my stomach when I see her. Blonde hair tied into a ponytail as usual, she smiles at me when I walk in, looking up from the wine glass that she's cleaning. I pat my back pocket out of habit to check that its precious cargo is still in there. It is.

"Curtis, Mr. Gregorio wanted you here early, remember?" she says gently, trying to be cross but failing to mask her grin.

"I am early. It's two-minutes to nine," I try to give her a cheeky smile and she rolls her eyes.

The restaurant doesn't open until 9:30am for the breakfast shift, but there's a lot to do before we can let customers through the doors.

I wipe the tables and chairs down and fetch the table cloths from their cupboard behind the bar. Ella is silent, which isn't unusual for her, and I wonder if now is the time for me to ask. A jolt of panic courses through my chest. No. Now is not the time —I need to wait until things are a little calmer. Right before we open the doors to dozens of hungry people is not the moment. I push the panic back down and put my mind on the task at hand.

I shake open the folded table cloths and place them on each table making sure the creases aren't visible. Mr. Gregorio, the manager, requires perfection if nothing else, and after two months I've just about gotten the hang of what that means.

The sound of the radio echoes through the kitchen hatch behind the bar into the dining area where we're working, and although when customers arrive it will be turned down and ambient Italian music will be played in its place, whilst we set up it is accepted that Federico will listen to Radio 2 as loudly as possible. Mr. Gregorio doesn't usually leave his office until ten minutes before opening, and I've never seen him argue with the chef. I figure they have some mutual agreement going on since they've been working together for about a decade.

The news jingle clangs out across the room and a demure sounding correspondent announces the day's headlines. *"An alleged Augur attack on the small town of Aylesbury is being investigated today by police. It has been confirmed that there were no fatalities, but residents are 'shocked and shaken',"* she says, following which one particular 'shocked and shaken' resident's squeaking voice comes over the airwaves.

"We are really worried for our lives, you know? What if things had gotten out of hand? I'm scared for my children," comes the shrill voice of a panicked woman.

Ella tuts loudly from behind the bar, although I can't be sure if this is from the ridiculous news report or because there is a water spot on a glass she can't get off.

"In other news, the Prime Minister has agreed to hold hearings in parliament regarding the legal testing and segregation of Augurs in major cities, including London, Manchester and parts of Scotland and Wales. If the hearings are successful, Augurs will be legally

required to register themselves which may cause them
difficulties in obtaining housing, school places, and jobs
in the future."

Another snippet of some outraged citizen, this time an Augur themselves, comes over the radio, but the sound is cut short by Federico slamming a cooking pot down on the stove and then abruptly turning the radio off. The noise makes me jump. I had only been half-listening, but the sudden silence makes me glance right up at Ella, and what I see surprises me. She stands behind the bar, eyes wide and fierce and her face paler than usual, a slightly shocked expression on her face.

"You okay?" I ask, coming over to get the silverware from its drawer and beginning to place it on the tables.

She shakes her head, more as if trying to remove some thought, and looks back at me.

"I'm fine. Just got a lot on my mind," she replies, not unkindly but certainly distracted. I guess that Federico's thrashing about in the kitchen just startled her. I finish my cutlery placement and go back to retrieve the now shining glasses from the bar where she has placed them. The morning preparations are a well-drilled set up for us, and without asking Ella has handed me over four wine glasses for me to take by the stems and place on each table. Then follows the water glasses and finally the table placements, flowers of some kind or another that Ella's picked up during the week and painstakingly arranged for each table. We are just finishing up when Mr. Gregorio himself appears from his back office.

"Good morning, Mr. Gregorio," we say almost in unison.

He smiles pleasantly at Ella but barely nods at me. Having been here for over eight weeks I sort of hope that he'll give me some hint of appreciation, but when I've broached the subject with other staff they just say, "He pays you, doesn't he? What more do you want?"

Apart from the obvious benefit of being able to work with Ella, which is the highlight of my day, I stick it out because otherwise I'd be home every evening and weekend and so would Dad. I prefer to avoid being under the same roof as him other than to sleep if I can help it. Plus, I have an empty house to myself during the day which means I can pretty much do what I want, which largely involves playing video games.

"Should be a busy day what with our ad in the local magazine having reached everyone a few days ago. Let's have a good one, okay?" Mr. Gregorio's pep talks are usually short and sweet, with minimal hand gesticulations and only his thick black hair, dark features and strong accent to show for his nationality. He seems to lack the buoyant enthusiasm that I had always associated with Italians growing up. But then, so does Fred, so maybe the pasta adverts were misleading.

"Oh, and Curtis?" he addresses me directly which I find surprising.

"Yes, Mr. Gregorio?"

"Clean your shoes. They look like you walked through a swamp to get to work." And with that he leaves. I look down. It's true, they don't look great, so I grab some damp kitchen towel and try to clean them as best I can. I can see that Ella is failing to disguise her desire to laugh as she reaches behind the bar to play the restaurant playlist on the sound system whilst I unlock the doors and raise the blinds.

She's not the talkative type, but underneath the silences and often long periods of deep thought that I usually find her in, she's funny, smart and kind. Even if Mr. Gregorio and Fred aren't that taken with me, at least she shows some softness, even if it's hidden behind a lot of teasing and holding me at arm's length.

The brunch arrivals wander in a few minutes later and the morning follows with a steady stream of customers. A few people come in and I show them to their tables, take their orders and send the slips of paper through to the kitchen. Ella makes coffees and teas behind the bar and helps to carry food through when needed. There are only ten tables in the place so there are rarely more than twenty or thirty people to serve even at its busiest in the morning, and most of the regulars know not to be in a hurry when they come with one man working in the kitchen.

Mr. Gregorio always fills in where he feels he is best needed. This morning it's helping to take orders and serve food in his smart suit, chat to the customers and generally ensure that everything is going smoothly. At busy times he actually swaps the suit for an apron and helps in the kitchen, although I consider him extremely brave to step into Federico's territory when he does that.

By mid-afternoon I'm exhausted and starving. Thanks to some heavy persuasion from Ella, Federico makes us sandwiches. The cold Italian meats and cheese are like the best thing I've ever eaten, I'm so hungry.

I'm grateful when Federico steps out of the kitchen to the back alley to have a cigarette and Mr. Gregorio retires to his office to eat his lunch. It leaves just Ella and me on the restaurant floor, and we clean a table to sit and eat at together. This is how lunchtime has gone for almost every weekend that I've been here. Her and I, sitting at a table in the solitude of the empty restaurant, me trying desperately to flirt and gauge whether or not I'm getting a response.

I can feel that bubble of panic rising up in my chest again now. This is the perfect time, I can tell. Those tickets that I was up until 3am trying to get are for her favourite band. No one in the universe could say 'no' after being offered these, I hope.

The fact that we share the same taste in music feels to me like a sign that we are 'Meant To Be'. But it seems that fifty-thousand other people also share that same taste, and all of them have been trying to get tickets for this London show, so either they too are Meant To Be with me or my theory is possibly a little flawed.

My heart feels like it's about to beat out of my chest and my mouth suddenly becomes incredibly dry. I curse myself and take a gulp of water from a glass that she has placed on table for me.

"You okay?" it's her turn to ask.

"I, er, yeah. I was wondering," I start to say between another mouthful, trying to sound as casual as possible and not get a piece of salami stuck in my throat, "if you'd like to come with me to see the Flaming Fools of the Azure Octopus next week?"

Ella looks slightly surprised and chews a little slower, but her eyes are discernibly wide with excitement that she can't hide. Then she raises an eyebrow. "Like a date?" she asks.

"Er, no," I panic and reply a little too quickly. "I mean, do you, er, want it to be? It could be?" She starts to frown, and I quickly try to backpedal. Oh God. Is the frown because she doesn't want it to be a date or because she does? "Date? Pfft, no, of course not. Just two friends, er, colleagues hanging out and seeing their favourite band." The heat creeps up my neck and into my cheeks. Am I blushing? How embarrassing. That bubble of panic I had pushed down inside is now about ready to explode.

"Do you really have tickets though? I heard they sold out weeks ago."

I pull out the precious goods from my back pocket —two genuine printed out tickets that someone kindly emailed me over in the small hours of the morning. I slide them across the table as if showing her the map to the Holy Grail and she studies them for a moment, nodding to herself. My hopes lift, and then she says, "So, not a date?" she asks again. I'm so confused as to what answer she's hoping for that I shake my head on instinct. She leans back in her chair and studies me for a moment, skeptically. "I don't think it would go down well if Mr. Gregorio found out we were going on an actual date," she explains quietly. It had never occurred to me that it would be a problem, so I shrug.

"Not a date, okay?" She seems to relax a little even though saying it almost, *almost* kills my excitement. "So, what do you say?"

"I'm coming. You'd be hard pushed to keep me away," she grins and I feel a wave of relief wash over me. "But how are we going to get the night off? I doubt Mr. Gregorio will let us both off at the same time and I'm sure they aren't doing matinee performances."

I've been thinking about this long and hard, figuring that it will only work if I can get the staff on other shifts to cover us. I say as much and she nods in vague agreement but I can see that she's not sure how that will be possible.

The restaurant is grossly under-staffed, and I think the only reason that I've been kept on is because they have been steadily losing waiters over the past year. I've often wondered if this is because Federico is impossible to get on with or the previous staff haven't been able to put up with the lack of appreciation from the management, but now there are only six of us plus a cleaner who comes at the end of the day, which I know isn't enough to cover the workload.

I have a plan to solve this dilemma though.

Ella and I do evenings and weekend lunch times and two of Mr. Gregorio's nephews, Marco and Giovanni, do the weekday lunch and weekend evening shift, with the occasional need for us all to work together during busy times.

With the lack of staff, Mr. Gregorio is forced to close up for us to have lunch, but he tries to keep it at the minimum and I've barely finished my sandwich before he's out on the restaurant floor unlocking the doors and telling us to get back to it. With the Asking On A Date out of the way we're pretty much straight back into work, but Ella seems a little chirpier than usual. She can go days without smiling, I've noticed, and I always try and make the effort to get her to laugh even if I'm not a naturally funny guy. I'm the first to admit that.

It isn't until Marco and Giovanni come in at 5pm that I can do anything more about the date-not-a-date planning, and I get right to it as soon as I see the two of them walk in the kitchen door.

"Hey, Gio," I say jovially. Giovanni Gregorio is a friendly 20-something aspiring graphic designer, but without too much work being thrown his way he spends his afternoons and Saturday nights at his uncle's restaurant making a bit of money whilst he works graphic design in the evenings from home. His brother, Marco, is doing the same shifts but with the goal of saving up to travel the world by his twentieth birthday.

"Curtis, *come stai?*" he asks, slapping me on the shoulder in a friendly manner. He has a similar London accent to me but throws in the odd Italian just to remind everyone where he's actually from.

"All good, mate, thanks. Listen, I have a huge favour to ask you."

"Go on then," Gio replies, removing his jacket and putting on a serving apron just as I'm removing mine.

"Do you think you and Marco could cover mine and Ella's shifts on Friday night? I got us tickets to a concert and I was hoping I could get your help," I say, knowing that if Gio is on board then Marco will follow suit.

I know that Gio, who asked Ella out well over a year ago, had been painfully rebutted, so he looks surprised for a moment but recovers quickly with a huge grin. He slaps me on the shoulder for a second time and laughs heartily.

"Of course, although in exchange I'd like to know your secret for getting her to say yes to a date with you of all people." With his Italian dark hair and deep brown eyes, and always with the hint of a tan, Giovanni is probably a more appropriate match in terms of looks for Ella, compared to me, for whom the word scrawny was invented. I'm not totally sure what colour my eyes are, thinking they are some colour not that dissimilar to mud. I've gone through phases of trying to make my hair do anything but look like a bird's nest through my teens, but in the end copious amounts of hair gel are all that will put it into some semblance of hairstyle (which I rarely, if ever, bother with), and underneath my half West Indian heritage I'm probably an unhealthy shade of grey.

"Well, it's not totally a date so I can't tell you any secrets, but in exchange we'll cover any shift you need," I reply, confident that I can get Ella on board with that.

Gio is easily pleased and already has a date in mind for us to cover. I shake his hand and get ready to go.

The restaurant closes at midnight on Saturdays and opens early on Sunday for breakfast, so knowing I have an early start tomorrow I don't want to hang around longer than I need to. I find Ella in the kitchen talking to Federico in hushed tones, but she sees me and gives me a wide smile. I feel disarmed for a moment but welcome the sight all the same. I tell her I've sorted it all out and that we'll have to cover the others' shifts next Saturday evening, but she shrugs happily and says it's no problem. Federico gives me a slightly dirty look with narrowed eyes, as if somehow he knows I'm up to no good, which makes me feel guilty for no particular reason.

Ella doesn't seem to be wanting to go home herself, so I give her a small wave goodbye and head out into the crisp November air, pulling my jacket collar up around my neck.

I walk home with a bounce in my step and a permanent flutter in my stomach. I don't even mind when my Dad makes some snide comment as I walk in the house. He's watching the TV but manages to take his attention off it for a second to tell me how I'm wasting my life. I don't care. I'm going out with Ella, date or not. My heart does another somersault and I go upstairs to my room to get an early night, but all I can now think about is her. I fall asleep with thoughts of how to turn the 'not a date' status into a proper date, and a smile on my face.

The remaining days of the week feel like a little bit of a blur until Thursday night. Unfortunately, some time during the day the dish washer in the restaurant decides to pack up and the cleaner calls in sick. Mr. Gregorio breaks the news to us half way through the evening shift and promises to pay us over time if we will stay late to clean up.

Although I wouldn't usually agree, Ella seems to be happy enough to stay so I volunteer to help her, even though I realise that means washing a hundred plates, knives and forks by hand.

As soon as the last customers leave the shop we set about clearing the restaurant, which is the reverse exercise of what we have to do on weekend mornings. The table cloths go in the washing machine, all the dirty dishes go in a huge sink in the kitchen and I don a rubber apron to start tackling the pile.

Ella offers to clean the bar and coffee machine as she knows better than I how to take it all apart, and Mr. Gregorio undoubtedly trusts her more with a £3000 piece of equipment like his espresso maker. I didn't even drink coffee before I worked here and now I'm on two cups a day thanks to the restaurant.

"Shall I put on some music?" she asks, putting a CD on without consulting me on what to listen to. I nod happily when I hear the familiar sound of the Flaming Fools of the Azure Octopus come over the sound system.

We chat briefly as she brings in more and more dishes for me to wash and I get to scrubbing them, but she leaves me to it before long to clean out the coffee machine. After fifteen minutes my fingers and arms are starting to hurt from being immersed in soap suds. I pull my hands out and my fingers are completely pruney. I search around for some rubber gloves to no avail, but then I remember that Giovanni is a little bit obsessive about doing the dishes and keeps a hidden stash somewhere.

I remember hearing him complain loudly about the fact that the cleaner conspires against him to throw away or lose all the washing up gloves, and that he had bought his own pair for the odd occasions that he needs them. Feeling a tiny bit guilty I decide that my fingers can't bear it anymore.

I search all the drawers in the kitchen. Nothing. I check on top of the shelves and in the cupboards. Nope. The only place that I can think he would hide something like that is perhaps the staff cloakroom that we are supposed to use as an office but never do.

I don't really want Ella to see me steal a pair of Gio's rubber gloves. Something inside me gives me the idea that she might think less of me for needing them. How dumb can I be? But rather than ask her outright I sneak quietly through the swinging double doors and slip into the staff room. I can see her side-on, standing at the coffee machine and wiggling her hips, still singing to the music that is blaring out from the kitchen. It's a sight that makes me want to go over and dance with her, if I could dance.

Sensing that I'm safe for at least a few more minutes, I begin to rummage. After several minutes I've still come up with nothing, even trying to break into the safety deposit box tucked away on the shelf. I reckon Gio would be paranoid enough to hide his rubber gloves in a locked box, but after wiggling a paperclip in the lock for several minutes I've had no luck. They make it look so much easier in movies to pick locks.

Sighing defeatedly I place it exactly where I found it. I know that if it's even moved a corner he'll probably notice.

Not trying to conceal myself any longer considering I actually have nothing to hide, I make to leave the room, but as Ella seems to be beautifully ignorant of my presence I admire her for a moment longer. Ponytail swinging, head and hips moving to the drum beats, she's almost irresistible. If we were dating I'd be able to go up behind her, swing her round and kiss her right now. She'd laugh, put her arms around my neck and kiss me back. I shake my head. One step at a time, Curtis. I realise this is probably a bit creepy and I should probably just slither back into the kitchen before she suspects I've been watching her. That could blow the whole date-not-a-date thing right out of the water then and there.

But right before I make my move to leave something bizarre happens.

There she is, taking everything apart and cleaning it quite happily, but obviously a little absentmindedly. As she air-drums a particularly good part of the chorus the jug we use to steam the milk flies off the counter. But rather than fall on the floor as I'm expecting it to do, she spots it quickly and it suspends itself in mid-air. She looks towards the kitchen as if checking for something. I realise that she's checking to see if I'm about to walk in the door. Of course I'm not, I'm hiding in the cloak room like an idiot. She waves her hand casually and the jug rights itself and lands gently back on the counter where it was a few moments before.

I blink. I shake my head. Did I imagine what just happened? I don't move for several seconds and she carries on as if nothing has changed.

She wipes down the front of the machine with a damp cloth and begins to remove the coffee taps, emptying the used-up coffee grinds into the bin we use. The first one comes off easy, the second one not so much. As I'm never allowed to use the machine I've never done much more than help her empty the bin once in a while, but I know that the right tap is stiff. She's told me on more than one occasion, or more accurately she's cursed it loudly while trying to prepare a customer's latte.

But rather than call me for help to loosen it she glances back at the kitchen doors, which are between where I'm standing and where she is. She still hasn't spotted me lurking in the shadows of the cloak room.

My heart sticks in my throat. What am I seeing here?

Her hand presses gently against the metal of the coffee tap. The whole thing starts to turn red with the extreme heat that seems to be coming from somewhere. Is the metal expanding? Impossible to tell for sure but then suddenly I know. She lets go and she points at it, as if she's about to tell it what to do. A small spark leaves her finger and the tap works itself loose, removing itself easily and tapping out the used-up coffee into the bin.

I nearly pass out with the blinding realisation; Ella is an Augur.

CHAPTER 2

I stand there for several minutes. The little display that she had been putting on for me unwittingly seems to have ended and she carries on wiping things down, washing them out and humming along to the music all the while.

Pretty soon she's going to need to empty that coffee bin. I do my best impression of a ninja, clinging to the shadow on the wall and slip back into the kitchen when her back is turned towards me.

I stand at the sink for a few moments, immersing my hands in the water and picking up where I left off but not really paying much attention to what I'm doing.

My head is completely swimming. I had seen her drop the milk jug. The milk jug didn't fall but seemed to just right itself without any effort.

Levitation. Telekinesis. I saw her struggle with the stiff coffee tap. Its lever had been stuck and I've known since I started working here that it's always been a problem for her. There had been redness from the heat. A spark had left her finger. The coffee tap had turned itself without her touching it, emptied itself into the bin and she had just carried on as if nothing was happening. The ability to channel energy.

I'm no expert but from what I've heard this is definitely Augur magic.

But it seems like a ridiculously risky thing for an Augur to do. Yet she thought she was effectively alone with me in here doing the dishes. She probably thinks nothing of doing Augur stuff when there's no one about.

I now feel guilty for even having seen it. But the guilt doesn't replace the biggest feeling of all: pity.

My mind wanders as I listlessly wash the dishes, slowly scrubbing each plate and rinsing it. How can someone go their whole lives having to hide like that? Has she always had to hide? Did she always know she had powers? You'd think that people would be used to the concept by now, but there are probably only one in a thousand Augurs that I've heard. Then the thought occurs to me: what if there are more but they've just never revealed themselves? What if the statistic is more like one in a hundred but they've been clever enough just not to come out into the open about it, for fear of being rejected by society?

"Curtis!" Ella's shocked voice breaks my train of thought and I nearly drop the plate I'm holding. I didn't hear her come in. I look at her and the surprise must show on my face. She laughs and puts her hand on my shoulder, which in turn sends a little buzz through me. "God, I'm sorry to have frightened you. You look like you've seen a ghost."

"Er, n-no. Sorry. I was just… thinking," I say stupidly, trying to explain my expression.

"Must have been deep thoughts —have you been washing the same plate for the last half hour? It's nearly 1am!" she exclaims. I glance at the pile

42

I've still left to wash and realise she's right. I'll be here all night if I carry on this way.

She reaches up above the cooker and pulls out the kitchen first aid kit. Much to my dismay she pulls out a pair of bright yellow washing up gloves. The last place I'd think to look. She gives me a wink and puts on the gloves, nudging me out of the way of the sink with a gentle hip bump. This sends another course of energy through my body and I start to wonder if that's Augur related too.

"I'll wash, you dry. Just don't tell Gio I borrowed his gloves," she winks at me and I gratefully begin drying the dishes, thankful that my hands will finally get a rest.

"I'm sure he won't mind if you tell him," I say, trying to sound normal.

"Ah, but they're pretty secretive people, the Gregorios. Probably best not to let him realise that I know his hiding place or he'll put them under lock and key. Literally." She smiles at me and I feel completely disarmed. She starts chatting excitedly about the concert that we're both looking forward to so much and I let her talk, trying not to seem too preoccupied.

"Hey, are you okay? You seem distracted," she suddenly says, and I realise that I've probably just been staring at her oddly for the past few minutes rather than properly engaging in conversation.

"I'm just tired," I sigh convincingly, for lack of any better excuse.

"Can you keep a secret, Curtis?" she looks at me earnestly and my heart practically leaps through my shirt. Is she suddenly going to tell me that she's an Augur? Tell me how all her life she's wanted to find someone she could trust and now she's finally found me?

"Er, of course," I say lamely.

She seems to think for a moment. Then she says, "Okay, I think I can trust you. Come," and she removes the gloves and pulls me over to the huge walk-in fridge at the back of the kitchen. This wasn't quite what I was expecting as the ideal location for her to confide her biggest secret, but just being close to her is enough of an excuse to go with her. She yanks the huge door open that probably weighs the same as the both of us and steps in. I assume she wants me to follow her so I do, but rather than burst into an explanation of how she's hidden her powers from everyone around her she reaches for a small plastic container off the shelf and hands it to me.

To my disdain at first, and then delight shortly afterwards, I realise that it's the last two pieces of Federico's famous tiramisu. It is one of the things that he never lets me eat at the restaurant, most likely because he doesn't think my simpleton taste buds are good enough for it or something. I give her a huge grin and she ushers me out of the cold room quickly. Grabbing one of the plates that we've recently just washed and two forks, she carefully places the dessert on it and offers it up to me.

"I know that Federico would never let you have any. Hell, he doesn't let *me* have any, and he actually likes me," she says, not trying to hide the known fact that he can't stand me. "Go on. Have the first bite."

I take a fork and serve myself up a generous mouthful. It's the best thing I've ever eaten. The sponge melts in my mouth and the cream dissolves like butter. The combination of chocolate, cream and rum is perfect. I feel like I've been cheated for these past two months by not being allowed to have any. I'm not even particularly into food, but this is too good.

Between the two of us we finish off those last two helpings pretty quickly and wash everything up to try and hide the evidence. I don't want to think about what Federico will do tomorrow when he finds out. I hope that Ella won't get in trouble, but then I realise that there's no chance. She's everyone's golden girl, and for good reason too.

With a new lease of energy thanks to the sugar and small alcohol content in the tiramisu we finish the rest of the work quickly and pack everything away.

Ella dries the washing up gloves and puts them back in their hiding place. I turn off the sound system and the lights. We grab our coats from the cloakroom and she sets the alarm, ushering me out the back door so that she can lock up. The November air is like a slap in the face when I step out from the warm kitchen. The pavement sparkles with frost that has already set in and a biting wind travels down the alleyway. She shivers a little bit as she tucks the key in her bag and puts her gloves on. I resist the urge to put my arm around her as I think she'll probably think it a bit too forward. Even if we did just share tiramisu.

"Want me to walk you to the bus stop?" I ask, turning up my jacket collar. She nods as she knows I'll be walking in that direction anyway and we make our way there moving quickly to fight off the cold.

"Are you okay?" she asks me not for the first time.

"Me? Yeah. I'm fine. You?" I stop walking and hold her arm for a second. It's presumptuous, I guess, but I want to see her face when she answers. "You know you can tell me anything, Ella. I'll always be there for you," I look into her eyes as I say it and she seems to be caught off guard for a moment, but quickly recovers.

She replies with a nod and a shrug, "I'm excited about the concert tomorrow. And I've really enjoyed this past week working with you. More than before…" she lets that hang there for a minute and I'm not sure what to make of it.

"But I was asking you if you were okay because normally I can't hear myself think for you talking. Tonight you've been particularly quiet. Did I say something to upset you?" she presses me for an answer that isn't going to brush her off. I laugh at the thought of her upsetting me and shake my head.

"Far from it, Ella. Really. I'm excited about tomorrow too. I just have a lot on my mind, but nothing you need to worry about." The half-lie is easy when I think about all the things she really has to worry about. I'm the least of her troubles if all the Augur laws and regulations are about to come into effect. I realise she probably doesn't need me complicating things.

There are very few people out at this time of night, but still one or two stragglers. It doesn't matter the time of day in London, you'll never be alone. The odd car passes us, catching us briefly in its headlights as we walk down the high street.

I offer to wait with her until she's safely on a bus but she refuses. I know she can take care of herself, but I want just a few more minutes of her company if I can possibly get away with it. Her bus comes round the corner which spares me finding an excuse to stay with her any longer and she puts her hand out to call it. Before she boards she grabs my hand and squeezes it gently. The exhilaration runs through me again and I realise I could get used to this feeling.

"Night, Curtis. See you tomorrow," she gives me a little wave as the doors close and the bus pulls away. I watch it until it goes out of sight and then turn to walk home, hands deep in my pockets and teeth chattering.

My head is full of thoughts that fight for precedence. I had always planned to use the concert as an excuse for a date and try to win her over. I had known that if she had spent enough time with me she might just end up getting used to having me around. Like I could get her to date me by war of attrition. But now that I know what I do, I wonder if maybe she's just incredibly lonely and needs someone to confide in.

I've been so thoroughly friend-zoned by her for the past two months I never imagined I'd get to this point, but just as my chances are improving on the romantic front I have this extra complication to deal with.

Then I feel selfish for thinking about her powers that way. I roll my eyes at myself as I walk down my garden path, unlock the door as quietly as I can with my key and close it silently behind me.

The TV is droning in the front room even though it's nearly 2am.

I step through to see who could possibly be up at this time and see that Dad has fallen asleep in front of the telly in his pyjamas. A book rests across his oversized stomach and when I glance at the title I almost want to hit him with it. It says *The Roman Empire: Cesar and the Augur who Betrayed Him* by L. M. Sloane.

I go to turn the television set off but notice that it's quietly playing a 24-hour news channel. The show that seems to be playing now is where a group of journalists and 'experts' sit around on couches and discuss the latest headlines in ridiculous and excruciating detail.

"Well, Bob, the Augur threat is very real," a bespectacled man is saying to the news host. "The fact is that many of them are hiding their identities and so we have no way of ensuring public safety if one of them gets out of hand."

"Studies are showing an increase in Augur activity since the dawn of the digital era, so that would indicate that it is our own advancement in technology that's causing the greater number of

Augurs. Do you not think that forcing them to register is a violation of basic human rights?" the host questions.

"Look at it this way, Bob. We've never proven that Augurs are part of the human race at all. They could be another species all together. It's true, there are theories of human evolution that connect to Augurs but none of it has been properly documented and evidenced. The fact is that for the safety of everyone, Augurs included, we should really be testing them at the time of birth. That way there's no question of registration and people can sleep safe in their beds at night knowing that any Augur threat would be eliminated before it could escalate."

I feel the anger rising, but rather than kick the TV, which is what I feel like doing, I turn it off and leave my Dad snoring in the darkness of the living room.

I don't understand how people can be so stupid. I know I felt this way before I knew about Ella, but now that I do I want to tell them all where to shove their opinions. Augurs are just people. Plain and simple. Why can't they see that?

I try not to think about it as I brush my teeth and get ready for bed.

I lie there for a while, staring at the ceiling, pushing the anger away with the thought of Ella squeezing my hand before she got on the bus. It makes my heart do a little flip flop. I realise that this past week has been more eventful than any of the others since working at the restaurant, in all kinds of ways. At least I can't complain of being bored any more. Sleep eventually takes me, and I dream that I'm in the restaurant with Ella. The place is packed out with customers and she stands behind the bar, sparks flying from her hands sending full plates of food out to tables all at the same time. Everyone laughs and claps at the amazing service. Mr. Gregorio beams with pride and says to me, "Isn't she lovely?" I nod but in response he says, "Too good for you!" and storms off. I'm startled to find that I'm not wearing my work clothes but a police outfit. At that moment the doors burst open and a swarm of policemen storm into the restaurant and arrest Ella for using her powers in public. The dream fades and I sleep restlessly.

The following morning I wake up late. It's not unusual for me to get up after Mum and Dad have left, but it's nearly lunch time when I emerge from my room to forage the kitchen. Both of my parents are at work. Dad works in finance. Something to do with stocks or bonds or both. I don't know what any of it means and I've never been interested in it, which is probably one of the many reasons why he thinks I'm a terrible son. It's also probably one of the reasons he's made me pay rent since my eighteenth birthday.

Mum is a nurse at a care home. She gets weekends off but works long hours on weekdays and gets up at the crack of dawn. If she were here now I'd probably end up confiding in her, she's the kind of person who is easy to talk to. But because of that I'm quite glad she's not. After all, Ella's secret isn't mine to confide.

I have five hours until I meet Ella. I've asked for her phone number loads of times using various excuses but she's always found her own ways not to give it to me. I always thought she was trying to blow me off but now I realise that she probably couldn't have a phone. Augurs have this weird thing about energy. Something about them being able to channel electricity or the fact that electricity is very close to the kind of thing that gives them powers. So, carrying around small amounts of radiation and electricity in their pockets would probably be fatal for someone. I remember hearing about a guy on the news a few years ago who had been forced to carry a mobile phone for work. He had accidentally set fire to his office because his hands kept bursting into flames when it rang and it burnt most of the building down. No one has bothered to make 'Augur-friendly' phones yet but even if they did I doubt they'd use them.

Accidents like that one are what give Augurs a bad name.

I make myself some coffee but to my distaste we're out of milk, so I have it black. I find some bread in the freezer and settle for something simple. Dad has left a newspaper from yesterday on the kitchen table and I glance at it whilst I eat, almost reluctant to go past the first headline. I can't help but read it though.

THE MAGIC CIRCLE KILL INNOCENT FARMER
Small Town Left in Shock After Augur Attack

It is reported that one person has been killed and five more injured during an alleged Augur attack on the small town of Crimplewick. At 7:30pm last night explosions were heard coming from the outskirts of the town at the edge of Brimble Farm. Mr. Jonathan Brimble, owner and farmer, was said to have left his home to investigate the noise and was found mortally

wounded some hours later by his wife, Mrs. Alison
Brimble. Mr. Brimble, 45, died later from his injuries.
He leaves two children and his grieving wife.

Public are demanding answers from the authorities
as to how they propose to tackle this blatant violation of
the law. Sources say that the police are still
investigating the scene to determine how many
members of the Augur gang, The Magic Circle, were
involved and what exactly occurred.

In an exclusive interview with Civil Defence
Minister, MP Carlton Munday, we gained exclusive
comment that the government are 'stepping up' their
work to prevent Augur-related crime, including the
recent proposition to register all Augurs at birth and
demand by law that any Augur living in the UK or
Ireland register themselves on an immediate basis.
Munday has been proposing the creation of a task force
with the investigation of Augur related terrorism as its
primary concern.

"It is a fact that people do not feel safe with Augurs
being allowed to run rampant in our country. I'm not
saying that all Augurs are bad, I am a firm believer that

they are people just like the rest of us and that we must not give the satisfaction to this small faction that they are affecting us. The British people are a strong people and we will do our utmost to keep everyone safe. I am in talks with the Prime Minister and the House of Lords to pass a law shortly that will change the way that we perceive Augurs that will give correct precedence to tragic incidents such as these."

MP Carlton Munday, who's responsibilities include the domestic police and matters of local safety, is due to meet with the Prime Minister within a matter of days. For all of the exclusive news, make sure you read our updates daily.

I feel unsettled. I can't tell from the article if this MP is on the side of the Augurs or not, but it sounds very much like the latter. I think about Ella being forced to register as an Augur. Would Mr. Gregorio even keep her at the restaurant if he knew? Would people look at her differently? I know I do, but not in the way that others will. I respect her more for being able to keep that secret for so long.

One thing's for sure, I'm out of my depth and I need answers. I shower but don't bother to shave the tiniest bit of stubble I've managed to grow. I admire it for a minute in the mirror. It makes me look slightly older which is good for me as right now it all helps. I deliberate about what to wear for a moment but realise that I'm going to be crammed into a mosh pit with several thousand other people, so jeans and a red t-shirt is the way that I go, with my more comfortable trainers. Despite her trepidation, I've managed to convince Ella to meet me for a bit before the concert, so in my head I can pretend it's a date even if I'm the only one participating. Her spirits have definitely lifted since I asked her, so I know that she is looking forward to it. I'd always wondered why the hottest girl I knew was also the saddest person I knew. Underneath her chirpiness I had always felt that she wasn't being herself. I would get glimpses of this bright, radiant person between bouts of silence and looking like she might burst into tears. Now it dawns on me that she has probably been worried half to death most of the time and spent a lot of her life looking over her shoulder.

Augurs are ostracised, ignored, unemployed or at the very least suffer discrimination. People don't understand them, and what they don't understand they either fear or attack. I realise that I probably need to learn a bit more about them to truly appreciate what she's really going through, otherwise I might end up screwing things up, which for me is altogether too likely.

I decide to walk to the corner shop to get some milk, really just wanting an excuse to arrange my thoughts and get out of the house. There's not many places in London that a trip to the local shop isn't more than a few minutes away. Near the end of my street is my local newsagent where I collect the milk and a packet of chocolate digestives, just because they're on offer. As I thread my way through the aisle which has an odd combination of ant killer and pet supplies, my eye falls on a stack of newspapers that have been dumped by the till, evidently today's news.

AUGUR ATTACK IN TRAFALGAR SQUARE

Worried Londoners Demand Action from PM

I scan the article, not really wanting to read it at all, but the premise is the same as the one I read at home. People are scared, The Magic Circle are to blame. At least this time no one has been hurt, but of course there's the usual 'traumatised spectators'. Apparently during a busy tourist-filled afternoon in central London two Augurs channeled energy from an underground electricity line, turning off all the power for a square mile. Although it's difficult to tell from the way it has been reported how long this lasted for, I'm guessing it isn't for long as the culprits managed to escape before police could make an arrest.

Unfortunately, traffic lights and the London Underground were affected so people were late for meetings and chaos ensued. I tut and shake my head —what could they do with that quantity of energy? Surely it would take their heads off if they took it and didn't do anything with it? I realise there's a hell of a lot about Augurs I don't know or understand, but I resolve myself to find out.

"You gonna buy that, son?" the shopkeeper says in his gravelly voice, breaking my concentration.

"Oh, er, sorry. No, just these thanks." I show him the milk and biscuits and pay him the £2.70, leaving him slightly disgruntled that I haven't paid for the newspaper I've been staring at for a good five minutes.

I walk home shaking my head and decide that I need a much nicer cup of coffee, with milk and a chocolate digestive or two or three.

I notice the man with the cigarette standing on his doorstep again, the same surly look on his face as last Saturday, but this time in jeans and a jumper. Just like the other day he gives me a perfunctory glance before looking off into the middle-distance. I give him a little nod as I walk past but he's now stubbing out the cigarette and walking back inside. I wonder what a bloke like that does for a living that he's not at work during a weekday. Not the type to pop over and borrow a cup of sugar, it seems.

At home with coffee and the entire packet of biscuits in hand I sit at the kitchen table with my laptop. If I'm going to even begin to approach Ella on the subject of her being an Augur I want to be armed with information, and there's only one place I know I can safely get it. The internet search bar blinks in anticipation of my first question and I realise I'm not sure where to start.

I type: *Where did Augurs come from?*

There are millions of results, and after reading dozens of articles I don't know if I'm any the wiser.

I've covered everything from theories on human evolution to the fact that they're from space, but all of it seems implausible. There's talk of Augurs being around thousands of years ago alongside articles about the sudden upsurge in

Augur activity, just as that guy on TV was saying last night.

I feel like I'm disappearing down a well of unsubstantiated speculation, writers just making things up as they go along, when I see a link to something that interests me even more: *Augurs — the First Men of Earth?*

I'm not sure why this grabs my attention, but I click it and find myself on a blog written by a self-proclaimed Augur expert who seems to have written a number of posts on the subject of their history, their abilities and what it's like to actually be an Augur.

According to the writer, Augurs have been a part of the world since it was formed. They have been responsible for everything from the building of the pyramids to the rise of the Western culture.

What are Normals, he writes, *but perhaps Augurs that have lost their ability to utilise energy properly?*

He seems to think that they have been strategically posted everywhere from military units to government bodies, but that due to the unannounced 'War on Magic' that seems to exist below the surface of society, most of these people have held their posts in hiding or under the guise of being a Normal.

I read several of his articles going back a few years. I even find one where he talks about why the media 'hates Augurs'.

He makes the interesting observation that often Augur powers are hereditary, passed from parent to child, even if the other parent is normal. He also points out that in the '70s a group of inquisitive scientists decided to prove whether or not Augur powers are weakened when the genetic line is 'watered down' by Augurs marrying Normals, and those subsequent children also marrying Normals. Apparently, the outcome of their tests resulted in a lab explosion and all involved were killed. I'm not sure whether to smirk or squirm. I take issue with people being treated like animals. Something in my chest aches a little at the thought of Ella being experimented on like that.

Another blog post catches my eye: *Why are Augurs a problem?*

The title of the article should put me off, but as the blogger has up to now been kind of supportive in his writing, I decide to read it. It's not an article but a video, all of two minutes long. I click the play button and the face of a middle-aged man comes to view.

"Why are Augurs a problem?" he begins in a thick American accent.

"After years of research, I've discovered that Augurs have only really become a 'problem' in people's eyes since the development of more and more technology. The more clever we've become, the more we have used technology to solve our problems. But in doing so we've pushed out the people that for centuries were helping us.

"What do I mean by this? Well, for starters, Augurs were considered almost like deities up until the 18th Century, and certainly it was considered vital to employ at least one Augur in every business up until Victorian times. Even the monarchs of England would have an Augur advisor on their council.

"So what changed? Partly the fact that Normals developed more ways to do things that Augurs would have otherwise done. But the other fact is that with more energy and electricity at their fingertips, Augur powers began to change.

"Imagine a man in the olden days that used to be able to channel the energy of the sun to move objects. There's a small amount of energy that comes from living things, which is why we as people tend to go for the stronger but more destructive route of using fossil fuels, which produce more energy faster than natural sources.

"Say that same man now has access to thousands of volts of energy because there are power lines running under his feet and through every wall in almost every building in the country. Now he's going to be able to do a whole lot more than just move a few planks of wood about.

"So ultimately Augurs have become a problem for Normals because of their own attempt at pushing Augurs out.

"Folks, I'll let you formulate your own opinions about that, but thanks for watching and don't forget to like and subscribe."

The video ends and I sit there in silence for a moment. My eye falls on the clock at the bottom of the screen and realise that I've been staring at my computer for the best part of two hours. I must have read more than twenty articles by this guy.

I close the lid on my laptop and throw the empty biscuit packet in the bin. So much for restraint. I've got an hour before I'm meeting Ella but it can easily take that long on the tube, particularly if there are delays, so I need to get moving. I throw on a hoodie, then my jacket and a scarf I've found, knowing I'll probably be boiling by the time I get there but I'm anticipating the journey home as much as anything.

As I step out and close the front door behind me I realise that my next move is obvious. I can't help her if she doesn't know I'm there to help. Somehow, without scaring her off, I have to tell Ella that I know her secret.

CHAPTER 3

It's just after 5pm and I'm standing outside Greenwich station, our meeting place. I spot Ella coming out of the entrance and give her a wave, trying not to look too keen when in actual fact I'm almost bursting from the anticipation of seeing her again. You would think I'd get over it, considering we work together, but there's always that moment of excitement and fear every time we meet. Now I'm starting to think maybe it's related to her powers.

She approaches me and gives me a hug, which I'm not entirely prepared for. Her hair is out of its usual ponytail and falls to her shoulders, and it hits me in the face as she reaches her arms around my neck. I can't help but take a small breath inwards and inhale her familiar scent of flowers.

"Have you been waiting long?" she asks.

"Nah, about five minutes. You look amazing," I say, and she does. Black jeans, Flaming Fools t-shirt, leather jacket and her blonde hair loose and shining. She laughs and hits me playfully on the arm.

"Thanks, you too. You feeling alright though?" I realise I must look a bit red-eyed after hours of gorging on information in front of a screen, and I feel very preoccupied even though I'm trying to put it all out of my head.

"I'm great," I smile and gesture towards the massive dome that is the location of the concert for tonight.

We find some overpriced food, eat it standing up and head over to find a spot somewhere near the front. Obviously there have been people there since lunch time willing to sacrifice their day for a better spot, and I realise that maybe I should have done the same. Ella isn't disheartened though. She grabs my hand and manages to squeeze through enough people that she finds us a very decent position to see everything. She eventually lets go of my hand but it doesn't go unnoticed by me. Every time she touches me I feel like a pang of electricity courses through my body. Maybe an Augur thing? I've had girlfriends in the past and although it's been exciting and fun, I've never felt like this I don't think.

When the band walks out onto the stage the arena erupts with the excited screams of ten thousand people.

"Are you ready to have a good time?" they call to us, their voices amplified by their head mics. The audience practically explodes in response and there's an exhilaration in the air that is almost tangible. I kind of wish I could bottle it up and keep it for a time when I need a pick-me-up.

The concert isn't a 'sway and wave your lighter' affair and we jump up and down emphatically to every guitar solo, scream the lyrics to every song at the top of our lungs and try not to get knocked over by the knees and elbows flailing in every direction. I feel like the stage is going to light up in flames at any moment and almost in response a jet of sparks comes from somewhere above us and showers us in light. In all the sweaty, shouting bodies Ella stands out like a beacon, a bead of sweat running down her forehead and a huge grin on her face. I imagine kissing her now would be amazing. She catches me looking at her and smiles, with more feeling than I've ever seen before. She grabs my hand and squeezes it as we raise our fists in the air to one of the band's best-known anthems.

"Do you have time for one more?" the lead singer questions us after two amazing hours. We erupt in a chorus of agreement, and Ella takes my arm, our bodies hot and sticky from all the exertion.

"Any first dates out there tonight?" he asks the audience and to my surprise Ella screams 'yes' along with about a thousand other people. I crack up laughing and pull her closer as she suddenly looks at me sheepishly.

"Well, guys and girls, this one's for you," and with that the band strikes up for a final song. I don't want to let her go and she doesn't seem to either. My arm around her shoulders, almost a head shorter than me, we jump up and down in time to the beat and almost collapse in a heap once the song is over. When it's obvious they aren't coming back for a second encore, along with thousands of other people we exit the arena, throats hoarse and ears deafened.

It takes us nearly half an hour to work through the procession that is making its way to public transport and Ella suggests we walk a bit to save standing in the cold night air. I'll agree to anything that will let me spend more time with her.

My confidence boosted after her admitting to thousands of people, and our favourite band, that we *are* actually on a date, I take a chance.

"Hey, do you want to grab a drink while we wait for the crowds to clear?" I ask, suddenly nervous again. I pray that my luck with Ella, which up until now has been non-existent, doesn't run out.

"Absolutely," she replies with no hesitation, and I try not to smile like a fool as we thread our way through the masses to find a decent-looking pub tucked on the corner of a side street.

It's a Friday night so the place is busy and thick with people, but we manage to find a booth at the back that a group of lads have just vacated, so Ella slides in and I order drinks. I figure she might be hungry after all the jumping up and down, so I grab a packet of crisps too, it not being the kind of place that would serve food at 11pm. As we've got work tomorrow I order a couple of light beers. When I bring them over to the table she laughs at me, "What are you, sixteen?"

"No," I say defensively, "I just want to make sure you get home in one piece. Wouldn't want you thinking I was trying to get you drunk!" And we both laugh again, giddy and electrified by the events of the evening.

"I've had a really great time tonight," she says, suddenly changing the subject and looking at me with her blue eyes sparkling.

"Me too —I'm glad you agreed to come, even if you had to put up with me screaming in your ear half the time," I reply. She doesn't say anything for a moment and for some reason it feels like a bit of a rebuttal, so I drink my beer to fill the silence. She sighs deeply and finally she speaks up.

"I find it hard to make friends with new people. I've not meant any offence to you this past couple of months we've been working together, I just have a very tight group of friends and I'm not used to letting other people in." She sighs again and takes a sip of her drink, shaking her head a little.

"I understand. You know, I went to boarding school where my friends were scattered across the country in the end, and I spent the past year working odd jobs not really knowing where I was going with my life. I've found it hard to find a stable friend amongst it all, and to be honest the way everyone treated me at the restaurant I wasn't sure how long I'd last," I reply earnestly. It's true. Almost all of my mates are not from London and the few that are have gone to Uni, so I end up feeling like a loner most of the time.

Ella laughs gently, trying not to make light of the situation too much.

"You'll have to forgive Federico. He's worse than I am at letting people see his softer side. And as for Mr. Gregorio, I think he's just sore because you took the position his son had when he decided to leave. It's not much to do with you personally, although it wouldn't hurt for you to turn up early once in a while," she adds giving me a raised eyebrow.

I smile, relieved. I'm not one to dwell on things much but with the way everyone has been treating me at the restaurant I couldn't help but wonder what was wrong with me. It's been a tough few months since leaving school, that's for sure.

"Well, that's a relief. At least I know it's not just my terrible personality to blame," I joke. But something about the way she looks at me, so sincere, almost sympathetic, I figure she obviously knows how it feels to be an outcast.

She suddenly puts her glass down and stretches her hands across the table to mine. They're a little cool and a shiver runs up my arms and down my spine. There it is again, I think to myself.

She looks at me intently, her eyes the colour of a clear Autumn sky. There's a whole table between us but there's something else, too. An invisible barrier that she's had up since we met feels like it could be coming down a little and the hard edge that I've been accustomed to seems to be gone. Could I kiss her, right here and now in this crowded, noisy pub? I lean forward, thinking that maybe the combination of a great evening and a small amount of alcohol might have tipped the odds in my favour.

Then a thought strikes me like lightning. How can I confess to her that I know her secret only after trying to make a move? How dumb can I be? Surely she'd be mad that I knew and didn't say anything. She'd probably think I'm taking advantage. Maybe I'm being overcomplicated, but

I know that I'll look like an arse if I go for it now and she finds out later.

She must be seeing the conflict in my face, because she's frowning. She leans back a little, to my disappointment, but doesn't let go of my hands. I see a flicker of doubt and the colour rising in her cheeks. The fact that she's embarrassed makes me feel even worse. Whatever 'moment' we were having is gone and I've blown it.

"Ella, I'm sorry," I start to say but she cuts me off.

"No, God. I'm sorry —I feel like an idiot," she flusters trying to pull her hands away and making to reach for her jacket. I hold on to the hand that's still on mine tightly.

"No, you shouldn't feel like an idiot. I'm the idiot. And I have to tell you something," I blurt. I can feel my heart begin to pump loudly in my chest again with anticipation. Now or never.

She looks at me quizzically. Her eyebrow arches in suspicion of what I'm about to say. I take a swig of my drink to stop the inside of my mouth resembling a desert.

"There's no easy way to say this. I know. About you." I stop short, not really sure how else to explain myself. Glancing around it seems that no one else is listening in or even paying attention to the fact that we're there. Friday night pub-goers don't appear to have attention for much more than the people and drinks immediately in front of them.

She frowns at me and I can see from her expression that she is wondering if what I've just said means what she thinks it means.

"Yes," I confirm, "I know. I saw you at the coffee machine last night at the restaurant." Shock and then fear cross her face, "but *please*, Ella," I beg as she wrenches her hand free from mine and grabs her jacket. "Please, I don't care. I don't mind. I really, really, like you. Please don't leave," I say. Even I know I sound pathetic.

She doesn't say anything, but she stops trying to get her arm in her sleeve unsuccessfully and looks everywhere except for right at me. She opts for staring into her glass ponderously. Various expressions are fleeting across her face. Pain, worry, anguish. Eventually she says, so quietly that I can barely hear her, "Why didn't you say anything before?" She absentmindedly flips a beer mat over in her hands, her eyes downcast.

"Well, for starters I knew you wouldn't dare go out with me if you knew that I knew," I reply, getting the expected unimpressed look from her for that. "But also I didn't want to worry you. God, Ella, you've been the happiest I've ever seen you this past week. I didn't want you worrying that I was going to blab and feel like you had to leave the country or something." Her sad expression seems to soften at that and she pulls her eyes from the table to look up at me again.

"You don't want me, Curtis. No one should. I'm not safe to be around." Her voice is so quiet and so pained I have to strain my ears to hear her above the din. I shake my head emphatically.

"I really like you, Ella," I repeat. "You're the best person I've met, ever, for a number of reasons. You're intelligent, funny and beautiful. And if the past day that I've known about your secret has shown me anything, it's that you are also incredibly strong. So I'm sorry I didn't say anything before, really, but I hope that doesn't make you think less of me."

There's another loaded silence whilst she digests all of these compliments. She's obviously not used to them and is blushing hard. She doesn't seem to be surprised about anything I've said, but more curious, like she's weighing me up, pros and cons. It's starting to get a bit awkward after a while and the only thing I can do while she thinks is to drain my glass and try to seem like I'm not pressuring her in any way.

She finishes her drink too and then finally says, "Come on, why don't you walk me home?"

I practically leap out of my seat to help her get her arms into her jacket properly, and shrug on my own. We take the short walk back to the station in silence, the crowds from the concert long since gone. I let her think. I can feel she's mulling over her options in her head; I can't help but wonder what those options are. Pretend like it never happened? Get rid of me quickly and painlessly so that no one would notice? I shake that thought out of my head. It's unlikely that she's the kind of Augur that would hurt other people, although admittedly I don't know her as well as I like to think I do. From what I can tell there aren't many that would actually hurt people, except the idiots I hear about in the news.

We board the Jubilee line, which is still fairly crowded as usual on a Friday night, so we have to stand. To my surprise, Ella holds onto my arm instead of the hand rail and I feel that same tingle course up my arm. Maybe she's coming round to the idea that I'm not so bad after all. My stomach is starting to tie itself into knots thanks to the proposition of walking her home. I've never heard her mention her parents —does she live alone? Unusual for a nineteen-year-old. Would she invite me in? That thought makes my insides flip flop and I try to push the thought out of my mind. The idea of getting lucky with a girl that, up until less than an hour ago, hadn't looked at me for more than a few seconds at a time seems incredibly unlikely. Plus, in her current mood, which I can't quite decipher, the possibility of her dumping my lifeless body in a ditch so that I don't tell anyone her secret is still entirely possible.

But when we emerge from the tube station she is still holding onto my arm, as if stabilising herself, and I realise she is gently guiding me in the direction of her house. I vaguely recall her telling me it's twenty minutes between the station and her house, and the information surfaces now while we walk through the empty streets.

She hasn't said a word since we left the pub, so I'm relieved when she finally breaks the silence.

"Thank you," she says, and I realise that I've been holding my breath for a long time.

"What for?" I exhale.

"For not being like everyone else, I guess. For not immediately deciding I was dangerous or evil. For giving me some sort of a chance. And for telling me you knew. That's actually pretty brave of you. Oh, and for tonight, which has been the most fun I've had a in a long time."

"That's a lot of things to be thanking me for," I grin. "But you're welcome. I guess I should be the one thanking you for giving me a chance. I mean, if you're not planning to kill me, that is," I smile nervously. She gives me a wry laugh in response.

"The night is young as far as that goes," she winks. "But in all seriousness, I can't invite you in just yet. My, er, flat mate probably wouldn't appreciate an unexpected visitor…"

I notice that we've stopped outside a fairly plain-looking Victorian house that must be split into flats. It sits on a street of identical terraced houses, lit by the yellow street lamps, the houses obscured by large Plane trees on each side.

She lets go of my arm and steps through the gate, which leads up a short path to her front door.

The house is slightly concealed by large bushes and there's a moped in the front garden which looks yellow in the eerie phosphorescent glow. There's a light on in the hall and I can hear voices coming from inside, so rather than make any presumptions I stay right where I am on the pavement. She pulls her keys out and turns to me.

"Goodnight, Curtis. Thanks for walking me home."

"Ah, there you go again, thanking me for things," I joke, but my heart sinks now that she's let go of me. I raise my hand and give her a little wave, standing there like a pillock while I wait for her to unlock her door. I assume that the correct thing to do is to wait until she's safely indoors, but in practice it seems a bit creepy. I see her place her key in the lock, hesitate for a moment and then spin around, bridging the gap between us in three steps. She leans up to me and kisses me softly on the lips. I'm caught off-guard, but it only takes me a second to respond, putting my arms around her and kissing her back. I breathe her in and feel the tingling sensation run through my face and into my chest this time. She reaches her arms around my neck and pulls me in tighter, the cold metal of the keys still in her hand pushing against the back of my head. For what could be several minutes I feel completely consumed by her. Finally, she pulls away and looks at me with that familiar sparkle back in her eyes. She kisses me quickly on the cheek, then runs up and unlocks her door. Loud noises spill out and she hurriedly steps inside, giving me a wave before closing it behind her.

I stand there slightly stunned for a moment. A wind picks up and ruffles my hair, and something stirs me to move. All the way home I tingle.

CHAPTER 4

I wake up to the lingering feeling of my face tingling. I think I was dreaming about Ella but as I try to grasp the fleeting remainders of the thought it disappears. I'm tempted to pinch myself, just to see if I'm really awake and if last night really happened, but the memory is so clear in my mind that there's no way I imagined it. Her lips moving against mine, her smell, the feel of her hands on my neck. I sigh happily as my alarm clock goes off, but rather than hit it repeatedly to snooze I leap out of bed, despite the late night. I shower, dress and race downstairs to the familiar Saturday morning scene.

"Morning, love. I haven't done your breakfast yet —you're a bit earlier than usual," Mum says.

"Don't worry Mum, I've got to be at the restaurant early, so I'll grab something on the way," I reply, kissing her on the cheek.

"It was a late one last night —how was the concert?" Dad asks, sounding genuinely interested for some reason.

"Brilliant, Dad. Best one I've ever been to," I smile and throw my coat on.

"It's icy out today darling, pop your gloves and hat on, won't you?" Mum warns. I try not to roll my eyes and dig my gloves out of the cupboard under the stairs where all the coats are kept.

"Don't forget we're off to Spain on Monday," she adds as I retrieve them.

"Got it, Mum. I've got to go, alright?" As I turn to wave goodbye to them both I notice yet another newspaper headline Dad is reading, splashed across the front page.

SAFETY CONCERNS
AS AUGURS ATTACK PM

I want to get out of the house but something about the line draws me in. I read the article over Dad's shoulder. An Augur allegedly set fire to the Prime Minister's car, although the PM wasn't in it at the time but had sent her chauffeur to collect her husband and son from their home. A young male had stood in front of the car at a red traffic light and placed his hands on the bonnet. Witnesses then reported that smoke began billowing from the engine. The chauffeur was quick-thinking enough to move the PM's husband and son from the car to safety before it went completely up in flames. No one was injured but the family were being treated for shock.

I sigh angrily. There are obviously antisocial Augurs just as much as there are antisocial Normals. Why the newspapers don't bother to mention that beats me.

It makes me worry that someone is trying to goad the PM into triggering the anti-Augur laws sooner and what that might mean for Ella.

"It's bloody ridiculous," says Dad, taking my sigh as an indication that I am upset with the news story for different reasons. "How can they let Augurs run around the streets when they are an obvious threat to society?"

I shouldn't say anything, but the anger inside my chest flares. "Oh my God. I bet you think they should be locked up or given dog collars or something," I say, venomously.

"Well, it wouldn't hurt," Dad bristles in response.

"Unbelievable! Don't you think it would hurt the human beings that have to call themselves Augurs?" Dad gives me a warning look. I'm overstepping some precious invisible boundary once again, which I've done many times before and has never ended well for either of us.

"Didn't you say you had to be off early, love?" Mum chimes in gently, trying to ease the tension. I give a superficial nod and an angry glare at Dad before storming out the door. As I close it behind me I hear her say, "You and your big bloody mouth. He was the happiest I'd seen him in months…" but rather than linger to hear what he has to say for himself I walk briskly to the restaurant.

I swear I have to move out. After Christmas, maybe. But that's only a few weeks away, so it might have to be in the new year at this rate.

I try not to think about the world's problems. Or more specifically Augur problems. I can think about one in particular, and that's Ella. My heart does a little leap when I think about our kiss last night. She put her heart and soul into it, and I hope that I made it seem that way too. It was a bit like having the wind knocked out of me on a rollercoaster. Scary, exhilarating and a bit hard to breathe. God knows she's the only thing keeping me going at the moment.

Mum was right; it is cold, and I pull my collar up around my ears and thrust my hands deep into my pockets. The last of the leaves are being blown off the trees by a keen wind and they crunch underfoot in the frost.

The high street is quieter than usual thanks to the cold and earliness of the hour. There's only one or two other people out and about.

By the time I reach the restaurant I have managed to push Dad's narrow-mindedness out of my head and have filled it with thoughts of Ella. There had been no 'let's do this again sometime' conversation and a small pang of fear makes me wonder if she will have completely regretted it afterwards.

But when I walk in the back door of the kitchen she is standing by the ovens deep in conversation with Federico. When she spots me walk in her face lights up. There is no sign of doubt at all, just that beautiful sparkle that I find myself constantly looking for.

I say good morning to the both of them, trying not to grin like an idiot as I squeeze past, touching her arm lightly as I go by.

I set up the dining room as usual and she joins me shortly afterwards, happily slipping into our routine of laying out the cutlery, folding napkins and polishing wine glasses. We don't say much, but there's no need. Apart from the fact that I wouldn't want to talk about last night in front of anyone that might be listening, Mr. Gregorio included, we are happy enough just to share each other's company and work together.

I look back at the past few months, no, years of my life. This is the happiest I've been in a long time and I didn't even realise I was miserable before. And all I'm doing is waiting tables. Maybe I'm too easy to please, but this is the best feeling ever as far as I'm concerned.

The day is hectic. In the run up to Christmas Mr. Gregorio has decided to start a seasonal menu, and the punters seem to be completely up for drowning themselves in turkey with all the trimmings and festive alcohol whenever possible.

We don't even have time to close for lunch, and Ella and I have to take it in turns to eat in the back of the kitchen whilst Mr. Gregorio covers for each of us in turn on the restaurant floor.

There's an odd incident during the dinner shift where a group of middle-aged women come in for a ladies drinks evening and one of them drinks so much wine she falls off her chair, but Ella and I recover her quickly and send them on their way, giggling and cackling all the way home.

When we finally lower the bolts on the front door, Ella makes sure that there's no one within earshot before engaging with me.

"I'm sorry I haven't had much of a chance to say anything today," she says.

"Ah, don't worry about it. It's been manic. Did you sleep okay after last night?" I ask. I know for me at least it took me ages to calm down and when I finally did I slept like a log.

"Yeah, really well, thanks. Last night was amazing. For the first time in a long time I feel a little lighter. Like some huge weight has been lifted off my shoulders. Like I can finally speak to someone that isn't just my sister," she says and takes my hand in hers. For some reason the gesture surprises me and my heart does a little flip flop. I mentally tell myself to calm the hell down.

"You have no idea how good it is to hear that," I say, smiling. "I didn't know you had a sister, what's she like?"

"Oh, er, she's a bit… interesting. But can we not spoil this moment by talking about her? I thought maybe we could do something on Monday afternoon," she suggests.

"Like a date?" I tease, and she punches me playfully on the arm.

"*Like a date,*" she whispers, her lips just a few inches from my ear sending another shiver up my spine.

"Are you sure? I mean, spending all this time with me outside of work you might get bored of me pretty soon," I joke, internally praying that she won't.

"I wouldn't ask if I didn't want to spend more time with you, silly. So, do you want to hang out?"

"Couldn't think of anything better to do with my Monday," I grin. Honestly, I can't think of anything better to do with the rest of my life than spend time with her. Hopeless, I silently tell myself.

I walk her to the bus stop, even though she tells me not to bother, and wait to see her off. I'm hoping for a revisit of our kiss, but she merely squeezes my hand and waves goodbye. Even that doesn't stop me from feeling elated to be in her company.

As I watch the bus take off and see her take a seat through the back window the hair stands up on the back of my neck. I wonder if it's a delayed reaction from her touching me but this is something else. I begin to get the feeling that someone is watching me. I turn around and look up and down the street. Other than a pedestrian huddled over and walking home there isn't much happening on the high street. In the headlights of a car I notice two orbs glowing in the darkness of an alleyway. What are they? I move closer for a better look. It takes me a moment to register that a pair of eyes are staring at me intently. I try not to jump in fright when I realise that it's just a very black cat.

"Jesus, you scared me," I say to it as I pass it. It gives me an unimpressed look before proceeding to clean itself. I must be losing it. Evidently, dating-not-dating an Augur has put me on edge.

I walk home, collar turned up, and try to ignore the continued sensation that I'm being watched. I think I see another pair of glowing eyes scanter down the street as I turn into my road, but I assume that it's probably a fox. The 'cigarette man', as I have mentally dubbed him, is not standing outside his house but there's a light on in the window upstairs and I notice a twitch of curtains as I walk by. I wonder if I'm becoming paranoid. Now that I know Ella's secret it is, of course, mine to keep as well, and I surmise that the weight of it is taking its toll already.

As I open my front door I notice the blue glow coming from the living room. It's late so I imagine that Dad as fallen asleep in front of the TV again. I quietly remove my coat and walk in, expecting to see him sprawled out on the sofa with the remote dangling from one hand. But the room is empty. The TV is silent, but the pictures show a late-night news program of people protesting, some for the freedom of Augurs, others against it, outside the Houses of Parliament. I go to turn it off when I notice a note, taped crudely over the button. It has my name on it and I yank it off, unfolding it in my cold hands.

Curtis. I know you know. Keep away from Ella. Or else.

I don't really know what to make of it, but it sends a chill through my body all the same. What the hell does it even mean? The only people that have access to my house are Mum and Dad and I doubt they would write a note like this. It's in a child-like handwriting that I don't recognise. I scrunch it up in my hand and turn the TV off. I don't know whether to toss it in the bin or keep it, but I decide that just in case one day there's an investigation into my mysterious murder it might come in handy as evidence.

I shake my head at my own morbid joke as I head up to bed. Not even I'm laughing at that one.

One thing I do know though, is that there's no way I can tell Ella about this. If she realises I'm getting threatening notes about her she'll freak out immediately and either stop talking to me, or disappear, or worse.

I shove the crumpled note in a drawer in my room and get ready for bed. Laying my head on my pillow in the darkness, I try to clear my mind of threatening notes, black cats and weird men standing on doorsteps and instead try to fill it with thoughts of her. But when I do finally get to sleep I dream that we're running, this time from the crazy robe-wearing cigarette man and his fire-breathing black cat. Ella is trying to drag me along, but I weigh ten tons and she has to leave me behind to save herself. Then a woman's voice that I don't recognise comes from somewhere and says *I told you so,* and I fall into blackness.

Monday can't come too soon. Rather than try to brave any shops this close to Christmas, I decide I'm going to treat Ella to a day of activities I think she'll like. We meet in Queensway because I know there's a skating rink, bowling alley and arcade all under one roof. Being a Monday they're fairly empty and Ella is pleasantly surprised when I tell her about my plan for the afternoon.

I discover that she's never ice skated before, but she takes to it pretty quickly. I'm not bad myself and she holds onto my arm the whole way round the rink, which makes me smile inside and out. After half an hour our legs are aching and I realise that I'm going to have to show off my bowling skills pretty soon. As it turns out, she's bowled plenty of times before and puts me to shame with her spares and strikes each time. The worst thing isn't that she's mopping the floor with me, but that she does it so nonchalantly, asking me questions about my family, my school and everything in between the whole time whilst knocking down pins left, right and centre. After three games I realise I'm fighting a losing battle and suggest we get a bite to eat.

We find a coffee place that seems to serve decent food whilst also being conveniently empty, and as we settle down I try to fire a few questions in her direction in exchange for the Spanish Inquisition she's been giving me.

"So, are your parents from London originally?" I ask her whilst tearing off a piece of toast.

"Yep, London born and bred, both of them. They died when I was eleven and it's been me and Agnes ever since. She's eight years older than me so she kind of took me under her wing, although I don't know whether that was to my benefit or not." Surprised to hear so much about her life in one go, I try not to bombard her with the questions I suddenly have.

"I'm so sorry. I didn't realise."

"It's okay, I guess," she shrugs. "I still miss them, but there's not much to be done about it now. Agnes and I rent a house with several other people and I started paying my way as soon as I could, so we manage okay," she sounds flat, monotonous even. But I can tell from the way she intentionally keeps her eyes down that she doesn't want to confront me when mentioning it. I feel lucky for a moment to have two very much alive parents. Although Dad and I have major differences and generally can't stand each other, Mum will always be there for me.

"You can tell me to bugger off, but how did it happen if you don't mind my asking?"

"Er, difficult. I want to tell you, but in case of waterworks it's probably best we save that tragic story for some other time," she replies and when she looks up I can see her cheeks are getting a little red, so I don't push it further.

"No problem. Some other time." I reach over and put my hand on hers and she smiles at me.

"But I will tell you. I've not spoken about it to anyone. Ever. But I feel like I can somehow trust you. I know you'll be honest with me no matter what happens." I mentally kick myself as I think about the creepy note from last night, but I tell myself that I'm protecting her by keeping it quiet.

"Of course," I say and try to smile to cover my internal debate.

"I know it's going to sound really corny, but you have no idea how glad I am that you asked me out, Curtis," she says. It doesn't sound corny at all. It makes me smile idiotically.

"Well, all I can say is that you've no idea how glad I am that you said 'yes'. To be honest, my life wasn't particularly going anywhere good, and if nothing else you've made it interesting," I say, trying to make light of it.

"Unfortunately, I think I'm going to end up making it a whole lot more 'interesting'. There are some people I really want you to meet. I think you'd like them if you got to know them. But they aren't the trusting types and I think it would be best that you meet my sister first, as much as I hate to admit it. If you can get into Agnes's good books, you're half way there," she grips my hand in hers and I give her my best lopsided grin.

"You make your sister sound like some terrifying boss beast that I've got to defeat before I can move up a level," I joke. She rolls her eyes, but I can see that I'm not totally wrong.

"The thing is, now you know about, er, me, you're inevitably going to end up meeting other people like me, and I'd rather you be prepared. We're not a trusting sort of people generally."

"And for obvious reasons," I say, briefly mentioning the research that I'd done before the concert. She looks surprised but in a good way.

"You've been doing your homework on us," she says, and I hope that she's impressed. "But don't believe everything you read on the internet. I'm sure that there are plenty of 'experts' that probably don't have the faintest clue about what they're writing but are more than happy to sound like they do. Take the Civil Defence Minister, for example."

"That Carlton Munday guy?"

"Yeah. Total pillock. No idea what he's talking about, but he's the government's leading 'expert' on Augurs and is bound to get a law passed for us to all be registered and microchipped or something if we're not careful."

She's raised her voice a little and I'm worried that someone is going to be listening in, but the place is virtually empty and the barista behind the counter is in deep conversation on her phone. It seems our own discussion isn't going beyond the two of us and our lattes.

"You seem to have some serious political opinions there, missy," I say, not unkindly.

"Yeah, I bloody well do, but just wait until you meet my sister," she smirks and then gives my hand another squeeze.

"Can I ask you something, completely changing the subject?"

"Oh, please do," she says.

"What's it like? When you, you know, do your Augur stuff?"

She laughs, and the sound is like music to my ears. I don't hear it often enough.

"I don't really know how to explain it, but I could probably show you."

"Show me? Really? How?" My curiosity is piqued.

"Well, I'm guessing that we're in far too deep now for me to try and hide anything from you. There's a place I want to take you, but it'll have to wait until after work. Do you fancy a late night?" she looks expectantly at me.

"With you? How could I say no?" My stomach does that flip flop thing and I try to push the feeling of anticipation down so that I don't start acting like a nervous wreck.

We finish up our coffees and food and head for the tube station, which takes us all the way up to Hampstead and a short walk to the restaurant. With a bit of aforethought I left some spare clothes in the cloakroom the day before, so I change quickly and we dive straight into the dinner shift.

The evening seems to drag on and I can't wait for the picky orderers, slow eaters and mean tippers to leave.

We lock up the restaurant and put our coats on, heading out into a damp December night. The streets are lit by Christmas lights hanging from every other lamppost, and the shops that have decided to make an effort have their decorations flickering all night long. If it weren't for the drizzle and having to trudge through leafy sludge that comes from a mixture of dead leaves and rain, it would almost feel like a Christmas card scene. She puts her gloved hand in my large pocket and I hold onto it like a lifeline.

We walk some fifteen minutes to an open park that sits in the middle of a council estate. It's the sort that has a low metal fence that anyone can jump over but is symbolically locked every night anyway. The equipment in the fenced-off playground is sad and dreary-looking. Small drops of rain slap onto the softened tarmac from the swings, and the rusted metal glints in the light of the singular streetlamp that stands like a sentinel at the entrance.

"This doesn't seem like the best place for a demonstration," I whisper, looking up at the looming block of flats with its few lit windows. Other than the rain and our footsteps on the squelching pavement, there's little noise. A car passes somewhere on a distant road, the sound of it wetly rumbling past just audible from here.

"This is the perfect place, come over here," she leaps the fence agilely and I follow suit as she leads me to a small covering of bushes and trees. The surrounding buildings are still visible but there's no one in sight from what I can tell.

Under the cover of a low tree she pulls me close and removes her gloves.

"Ready?" she asks, and I nod nervously, not really sure of what to expect.

She takes my hand and pulls me into a crouching position on the wet ground, placing my palm downwards between the few tufts of grass that are trying to grow in such a poorly kept area. She puts her hand next to mine and a slight look of concentration crosses her face for a second. To my surprise the soggy dirt becomes very dry right where we stand. What was, a moment before, a muddy patch of earth is now as dry as if it were a summer afternoon. But she's not done yet. She places her hand over mine and with the other she touches the tree we are standing next to. I feel the ground rumble beneath us almost imperceptibly and a feeling of what I can only describe as an energy impulse surges through my body. Between our fingers grass begins to grow as if it is on steroids. All round us small plants and seedlings are pushing their way to the surface, and within moments we are surrounded by shrubbery that reaches above our ankles. The single streetlamp that had lit the playground flickers on and off a few times, and she takes her hand off the tree. I feel like my hand has been put in a plug socket with the way it tingles, but it's not an unpleasant feeling.

"Wow. That was amazing. Is that what it feels like for you too?" I ask a little breathlessly. She grins with satisfaction at her handy work.

"I'm guessing so. From the look on your face yeah, that's how it feels for me too, but possibly more intense."

"Why did you pick here of all places?" I ask curiously.

"A shabby council estate? No one's going to complain about a bunch of plants sprouting up in the park. They'll just dismiss it, and there's no CCTV which means no one is about to catch us. Besides, there's plenty of energy beneath the ground here thanks to the blocks of flats so close by."

I look up curiously at the ugly buildings that surround us. "So you have to use electricity to make your powers work?"

"Me? Not really. But all Augur power is just energy transference of one kind or another. Most Augurs need to channel something in order to make something else happen. I happen to be one of the few that doesn't need much at all. I'm kind of a walking energy source all of my own," she shrugs and leads me away from the small garden that she has created, much to the council estate's benefit.

"Does that mean you're more powerful than other Augurs?"

"Sort of. Some at least. Not all of them. Plus, lots of Augurs have different kinds of powers. My sister, for example, could never do any of the things that I could do, but she sees things. In terms of making things grow or move or objects obeying her she can't do much, but she can tell you what you're going to eat for breakfast in six months' time on a Tuesday."

"I can probably work that out. It'll be a bowl of cereal and a cup of coffee. What? I'm a creature of habit," I say as she gives me a look. "So, when can I meet this mystery sister of yours? She sounds like quite a character."

"As soon as you like. But I warn you, once Agnes has gotten under your skin she doesn't get out. She isn't easy to get on with," Ella warns me with a serious expression.

"And when am I going to have the honour of meeting your parents?" she suddenly accuses more than asks.

"Oh, you don't want to meet my Dad. He's awful. I told you, a total Augurist and not a drop of humour in him. Mum would like you though, she's a nurse," I explain.

"I think I can handle your Dad. He won't be the first Augurist I've ever met and besides, there's no reason to tell him what I am now, is there? I don't have any intention of letting the cat out of the bag, so I don't suppose you will."

With the mention of a cat I think about the odd encounter with the black cat I had the other day. That's something I do tell Ella as it seems weird enough to bear a mention.

"A black cat you say? Hmm. Could be suspicious," she says looking contemplative as we walk back to the high street.

"Really? Do you think it's an omen?" I ask quickly, my thoughts flitting to the note on my telly which came immediately after the cat sighting.

"Oh yeah. There's definitely someone who wishes you ill will," she says seriously. "Maybe I should read your palm just to be sure," she offers a hand and I look gravely at her, putting my hand in hers right before she cracks up and playfully hits me on the arm.

"Curtis don't be silly. Black cats are just cats that are black. There's no such thing as omens and I don't think you've got a feline stalker, so don't worry about it."

I try to feel relieved, but the fact that I had what can only count as a threatening letter after my cat sighting doesn't make me feel any better.

"I think I'll take a bus tonight too. It's late and it'll take me ages to get home otherwise," I say as we walk to the nearest bus stop.

"Well, there's that and the fact that you don't want anyone to be following you," she grins. It's my turn to roll my eyes as I try not to feel foolish.

"Listen, do you want to come over to mine tomorrow? I'll be home alone until it's time to go to work and it would be nice to have the company," I ask, changing the subject.

"Sure, I'd love to," she replies, and I feel like pinching myself. It's ridiculous to think that I can be lucky enough to have a girl like her in my life. That actually wants to spend time with me, that is.

As we wait under the cover of the bus shelter, she takes my freezing hands in hers and rests her head against my shoulder. Although there are many layers between us, I feel like she can probably feel my heart thudding in my chest. In spite of the cold and the dampness, I can't help but feel warm inside, and before I know it she's looking up at me, our noses almost touching. Without warning she leans up and kisses me, her warm lips on my cold ones. I wrap my arms around her waist and feel her hands slide up around my neck and into my hair. Every inch of me feels like it's lighting up like a Christmas tree. For over a glorious minute we stand there, her mouth on mine, filling me up inside. The only thing that breaks us apart is the sound of a bus approaching and, reluctantly, I have to let her go. I wave at her through the window, grinning stupidly until she's out of sight, and to my relief I don't have to wait long for my own bus.

I feel bad about not telling her about the note, but I can't currently see what good it would do other than worry her. It could be nothing, just like the cat, right?

When I get off just a few minutes from my house I get that horrible sensation of someone following me again. But far worse. For reasons I can't explain I feel a nervous pull in my gut, like I'm walking into danger. I shake my head, as if that will shake out the fear with it. My road is in unexpected darkness. No street lamps, no glow from inside any houses. If it's possible to feel even more freaked out, I suddenly am. I walk hurriedly to my front door. I can't help but think that maybe it's Augur related. Hell, everything is these days. But what if it's just an ordinary power cut? That seems like the more logical explanation I realise. But no part of this feels logical.

My hands are shaking as I find the key hole and fling the door open. The house is silent, and I march down the short corridor to the kitchen. There's a note on the table, and my heart freezes. My mystery stalker. It's a crude, folded-once torn page from a notepad.

I pick it up reluctantly and flip it open. The kitchen light won't turn on, so I use the light from my phone to read it.

Curtis,

Dad and I will be back from Spain on Saturday. There's a few dinners in the freezer if you get hungry but you'll need to do a little shopping if you run out of milk.

Don't forget to turn the heating off before you leave in the evening and make sure the back door is locked.

Lots of love,

Mum x

Relief floods through me. I completely forgot that Mum and Dad were heading for a winter break. There I was, worrying that they might have been kidnapped or worse. I feel like a total pillock.

I check the back door as instructed and notice the thermostat is turned down, so I leave it off for now. I'll wake up to a cold house in the morning but that doesn't bother me too much. I head into the living room to make sure all the windows are closed, not wanting to take any chances of a mysterious night visitor. Then I do the rounds upstairs and again make sure it's all shut. I think I read somewhere that the largest number of burglaries occur during power cuts as the home security alarms are always disconnected. I brush my teeth and head to my room, grateful that I don't have an early start tomorrow.

With no electricity I have to fumble around in the dark, undressing and pulling on some tracksuit bottoms and a t-shirt to sleep in.

I nearly have a heart attack as I pull the covers off my bed and something black shoots off it and across the room. I swear loudly and grab the nearest thing I can find, which happens to be a book, pointing it accusingly at the mysterious creature that I can barely make out in the darkness. I grab my phone and point it at what looks like a darker area of shadow. It's too dark even for the light from my screen to make out. I feel sick with terror, no matter how hard I try to calm myself down. Fumbling with the touch screen I finally get the torch function working, cursing all the while. A pair of yellow eyes glares at me menacingly.

"Are you kidding me?" I shout at the cat, who only narrows its eyes further.

"How the bloody hell did you get in here? I nearly died!" The cat seems not to care that it was almost responsible for my untimely demise and leaps back onto the bed.

"Oh no you don't," I say, trying to get my window open and remove the intruder. It's not having any of it and digs it's claws deeper into my duvet. No amount of cursing or pushing will make it move, and in the end I give up.

"Defeated by a cat. Unbelievable."

The cat gives me another unimpressed look and curls itself into a ball. I climb under my freshly clawed blanket and try to calm my heart rate down enough to get to sleep.

The window was locked when I came into my room. In fact, everything in the house was shut and locked from what I can tell. How did it get in?

With no electricity I can't charge my phone at all and have to hope the battery will last me until tomorrow.

When I finally do fall asleep I dream that Ella is the cat, sleeping on the end of my bed. I ask her why she keeps following me, but my Dad storms in and tells me to stop talking to cats or he'll tell everyone I'm an Augur. I try to point out that it's the cat who's the Augur, at which point he grabs it and throws it out the window. I scream that he's thrown my girlfriend out of the window and wake up shouting.

The comforting feeling of the cat at the end of my bed is gone. I open my eyes to see it sitting on my window sill, staring down the street below. It's freezing in the room and I shiver.

"What are you looking at?" I ask it. It's ear flicks as if to register the sound of my voice but it doesn't take its gaze away from the spot in the distance.

I'm not sure why but I something makes me feel uneasy, so I throw my covers off and peer out the window myself. I follow the cat's line of sight down to the end of the road. I freeze in sudden horror.

Standing at the end of the street, in a dressing gown and leaning against his garden gate is the cigarette man, returning my gaze. But it's not the cigarette man that shocks me. It's the fact that despite the distance I can clearly see his hand, hanging down by his side. His hand is a glowing ball of fire.

CHAPTER 5

I swear and duck down from the window. I dive under my covers, not being able to think of anything else to do. The cat doesn't seem to be perturbed by either the suspicious Augur at the end of the road, nor my failure at any sort of bravery.

The dream I had woken up from suddenly dawns on me.

"Hey, who are you? Or what are you? Are you an Augur cat?" I ask it, trying to sound calm. The cat blinks and twitches its ear again as if to say *I heard you but I'm not taking my eyes off this guy.*

"Fair enough," I answer it, feeling a little stupid for speaking to a cat. It's at this point that I wish I had some way of contacting Ella. The fact that she doesn't have a mobile phone is infuriating now more than ever. She'd know what to do about a scary Augur standing at the end of my road, staring into my bedroom window.

I try to take some deep breaths and calm myself. Can I even call the police? The guy isn't doing anything, and I wonder if I'm just as bad as the rest of the Augurists if I do that. Does 'standing creepily at the end of my road with a ball of fire in his hand' count as some kind of inappropriate behaviour?

It looks like the power is still out because the only light coming from outside is from the light pollution in the sky. Oh, well, that and the Augur's hand, which isn't bright enough to reach all the way to my room.

After ten minutes of sitting at the edge of my bed, shaking both from cold and fear I decide to take another look. The cat is still on guard although that doesn't particularly make me feel any better. I peer over the window sill as stealthily as I can, but Cigarette guy seems to have disappeared. Climbing back under the duvet seems to be my only course of action.

Really? This is how you're going to handle the situation right now? I ask myself.

A hurried knock at the back door nearly sends me shooting out of my skin. I swear under my breath repeatedly whilst pulling on a jumper and a pair of trainers. The knocking comes again, urgent and persistent. I cast my eyes frantically around the room for some kind of weapon. Crap. Crap, crap, crap. The Augur-Cigarette-man is probably waiting on the other side of the door with his burning hand ready to put me down as soon as I open the door. The sleep in my head doesn't allow me to work out what I might have done to offend him.

The only thing that is heavy enough to do any damage is a trophy I won as Man of the Match in a high school football game. It's the sort which has a little metal footballer on top of a faux marble plinth. I pick it up and weigh it in my hand, trying to figure out if it would knock someone out with enough force for me to get away.

When I open the door, the cat is out of there like a bullet. Damn. Maybe it'll blow my cover. I try to sneak quietly down the stairs and into the kitchen, ducking behind the door frame so that I can unlock and open it from behind and hit whomever barges in over the head.

The bevelled glass shows the silhouette of someone tall and thin. Not the cigarette man?

"Curtis, bloody hell, it's freezing out here. Would you open the door?" It's Ella.

I nearly faint with relief. With shaking hands I unlock the door and let her in. She tiptoes to give me a kiss on the cheek, but I push her into the house and hastily lock the door behind her.

"What are you doing with that?" she asks, frowning at the trophy in my hand.

"I, er, oh. I thought you were someone else. Sorry." I put the trophy down on the kitchen counter and peer out the back window.

"There wasn't anyone following you was there?" I ask hurriedly.

"No, why?" she laughs at my obvious hysteria.

"Because, er, I hate to have to tell you like this, but I just found out there's an Augur living at the end of my street and I think he's been spying on me," I say, the words tumbling out.

I can see she wants to laugh again but she feigns seriousness for a moment.

"Hang on a minute, Curtis, how do you know he's an Augur?"

"Well, there was a power cut last night —I was having this dream and when I woke up the cat was staring at him on the street, and when I looked out the window he was standing there in his dressing gown with a glowing hand. A glowing hand! And the other night when I came home he'd been watching me from his window and then there was the note, and the cat, and oh my God, Ella, I think he knows that I know that you know—"

"Curtis, you aren't making any sense. Come, let me make you a cup of tea and you can tell me all about it. But do you think we could get the heating on in here? I can almost see my breath," she fills the kettle while I go and turn up the thermostat.

When I come back she's already found the teabags, milk and sugar, but I have to tell her that I don't drink tea, so I make myself coffee while she fixes herself one.

When we're seated with our drinks at the table, the cat decides to make its entrance. It comes over to Ella and rubs itself against her leg, purring like a motorbike engine.

"Well, hello you," she strokes it behind the ears while I try to calm my nerves. "You didn't tell me you had a cat. He's lovely," she says to me.

"I don't. I didn't even know it was a 'he'. Just turned up last night completely out of the blue. But he's the one that had been watching me a few nights ago, and then I dreamed that he was an Augur." She gives me another one of her raised eyebrow looks and tells me to start from the beginning.

I fill her in, but when I get to the bit about the note she stops me.

"Do you still have it?" she asks, completely serious now.

"Yeah, I do, actually." I fetch it from my room and place my football trophy back in its rightful spot on my shelf. When I hand it to her, she reads it several times before fixing me with a glare with an emotion behind it that I've never seen before.

"You should have told me about this," she says, laying it flat on the table between us. She looks at it like it's some sort of dead animal, there's so much disdain on her face.

"Honestly, I would have, but I didn't want to worry you."

"Curtis, this is *my* world. There is so much going on here that you don't know, don't understand. If people start threatening you about me, I need you to tell me," she says. I can tell she's angry, but she talks to me as if I'm some kind of child that has stolen from the cookie jar rather than her boyfriend, if I can call myself that yet.

"I got it. I'm sorry. Really, I am. I promise it won't happen again." Christ, if she dumped me over something like this I'd never forgive myself.

Satisfied with the apology, she folds the note up and puts it in her jacket pocket.

"And now to the Augur living on the end of your street. You said there was a power cut last night?" I nod in reply. "And that when you woke up this Augur had energy in his hand?" I nod again. She thinks for a minute. "Could be related, could be a coincidence. But if I can get a look at him I can probably identify him, or know someone who can."

"Seriously? Is the Augur community that small?"

"Sort of. I mean it isn't, but I have a friend who has a knack for 'identifying people', shall we say."

"Wow, so that's an ability too?" I can't help but be fascinated by that thought.

"Yeah, everyone has a little specialist skill. Some don't have much more than a better ability to fry eggs than other people, but every Augur leaves a little signature when they use their abilities, so even if I can't ID him myself, Jer could probably do it by standing outside your neighbour's house."

"Jer? Is that a guy or a girl?" I don't know why I ask.

"Jer is short for Jeremy as far as I know, so definitely a bloke," she replies casually.

"And is he an old, ugly bloke by any chance?" I know it's stupid to feel jealous. Of course Ella will have Augur friends who are guys. She said something about there being a whole group of them. I'd just thought they'd all be really hot girls.

"No, Curtis. Jer is about our age, a bit older perhaps," she's trying not to laugh at me again. "But he's not my type," she says and picks up our empty cups, kissing me on the cheek playfully as she does so. I don't feel any better for it, really, but the kiss helped.

"Now, I don't know what plans you had for us today but I'm afraid your note kind of throws it all out the window," she says, washing the cups and placing them on the draining board. I love how she acts like she belongs here, which to me she completely does.

"Oh, that's a shame. I'd had a great day planned of binging on popcorn, chocolate biscuits and watching movies," I smile and wrap my hands around her waist.

"That sounds like a wonderful idea. Maybe next time," she turns from the sink and kisses me hard, placing her still-wet hands on the sides of my face. When she pulls away, my entire body feels like it's going to explode. I haven't quite gotten used to being kissed by her like that. "But first, go take a shower and put something on that's a bit more presentable."

"Why, what's wrong with the jogging bottoms I sleep in?" I joke.

"Well, thanks to all the excitement and attention that's now on you, Curtis Mayes, I'm afraid I'm going to have to introduce you to my sister."

I do as I'm told and head upstairs. Ella and the cat stay downstairs and she finds one of Mum's magazines to flick through while I get ready. I feel weirdly nervous. It's almost like meeting her parents, but worse because her sister is an Augur.

Dressed in black jeans, trainers and a slightly better-looking jumper, I come downstairs.

"Ooh, you even combed your hair," she says as I come back into the kitchen.

"Yeah, I really went the extra mile for her. I hope she appreciates it." I grab my jacket and, on her advice, I take my scarf and gloves too.

Ella agrees to leave the house before me to check that the coast is clear of any ill-doers or smoking Augurs that might be outside. I follow a few steps behind, feeling calmer with her there. As we walk to the bus stop, she threads her arm through mine, which calms my nerves like some kind of human security blanket. Despite the earliness of the hour, it's Monday and of course there are people everywhere heading to work or school or wherever. The bus stop is full and the bus even more so, but we squeeze our way upstairs and sit at the back of the double decker, taking heart in the fact that we've got at least twenty minutes undisturbed in front of us.

She threads her fingers through mine and rests her head on my shoulder the entire way as we look out of the window at the passing buildings, a blur of greys and browns.

The route we followed on Friday night is pleasant in the daylight and I spot her road from where we get off the bus immediately.

"Just be yourself, but don't let her get into your head, okay?" Ella says as a word of warning.

"You make her sound like she's going to interrogate me," I laugh, but she doesn't answer which is disconcerting. We walk briskly up the path to the front door that we had kissed in front of what feels like a lifetime ago but in reality was only a few nights ago.

Without hesitation, Ella puts her key in the lock and turns it. Rather than the bubble of noise I heard escape last time, the house seems silent. There are lights on somewhere upstairs that spill onto the staircase, illuminating the dull green carpet and a few paintings hanging on the walls.

I don't have much time to take it in though. Ella puts her finger to her lips and looks at me urgently, pulling me to one side. We creep up the first flight of stairs, me copying her tiptoes as best I can past the cracked-open door on the first landing.

"Is that you, Ella?" comes a quavering voice from inside.

Ella motions for me to stay put and keep quiet.

"I know he's here too, so you might as well bring him in," comes the voice. Ella rolls her eyes and ushers me into the room, following closely behind.

"Aggie, I wanted to introduce you. Why'd you have to go and ruin it?" Ella says as I enter a strange, chintzy room.

Floral wallpaper on every wall, a large Persian rug on the floor and flanked on all sides by furniture, the room looks like something out of the late eighties that has never been updated.

Its single inhabitant is a short, squat blonde woman whom I assume is Ella's sister only because they share the same sky-coloured eyes. She stands in the centre of the outdated chaos with both hands on her hips, hair every which way, a little like she lost her hair brush several months ago. In a peculiar flowery dress and cardigan that looks like something my grandmother would wear, she examines me, and I feel strangely stupid, unable to stop staring at this interesting person.

"I've *seen* him, Ella. I'm not stupid, and neither are you, so I'm not sure why you brought him here," she says, not unkindly, but there's a disappointment in her voice.

"Curtis, this is my sister, Agnes," Ella introduces me, ignoring that last comment.

I extend my now sweaty hand to shake hers, but she doesn't take it.

"And you're trouble," she says to me before I can open my mouth.

"Excuse me?" I reply, a little unsure of myself. Something about this young woman is very unnerving. I'm not sure if it's the fact that I know she's not even thirty but looks like a fifty-year-old, or that she has obviously taken a dislike to me before I've had a chance to say 'hello'.

"You might as well come in and stop standing there like a banana," says Agnes, retiring to a scruffy armchair in the corner. I look puzzlingly at Ella, mouthing 'banana?', but she rolls her eyes and makes a 'crazy' circular gesture with her finger.

"I know what you're doing," calls Agnes, and Ella abruptly stops.

Following her lead, we take a seat on a short chaise lounge which is pushed against the window. We're wedged between Agnes and an ancient TV set which is silently spilling images of the news.

I take in the scene. A large cork board is pinned to the wall opposite a small bed, with multiple pictures tacked to it and pieces of string connecting words written on scraps of paper connecting bits of information to each other. A conspiracy theorist, I'm thinking.

There's a small wardrobe, a table and a chest of drawers. On pretty much every flat surface there are piles of paper. I take it all in; the rough drawings scrawled on napkins, large words circled multiple times that, on their own, mean nothing, like 'chaos', 'chipped', and 'hospital'.

One name appears multiple times and, surprisingly, I recognise it.

"Carlton Munday?" I say out loud. Ella hits me on the leg, but apparently it's too late.

Agnes's eyes light up and she takes them off the television for a moment.

"You know him! Yes, yes indeed," she says fixing me with an excited stare.

"Oh God," Ella says under her breath.

"Carlton Munday, Civil Defence Minister. Also an Augurist. Single-handedly responsible for the new legislation which, by the end of tomorrow, will force us all to register, and there begins the slippery slope for Augurs everywhere," Agnes's quavering voice is quite angry now.

"But you said he's an Augurist. Wouldn't that be grounds to lose his job?" I question.

"Indeed, but first and foremost he's a politician. And I'm afraid that his political aspirations will rise above his need to protect his people, if indeed he cares one little bit for us."

Ella sighs and pulls out a piece of paper from her pocket. "Aggie, the reason we're here isn't to discuss your theories about Munday. Curtis received this shortly after we started, um, seeing each other." My heart does that little flip flop thing when she says that. I mean, it's ridiculous because we're obviously seeing each other. But the dark voices of doubt always creep in and say that she's going to turn around one day and say it was just a bit of fun. She's a ten. I'm barely scraping a six. But that feeling of unreality I've had these past few days is finally starting to fade.

"Is he alright?" Agnes's voice pulls me out of my reverie.

"Sorry, yeah. I'm fine," I say and run my hand through my hair nervously. Agnes looks unconvinced but takes a look at the note in Ella's hand, reading over it with interest.

"Probably best not to further contaminate it. Give it back to Curtis and we'll get Jer to look at it."

Ella hands it back to me and I carefully fold it and slip it into my pocket. There's that guy's name again.

"There's also an Augur living at the end of Curtis's street that I'd like to get checked out," Ella says. Agnes nods in agreement.

"I'll get Jer onto it," she replies.

"When can I meet this Jer guy that everyone is so keen to talk about?" There's a silence while Ella and Agnes seem to have a silent conversation between themselves and I sit in between them like some petulant child that asks too many questions. After a few moments Ella says, "Ugh, fine. Go easy on him though, will you?" And she gets up to leave.

"Wait, what? Where are you going?" I ask, suddenly panicked to be left alone with Agnes.

"I don't bite. We just need to have a little heart to heart," Agnes says as Ella closes the door behind her when she leaves.

Agnes turns herself towards me, fixing her large blue eyes on me. I feel pinned to my seat, a hare in the headlights.

"You are a total nuisance, Curtis Mayes," she starts. "Not only did you have to get under the feet of Ella, who is more important to our cause than you probably have any notion of, but somehow you managed to make her fall in love with you." My heart skips a beat.

"She's in love with me?" I ask hopefully.

"Don't be a pillock. Of course she is. But the ramifications of that are far greater than your little mind understands. I've *seen* you. I know, sadly, everything that is going to happen. If I could make you disappear here and now, knowing that it would change the events of the future, I'd do just that. It would be easy enough." I suddenly feel threatened. This peculiar, mad-looking woman who happens to be related to the girl I'm crazy about is talking about killing me to get me out of the way. I have no doubt she's capable of it.

"But I fear that getting rid of you would set another course of events into play that I don't think will benefit us or the rest of the world. No. Instead I'll have to work with what I've got," she sighs and slaps her knees as if she's concluded an argument with herself and is resigned to the outcome. I feel as though I'm a spectator in a one-sided conversation that I'm not privy to.

"So, young man, the only question I have for you is: do you have what it takes?"

"I'm sorry, have what it takes to what?"

"To raise a child!"

"Excuse me?" I'm completely perplexed.

"You heard me," replies Agnes and folds her arms, unwilling to clarify the bizarre statement further.

"I, er, I dunno really. I've not given it much thought," I say, wondering if this is some kind of strange test that she's putting me through.

'Let's put it this way: if Ella is stupid enough to get herself pregnant would you raise the child?"

I feel a little ill. Agnes sees things. Future things. Has she seen that Ella and I have a baby together? That would mean that we'd have to sleep together. And the thought of that sends sensations through my body that I can't think about right now.

"I've evidently lost you to one of your little trains of thought. Just answer the question with the first thing that comes to your mind. Would you be able to raise a child with my sister?" Agnes snaps her fingers in front of my face and I respond immediately.

"Yes. I love her. I'd do whatever it takes," the answer seems to please Agnes. "But does that mean…?" I leave the question hanging between us.

"Well, it's one of some thirty outcomes that I've seen, half of which end up with you dead, a quarter with Ella pregnant and the rest, well, let's just say I've only seen one scenario where we all win. That's what I'm worried about, Curtis. Between you and me, the whole bloody fate and lives of Augurs in this country, and other countries too, rests on Ella's shoulders. At the moment you're a distraction. I'm hoping that you'll become more than just the boy who inconveniently discovered her secret."

I digest the information for a moment.

"Can I ask why Ella is so special? Apart from the reasons that are obvious to me, does she have different powers or something?"

Agnes seems to debate whether to confide that information in me or not.

"Yes. She's very special. Just as there aren't any other Augurs I know of that can see visions of the future, she's the only one that doesn't need to channel much energy, if any at all, to use her gift. She's a self-sufficient energy source. She just doesn't want to do anything about it."

I nod, remembering how Ella so nonchalantly mentioned it last night. "So, all the stuff about transference of energy and particle displacement that I've read about doesn't apply to her?" Agnes looks impressed at my knowledge, if only briefly before giving me a grave nod.

"It does, but because she can constantly create her own energy she doesn't need to take it from outside sources. And the worst thing is she doesn't want to try it, yet without her cooperation we'll lose this war. Some time, very soon indeed, I'm going to need your assistance, Curtis. I'm going to need you to convince my sister to use her real gift. Not growing flowers or fixing coffee machines," she pauses for a second when I look surprised at that statement, "but her *real* powers."

I realise that I've been leaning so close to her that I'm almost falling off the chaise lounge. "What is this war all about though? Why is it so important?" I try not to sound idiotic but it's difficult when I only understand half of what she's talking about. She sighs. It seems I've asked a million-dollar question.

"For years Augurs have been ostracised. Cast out from the groups of Normals because they didn't understand us. Normals dislike anything that can't be immediately understood or broken down into atoms, molecules and hard evidence."

My mind flashes back to the boy that I failed to help just a few weeks ago and I feel painfully guilty. Up until now I had pushed it out of my mind. What would Ella think of me if she knew I'd done nothing more than get myself a black eye and ran away?

"She'd probably forgive you," Agnes blurts out, a look of slight annoyance on her face that I zoned out again.

"Sorry," I mutter as she clears her throat to continue.

"Where was I? Oh, yes. Augurs have been working next to Normals for as long as there have been people on Earth, progressing and building together. But as Normals advanced and produced more technology, first to replace having to do hard work themselves and then to replace needing us, Augurs themselves started becoming more powerful. Just as Normals needed technology to keep them going, and now rely on it fully, Augurs became reliant on the energy around them to use their powers. Ella is one of the few that hasn't been affected by the technological advances around us.

"At the same time, Normals have become more and more suspicious of us, knowing that with all the energy and power around us we could probably do the human race a huge amount of damage. The thought that a being could channel energy and use it for something else is unthinkable to them, despite us being, essentially, the same species."

"I don't think all Normals feel that way," I point out.

"You aren't wrong there, but the ones that need to change, the ones that control the media and send out messages of hate are more worried about votes than people, about money than compassion, well, they aren't as understanding as you, Curtis.

"I know that Ella isn't the first Augur you've known, and I realise she's not the only reason why you agree with our cause. But the fact that you two are together could be the very best or the very worst thing for us," she leans back and seems to give me a cool look, waiting whilst I adjust my reality to this new and peculiar situation. What could I possibly do to make things better? What could Ella do against potentially hundreds, thousands or millions of Normals that want nothing more than to get rid of Augurs?

"There's so much tension building between the two sides. To top it off there's the small group of idiots running around and aggravating the situation."

"The Magic Circle," I interject, satisfied that at least I know something about what is going on.

"That's right. If they carry on they may end up pushing Carlton Munday and the Prime Minister over the edge, getting us all registered, which would mean that Augurs would end up being targeted individually. They make us register, then they start treating us even more like outsiders. Eventually we end up like animals, slaves or worse. It's been tried before, and they almost won. Our basic human rights are at risk, our families and children for generations to come will be penalised. The only thing that is stopping all this from happening already is our anonymity, and to protect that we need Ella."

I realise that she hasn't told me what for yet, but I know that she probably won't now. She sighs heavily and closes her eyes, and after a few minutes I wonder if she's fallen asleep. I take it that our little chat is over and get up to leave, but as I walk past her chair she grips my hand. With eyes still closed she says, wearily, "You're one of us now, Curtis. Whether you like it or not, the fate of the Augurs and the Normals rest on your shoulders. Ella won't do it without you. Will you help us?"

I feel a shiver go down my spine.

"I promise," I say, not sure of my choice of words.

"We're relying on you, Normal," she says, and for some reason I feel slightly offended by the word. I nod, although I know technically she can't see me, but she lets go of my hand and allows me to leave. I feel an almost painful tension in the pit of my stomach like I've never experienced before. That, I tell myself, is the heavy weight of responsibility.

CHAPTER 6

I find Ella in her room, lying on her bed reading. "Oh God," she says when she sees my face, "what did she say to you? You look like you've seen a ghost."

"Ah, nothing much," I say, running a hand through my hair.

"Well, that's a lie," she smirks. "You know, I can tell when you're nervous because you always run your hand through your hair."

"I do?" I say, immediately dropping it to my side and trying not to look too guilty. She laughs.

"So really, what did she say?"

"She said a lot. Like, a *lot.* Half of which I didn't understand but most of which I got the general gist of. But, essentially, she wanted to make sure my intentions were good," I say, trying to make light of it.

"Ooh, well I hope they aren't all good," she winks at me and pulls me down onto the bed. I sit next to her awkwardly, but she wraps her arms around me and pulls me down towards her. I freeze up completely. Agnes's warnings are still fresh in my head, and although half of me would want nothing more than to lock the door and spend the next few hours here with Ella, I suddenly worry about what that would mean for us.

"What's the matter?" she asks as I slump down next to her.

"Something Agnes said. One of her, I dunno, premonitions?"

"Oh, Curtis, don't worry about it. Most of what she tells me is only one of multiple outcomes. If she's scared you off, I'm sorry. I can go speak to her if you like?" I look into her clear blue eyes and want to hold her, kiss her and shut the rest of the world out, but I realise I need to start getting clever if I'm going to live up to my promise to Agnes.

"Ella," I sit up on the bed and take one of her hands in mine, "I realise that this is a bit sudden, but my parents are away for a week. Do you want to stay with me for a few days?" It's the only thing I can think of. It will get her away from the watchful eye of her sister. Not only will I feel a whole lot less paranoid, but we'll be together for long enough that I can probably convince her to tap into her real powers. I feel weirdly guilty as her eyes light up.

"Really?" She asks, but she's doing a terrible job of hiding her smile. I nod and put my hand on her cheek. "How could I say no?" She says and kisses me again, and that electrifying feeling runs through me. When she's happy I feel it right down to my toes.

"One proviso," she says as she grabs a bag and puts some clean clothes into it.

"I'm pretty sure whatever it is I'll agree to it."

"Well, with the weirdness going on at yours, I think we should have Jer check out your creepy neighbour first," she says, grabbing a fistful of underwear that I can't help but notice and chucking it into her bag.

"Fine, fine," I wave my hand dismissively.

"Great. I'll get Aggie to contact him, and in the mean time we should probably get something to eat. I'm famished." She flings her bag over her shoulder and leaves me to inspect the inside of her room while she speaks to her sister. I'd like to avoid going back in there if I can at all help it.

The whole thing is painted with basic magnolia, but there are photos, paintings and pictures covering much of it. The bed is a basic single thing that one gets when they're about ten, and probably like mine it hasn't changed since then. Other than a small wardrobe and chest of drawers there's only one item in the room I find interesting. On a small desk in the corner sits an analogue camera and a couple of lenses. I get up from the floral bedspread and take a closer look. It's interesting to see something like this in an age so full of technology. I examine it, rub my thumb over the shiny lettering and weigh it in my hands. It's been well used, and I wonder if the little knocks and scratches are her imprint on it or if she bought it from a second hand shop. Maybe it belonged to a relative. I realise that I had no idea Ella liked photography. The images around the room make more sense now and I walk over to the photos adorning the wall closest to me. They're pinned or tacked neatly around a long mirror. Agnes appears in one or two. There's even a couple with the rest of the staff of Gregorio's. There are portraits of people looking off to the distance, close up shots of flowers, even one or two street scenes. All of them have a nostalgic look to them, evidently all taken on film rather than anything from the last decade.

A picture catches my eye. Just one shot of a couple, smiling at the camera. The woman looks remarkably like Ella, although older, and the man has the same blue eyes as her. I realise these must be her parents and I feel a pang of sadness in my chest. The image is older than the rest, a little dog-eared, but evidently cherished as it's pinned right above the mirror just above my head.

"Good news, Agnes says Jer can come over tonight..." Ella bounces in but when she sees me looking at the photo she stops. She walks up behind me and I see in the reflection of the mirror that she has that sad expression on her face I've seen hundreds of times before. "That was the first shot I took with my camera," she explains and takes it from my hand. I didn't realise I was still holding it. "Mum and Dad spent too much money that Christmas on a proper SLR for me. Being Augurs we've never gone in for the digital ones. They were killed just a few months later."

I turn around and hug her. "God, I'm so sorry," I say, as if that will make any difference.

"Don't be. But thank you," she sighs and puts the camera back in its place. "I never really mentioned that I like to take pictures, huh?" she says, and I shake my head. "You know, I used to want to be a photographer," she laughs wryly, and I smile.

"Me too, would you believe? I even took a GCSE in it. But Dad thought it was a crap job and refused to help me get a camera, so I gave up in the end. Thought maybe I'd find an office job where I could get paid to push paper around instead."

"Thank goodness you got a job working at the restaurant, huh?" She says, pulling me towards the door.

"Oh yeah, life is so much more interesting since I met you," I joke, but it's true. I grab her bag from her, which she seems to appreciate, and we head downstairs and out the front door, Ella shouting goodbye to Agnes as we leave.

I feel a weight come off me when I step outside. It sounds idiotic, but I felt like Agnes was watching our every move while we were in there, like she had eyes in the walls.

We catch a bus back to my place where I cook the only thing I really know how to: a full English. Mum was shrewd enough to leave me eggs, bacon, sausages and all the trimmings knowing that my culinary skills are limited, and while Ella changes I put it together. We sit at the kitchen table eating and Ella makes appreciative noises. I don't know if she's doing it for my benefit or if she's just really hungry, but I feel happy knowing that I've managed to do something right.

"Can I ask you a question?" I ask her as I take a bite of toast.

"That was one. But you can ask another," she says, getting up to put some coffee on.

"Well, Agnes seems to think that Carlton Munday is an Augurist, yet he's not actually doing anything, from what I can see at least, to hurt Augurs or oppress them out of existence. I don't believe the papers, but it looks like he's just doing his normal job," I say.

"So, what's the question?" she asks, setting down a cup of coffee for me in my favourite mug and sitting back down at the table.

"Well, why would she think he's an Augurist do you think? It makes no sense."

"I'm no politician, but I know people like him. He will do quite literally anything for power. I'm fairly sure there's an agenda here somewhere that we don't even know half of. My parents..." she goes quiet for a moment and I'm surprised to hear her mention them. "My parents were in the process of exposing a huge plan to oppress Augurs. Everything from an inoculation that could dampen powers to a special prison where energy transference would be impossible. Padded cells, no light or heat, that kind of thing."

"But that's inhumane!" I say, feeling disgusted at the thought of Ella imprisoned or worse.

"Damn right it is. But then I came along and things got complicated. I know Aggie told you about what I can do," she shoots me a look and I try not to appear too guilty. I thought if she knew her sister had confided in me it would be all the more difficult to get her to cooperate in using her powers. Apparently, I've underestimated how close they are. I run my hand through my hair and then stop myself, realising that it's my 'tell', and she laughs.

"Curtis, you are hilarious. It's okay that she told you. I can't say it makes any difference to where I stand on the whole situation, but I prefer you know everything before it's too late to go back," she leaves that statement hanging in the air and now I wonder if Agnes told her about the phantom baby too.

"If I haven't said this before, I'll say it now," I say as I take her warm hands in mine. "Nothing is going to take you away from me. Not Augurs, not your family, not even — other complications. I'm here to stay even if it's the last thing I do." She smiles at that, but it's a sad sort of smile.

"I never finished telling you what happened to my parents," she says.

"You don't have to if you don't want to."

"No, I need to say this. Really." I nod at her to go on, her hands still in mine. "When I was born it was apparent that I was different. I would use my powers anywhere and everywhere, and it became obvious that I was a Purist. That's what they call Augurs with abilities like mine. In some ways Aggie is too. She doesn't need big energy transference to get her visions, but she can't do it with anything else. Mum and Dad decided to keep me as far away as possible from the madness, and instead of fighting the good fight for Augurs they tried to keep their family safe. Their priorities changed, but not before they could get themselves noticed by all the wrong people. They'd exposed more corrupt politicians and bonkers scientists wanting to tear us apart than I can count. I know you did your own research on us, but you probably never heard that there were whole time periods where Augurs were used as slaves, and other time periods where we were experimented on to get to the bottom of our differences." I shake my head because no, I'd never heard that, although now that she says it I'm not actually surprised.

"Well, we moved out of town, into the countryside, and for years that worked perfectly in keeping us off the grid. Then Mum got wind of an Augur being experimented on by some nutcases calling themselves doctors. It looked like their work wasn't over after all. I was completely and idiotically oblivious to what was going on around me, and I went out with my camera one day. It was so stupid," she shakes her head, furious at herself. "If I'd stayed indoors, done my homework like they told me to, I might have prevented it all." A tear slides down her cheek and I brush it away with my thumb. I want to tell her it's okay, she doesn't have to tell me everything. But a selfish part of me wants to know. Like watching a horror movie that you hate but need to know the ending of.

"I was out in our field one day and decided I wanted to photograph a particular flower. Himalayan Blue Poppies. My Dad had told me about them and said how rare they were, but that he'd grown a patch once near the front gate. They'd died after the summer and he'd never seen them again, but to me that didn't feel like an issue. I was out there, camera in hand and so concentrated on finding a bit of life in those seeds under the soil, I didn't even realise there was someone watching me. By the time I'd grown the flowers a few inches high I was being knocked out and carted away.

"I woke up in a concrete cell, only eleven years old and completely terrified. There was no power, no lights, heat or even water. But, of course, that's no problem for me. I did exactly what I shouldn't have: I used my own energy to create a crack in a wall and escape. But I didn't realise that at the same time, Mum and Dad were on their way to get me out. The crack made half of the facility cave in and in the confusion of chaos they were killed by a Normal who probably thought it was them creating all the havoc. They were shot moments before I found them," she chokes back a sob and I get up to put my arms round her.

"I'm so, so sorry," is all I can think of to say. It feels feeble and weak in the face of so much grief and pain. I realise it doesn't matter if it was eight years ago or eight minutes ago, losing someone is one of the hardest trials we have to face.

"The thing is that even though so many people were arrested in connection to the experiments, my parents' deaths were swept under the rug, like it never happened. That makes it hard to get closure on it. But from that day onwards I promised myself I wouldn't use those abilities. Nothing good can come of them." She sounds resolute now, angry even. I don't want to push her to say any more, so I simply nod.

"Thank you for telling me. I know it can't be easy talking about it," I say. I'd had no idea her parents had been killed until she'd mentioned it earlier. I just thought they'd died in an accident or something. But now her sister's insistence to use Ella's powers makes as much sense as Ella's own reluctance to. They both lost parents that day and they both want to do what's right. I feel like a tiny and insignificant pawn in a giant game of chess.

She dries her eyes and finishes her coffee. It seems that she's able to recover pretty quickly, and I'm impressed at her ability to wipe her tears away and carry on, but I guess it's almost a routine habit of hers now.

I clean up the dishes and realise looking at the kitchen clock that time is pressing on.

"We'll need to get over to work pretty soon. You want to change while I do these?" I say, nodding to the washing up.

"Sure. I'll just take my stuff upstairs," she says and grabs her bag. I realise that I have no idea what state I left my room in this morning.

"Oh God, hang on a second," I say and run up the stairs before her. I throw open the door of my room and make my bed quickly. I kick a few shoes into the corner and close the drawers I left open. The pile of laundry isn't yet spilling over the top of the basket and it doesn't smell too bad in there. Hopefully it'll pass.

She slides in behind me and manages to smile.

"Cute room," she says, eyeing my football poster on the wall that's been there since I was ten.

"Crap. Sorry, I didn't really prepare for company," I say apologetically.

"It'll do just fine," she says and kisses me on the cheek, ushering me out the door so she can change.

I head back downstairs to clean up and when I return not only is she perfectly dressed in her black skirt and white shirt, but my room looks remarkably cleaner.

"Blimey, how long was I?" I ask, impressed.

"Ah, nothing a bit of Augur magic can't fix," she winks and sits down on the edge of my bed. "You going to change?" she asks.

"Er, yeah. Don't you want to turn round or something?"

"What? To preserve your dignity?" She laughs. Why do I feel sheepish? Because there's a ridiculously hot girl sitting on my bed who happens to now be my girlfriend that I now have to get semi undressed in front of, that's why. I shrug in an attempt to seem unbothered. Like, 'yeah, sure, I change in front of girls all the time.' I sigh and strip down to my underwear, pulling on a white t shirt and my black trousers. I try not to make eye contact with her so as not to make the whole thing even more awkward. Just that small routine of getting undressed in front of her is enough to put an aching knot of nerves in my stomach. Of course, I invited her to stay. What was I thinking? That she was going to sleep on the sofa? I need to focus on the more important matters at hand and try to push anything else out of the way right now.

"You okay?" she asks, giving me one of her expert smirks.

"Er, yeah. Fine. Shall we?" I ask, holding the door open for her whilst scanning the room for my shoes that I kicked somewhere few minutes ago.

When we finally leave the house there's a keen December chill in the air and I'm grateful for my coat and scarf. She looks like a model from a winter wear catalogue in her coat, pulling the hood up to cover her ears.

I lock the house behind me, and as we walk past the end of the road I see the curtains twitch again in cigarette-man's upper window. I mention it to Ella and she shrugs. "Honestly, if he's got something to say he can say it to my face. Anyway, we'll have Jer over after work and he'll be able to tell us if he's a threat or not, hopefully." As if to appease my instant jealousy at the mention of another guy's name she takes my hand in her gloved one and I feel reassured.

"You need to stop that," she says as if reading my mind again.

"Stop what?" I ask defensively.

"Stop worrying about Jer, or that I'm going to suddenly run off with someone or whatever. I'm just as committed to you as you are to me. In fact, I'd have more to lose if you suddenly decided to dump me, just so you know," she says, matter of factly.

"What do you mean?"

"I mean that you know everything about me. Like, everything. But also everything about my family and very soon you're going to be finding a lot more out about my friends. I trust you one hundred percent. Surely you can do the same for me?"

"My God, Ella, I trust you with my life. I would never do anything to wreck what we have. You have to know that. But you're so much better than me in so many ways I wonder why you're even my girlfriend. I can say that, right? I mean, either you're my girlfriend or you're a very close friend that I happen to be madly in love with—" then I stop myself short. I said it. Out loud.

She stops walking and turns to face me. "You mean it?" she says. Does she not know how much she means to me really? I'm sure she does but wants to hear me say it again. And it's true. I'm in love with her in a way I didn't think was possible. All that soppy ridiculous stuff I've seen in movies or read about pales in comparison to what I feel for her.

"I mean it. I love you, Ella Cooper. You're the best thing that has ever happened to me." Saying it makes me feel somehow lighter, and in response she throws her arms around me and kisses me hard.

"I love you too," she whispers, her forehead pressed against mine, smiling.

I feel like I'm floating all the way down the street, her hand in mine. There's something good happening in my life and it comes in the shape of a beautiful girl that loves me. I'm insanely lucky, I know.

We decide to walk all the way to the restaurant, rather than get a bus. It's cold but we've got a little time to spare and I'm glad just to be in her company. We talk the entire way about anything and everything. I tell her about my old school and how I couldn't stand to stay there a day longer when I left; she tells me how her parents had her homeschooled so that she wouldn't have to hide her abilities from everyone.

She tells me how Agnes has been trying to control her life since they were orphaned, which in a way I can understand. How the search for the mysterious Augur girl that destroyed an expensive facility kept them moving for a few years before Agnes found them a stable group of flatmates and a job in the busiest city in the country: London.

I tell her about my parents. How my Dad and I don't get on, but that Mum will really like her. I plan to introduce them when they get back from their holiday, although I tell her I probably won't mention she's an Augur just yet, and we laugh and joke at how my Dad would react to that.

As we turn into the high street I notice a commotion somewhere near the bottom. Something about it makes me feel uneasy. The lights from emergency service trucks bounce off every building and I hear sirens in the distance, although it's difficult to tell if they are coming or going. Smoke billows up into the bleak afternoon sky, tainting everything with an even greyer film.

"What do you think it is?" I ask as we pick up the pace to get nearer to the forming crowd. The road is cordoned off in one section and home time drivers are honking to get through. We squeeze through a line of cars which are almost bumper to bumper.

"Looks like a fire somewhere," Ella says, pointing out the fire engines that are blocking the traffic and causing chaos. It's true, there are fire fighters everywhere and a long hose that is gushing out water to put out any remaining flames.

As we get nearer my heart stops. I finally realise as I stare into the charred remains of the green awning and ruptured front window why I felt so uneasy. The building that caught fire is Gregorio's restaurant.

CHAPTER 7

We muscle our way through the crowds to find an ambulance, three paramedics and a score of firefighters around the building. A huddled shape in a safety blanket is curled up in the open back of the ambulance.

"Mr. Gregorio!" Ella runs over, and I follow on her heels. Mr. Gregorio, whom I've never seen look anything other than slightly stern, is almost unrecognisable. His pale face and wide, dark eyes stare out from the shiny plastic cover that he's been wrapped in. Ella throws her arms around him, and he does something I didn't expect: he breaks down and cries.

"What happened?" she asks softly. He whispers something in her ear and I see her nod, a shocked expression on her face. I feel like a spare part, knowing that Mr. Gregorio barely tolerates me as it is. The last thing he probably wants is me standing there while he has a nervous breakdown. They speak, heads together in hushed tones and I decide to walk towards the wreck that was my workplace for a closer look. Where's Federico? Or Gio and Marco? They should all have been here finishing their shifts, but I can't see a single recognisable face in the crowd.

Seeing that Ella and Mr. Gregorio are still in deep conversation, I walk around the side of the building down the side alley to the back kitchen entrance.

There are no emergency services staff here and no Federico in the kitchen. I expected that the kitchen would be the starting point for the blaze, but the place looks fairly intact. An electrical fire on the restaurant floor, perhaps? I probably shouldn't go in, but curiosity gets the better of me and I step through the open doorway. On the left everything is as it always is, with knives and utensils magnetically fixed to the wall. The central workstation still has meals in various stages of progress laid out on plates. The right wall is lined with cookers, and although there are pots and pans on many of the hobs, everything seems to have been switched off. It's an eery scene with everything looking as though someone has just stepped away for a second and will be back any second to finish off their work. Knowing the mess that's out the front of the building I'm sure that the restaurant will be out of commission for a while.

I walk further into the long room and notice that the door to the walk-in fridge in the corner is ajar. It seems odd so although I know I'll probably get told off any minute now by someone for snooping around, I can't help but go in for a closer look. I gently pull the door open further with a finger, and my heart stops.

A figure is reaching into a plastic container on the top shelf but stops suddenly at the sound of my shout.

"Who the hell are you?" I ask accusingly, but before I get an answer the stranger has pushed straight past me and out the kitchen door. I would chase after him, but another sight stops me dead.

Laying on the floor in a pool of blood is Federico. There's a spatula in his hand and spilled containers of food everywhere. Is he still alive? Not knowing what else to do, I run out through the double doors into the charred mess of the restaurant floor and run straight into a figure in full fire fighting gear.

"Whoa! Hold on there, son, what do you think you're doing in here?" he says in surprise, his voice muffled by his lowered helmet.

"My friend is hurt!" I say and point in panic at the kitchen. He calls to one of his colleagues who is putting out a small fire in the corner with an extinguisher and tells her to grab a paramedic. Following me through to the walk-in fridge, I take him to Federico and he tells me to clear the way in case they need to move him.

"Is he still alive?" I ask, my voice sounding unfamiliarly shrill to my own ears. He removes a glove and with no regard to the puddle of blood on the floor he reaches down to check his pulse.

"Yes, but barely," he nods, and as I sigh with relief a paramedic pushes her way past me, followed by another, and soon the fridge is overcrowded. My head is swimming with questions and I feel nauseous from the sight of so much blood and the smell of burnt wood and fabric. I step back into the alleyway to get out of their way and to clear my mind for a moment.

Was the fire in the restaurant an accident, or something more sinister? If Federico was brandishing a utensil around the fridge in an attempt to fight that guy off, then there was possibly more to it than someone just trying to steal food. I feel lucky I didn't end up in a confrontation with the hooded figure now as I look down at the crowd gathering around Federico. He's built like a tank, and if that skinny guy could do something like this, then he was a braver man than I am. Assuming that it was indeed a guy and not a tall skinny girl. I realise I didn't get a good look at the assailant at all, it all happened so fast. I look down at the unmoving shape of Federico, only his legs visible from this angle, and I feel terrible. We've never gotten on, but I wouldn't want anything bad to happen to him, and I start to get that feeling that I should have been there to help prevent it. I step outside realising that I'll be no good to anyone if I'm only getting in their way.

What could I have done? I ask myself repeatedly. Me? Nothing. Ella though. If Ella was here instead of with me she might've been able to stop it. I wasn't even supposed to be at work yet, but it doesn't stop me from running through it all in my head. This is what Ella must feel when she thinks about her parents. That odd survivor's guilt that we put ourselves through, which helps nobody but somehow tries to justify our lack of responsibility. What does my Mum say? Hindsight is a beautiful thing. In this case it doesn't feel so beautiful.

"There you are," Ella says, walking down the alleyway towards me.

"F-federico," I say, and tell her what I found. Her pale face grows even paler in the ever darkening winter afternoon.

"Oh God," she says quietly, looking preoccupied.

"I know, it's awful. There was so much blood everywhere and everything," I say, feeling sick again just thinking about it.

"It's not just that, Curtis," she says. "Federico had something that the Magic Circle wanted. The person you saw must have done this to try and get their hands on it." I'm surprised at the mention of the Magic Circle, but the figure I inadvertently bumped into was definitely looking for something.

"The weird Augur terrorist guys that wind up the media?"

She nods at me, and I wait for further explanation. "They're not just a bunch of idiots that create trouble in the media. As far as we know they work for someone important. Federico had some information on their ringleader and a whole lot more. It was all on a flash drive that he kept hidden in the restaurant and he'd been trying to find the right person to help leak it…" she trails off as the realisation dawns on me that Federico is an Augur. She nods again as she sees me arrive at the conclusion.

"And Mr. Gregorio. Basically, everyone at the restaurant except you," she says, and I suddenly realise the implications of that.

"Bloody hell. No wonder no one really liked me," I say, getting the idea that I've been a total outsider in more ways than I had previously noticed.

"Yeah. But I convinced Mr. Gregorio to keep you on because, well, you know, I liked you," she says looking sheepish.

"Are you kidding me? You liked me? But I was always the one chasing you!" I say shocked. For some reason I feel more surprised by this revelation than the fact that Mr. Gregorio is an Augur. I shake my head, realising that we're getting off the important subject. "Doesn't matter. What did Mr. Gregorio say to you just now?"

"Well, I had to explain first that you knew about me and that I'd have to let you in on everything else, but his main concern was for the flash drive. As soon as the paramedics are out, we're going to have to get in there and check if it's actually been taken. He told me where it was, so I know exactly where to look."

Knowing that the place is now probably considered a crime scene, we'll have to play it very cleverly, and Ella is likely to be the best person to look, but she insists that I come in for back up. What back up I could provide against the police, ambulance services and firefighters I'm not sure, but I'll provide moral support if nothing else.

As we walk back into the kitchen I see that they've managed to get a stretcher through the large double doors and have just about gotten Federico out of the cramped space and onto it. Somehow, we have to get back into that walk-in fridge without seeming too suspicious and without disturbing anything else. Scenarios of the police finding us in there snooping around flash through my mind and I have to hope it's me being overly cautious rather than some kind of premonition. As the paramedics leave the way they came, struggling to hold the hefty weight of Federico on the stretcher before lifting him onto a bed with wheels, Ella walks over looking like she's going to follow them out the door. But before anyone has the chance to notice, she slips into the walk-in fridge, the door still ajar and being held open by a tub of soft cheese. I follow a few steps behind, deciding to station myself outside the door in case of any trouble. I can see her searching for a particular container amongst the racks. I feel like a lot has happened in such a short space of time, and while she searches I try to take stock of the situation. Ella loves me, and that thought alone sends a quiver through my chest. The people I've been working for this past couple of months are all Augurs, and the only reason I managed to hold down the job is apparently because of Ella. They all seem to be part of some secret Augur group that are hell bent on exposing or stopping some terrible thing happening, most of which I don't understand. They want to stop Carlton Munday from implementing anti-Augur laws. I think I've probably bitten off way more than I can chew and will probably choke soon. How could someone set fire to a restaurant to get a flash drive?

"Got it!" Ella says triumphantly just as I snap into the present and realise there's someone coming through the double doors a moment too late.

"Ella!" I whisper frantically as a uniformed officer steps through the door. If I weren't immediately terrified I would probably smirk at the fact that I predicted this happening.

"Excuse me, lad, but this is a crime scene and I'm going to have to ask you to leave..." the policeman trails off as Ella steps out of the fridge with a large platter of tiramisu in her hands.

"Sorry, officer," she says to him a little breathlessly, "But I know Federico wouldn't want this to go bad." She nods at the plastic wrapped tray as the officer stares at her dumbfounded.

"Er, I'm afraid that's crime scene evidence, Miss, and tampering with it is actually a chargeable crime," he pulls out a notepad and pencil from his belt.

"Oh, no! I'm so sorry —he's just so precious about his secret recipe. It takes hours to make and I knew he'd hate it to go bad while he was in hospital." Her explanation seems so ridiculously sincere that I think for a moment the policeman is disarmed. After a moment's consideration he nods and I realise that I've been holding my breath, which I exhale as quietly as possible.

"All the same, miss, I'm going to have to ask you to leave it here, and I'm going to have to ask you both a few questions," he says, giving her a kind look and one that is slightly less so to me. I nod idiotically in the hopes that the questions won't be too demanding of my wits. Ella is evidently much better at coping in situations of pressure than I am.

"Which of you discovered the victim?" He starts.

"Er, I did officer," I volunteer. He looks a tad disappointed, as if he'd much rather speak to Ella than me. I understand those sentiments completely. After a few minutes of asking the expected: did I see anything unusual? Only a person in a hoodie that I couldn't describe and didn't get a look at. How well did I know the victim? Not that well, we're colleagues but he's a private man. And was there anything out of place in the kitchen? Not that I could tell. He goes on until he resigns himself to getting nothing useful out of me that will forward the investigation that is now turning out to be a case of both arson and grievous bodily harm. He takes my address and contact details, and when he asks Ella for hers she simply says, "We live together," and gives him the sweetest smile she can obviously muster. My stomach does its familiar flip flop as she takes my arm, thanks him and leads me out of the kitchen through the back door.

When finally in the clear I lean close to her and say, "That was a close one!" but she doesn't answer until we're so far out of earshot we're practically a block away.

"God, that was ridiculous," she fumes. "But at least I got this," she says as she pulls out a small silver oblong from her jacket pocket.

"What now?" I ask, realising suddenly that we've no work to go to.

"Now we go and visit a few of my friends," she says ominously.

"Why do you say that like we're about to attend a funeral?"

"Because, no offence, but bringing a Normal into a group of Augurs is a bit like bringing a plagued rat to a hospital."

"Oh, how could I be offended by that analogy?" I say sarcastically. But I know what she means, and I'm no more happy about it than she is. "Can't I just stay at home?" I plead.

"Curtis, you're a part of this almost as much as I am now. Yes, yes, you don't really know what 'this' is yet, but I think I'm going to need you there more than you realise."

Agnes's words and my promise to her run through my head. I promised to stay with Ella, no matter what. I promised to help her use her true potential or whatever you want to call it. For Augurs everywhere, even if I'm fairly clueless as to how that's going to come about.

"Yeah, yeah, okay. So, let's take this plagued rat to meet your friends, shall we?" I sigh as she loops her arm through mine and leads me to the tube station that sits off the main road. One of the good things about living in London is the vast underground network that connects one side of the city to the other. Yes, sometimes it smells. It's often hot, and one regularly has to suffer their journey cramped worse than a sardine under someone's armpit while trying to read another person's paper over their shoulder. In the winter when everyone is sick it feels like an incubator for germs. But hey, I'm grateful that I can get across several miles of road in under an hour.

We descend the stairs that take us to the Bakerloo line, passing a busker who tunefully gives us a rendition of 'Jingle Bells' on his accordion. That's when I realise it's only three weeks until Christmas, and although the thought of that would usually make no difference to my life at all, I now officially have a girlfriend. That involves a whole extra set of protocols that I'm unfamiliar with but somewhat aware of.

"Hey, where did you go?" Ella asks, snapping me back into the present as we stand on our platform waiting for the train.

"Ah, I just realised it's pretty close to Christmas. I didn't even realise it was December," I say sheepishly. She smiles, although there's a sadness behind it.

"We haven't really celebrated Christmas since I was a kid," she grimaces. "What do you normally do?" she asks me.

"Ah, parents make food, we open presents, drive to my uncle's house, eat more food, open more presents. Then my grandparents' for the same routine," I sigh at the thought of all the travelling and eating, not to mention the gifts of knitted jumpers and festive socks I have to endure, but when I look at Ella she's giving me this odd dreamy sort of look. "Sounds amazing," she says. I wrinkle my nose.

"I tend to try and stay out of everyone's way. My uncle is nice, but my Dad has a way to end the day in an argument with everyone. He'd argue with the weather if he could," I joke. It's true though —he always finds some way to tick people off, even his own brother. I usually end up playing video games with my uncle and ignoring everyone if I can.

Our train pulls in loudly and the wind blows papers and litter around the platform. We hop on and I prop myself up in a corner. Rather than take an available seat she comes and leans against me. There's a feeling I get when she does stuff like that, or when she asks me to do things for her. I think I've realised what it is: it's a feeling of being needed. I've never been needed before. It sort of hardens my resolve to do whatever I can to help her and the Augurs. Okay, so mainly her. But I know that to someone I'm important, and that seems to have changed something inside me.

We rattle through London's underground and after twenty minutes or, so we end up in Oxford Circus. I'm surprised when Ella squeezes my hand and motions us to get off, as I didn't expect the Augur meeting place to be quite so, well, central. I say as much to her as we climb the escalators, missing out the word 'Augur' in such a crowded place, but she just smiles and says, "You'll see."

We navigate through the throngs of Christmas shoppers and tourists and she guides me down a side road. Oxford Street is lined with shops but between each block there are streets that branch off. The inquisitive tourist might venture down one and get completely lost, but the streets themselves contain specialist boutiques, restaurants and very posh offices, as well as hidden treasures. Ella guides me to an upmarket square, the kind that has a private communal garden in the middle. I feel out of place amongst the smart businessmen and women in their suits and wool coats, carrying briefcases and hailing taxis to take them home. I look down at my worn puffa jacket and scuffed shoes and wonder how long these people had to stay in school to get the jobs they did and the pay checks they take home. But as my uncle would say, it's not what you know, it's who you know. Impressive CVs and a nudge from the right person, and someone like me might even be able to land a job at one of these places.

Ella leads me up a short set of steps and uses the impressive door knocker in the shape of a lion's head holding a brass ring in its mouth. The sound--three precise and clipped knocks--reverberates around the square and I look around nervously, worried that someone might be watching us. The few people that are around couldn't care less about us —they're too busy trying to get home or catch their taxi to notice.

The door opens slowly and a man in a Butler's uniform shows us in.

"Good evening, miss, may I take your coat?" He helps Ella remove it and stands back. I wonder why he hasn't asked me for mine, but I realise he's looking at Ella for an explanation for this stranger standing on his doorstep.

"Oh, Mulberry, this is Curtis Mayes. He's a, er, friend of mine," she says gesturing towards me. Is she blushing? "He and I need to speak to the Duke about a very urgent matter," she explains. I try not to let my eyes roll out of their sockets with shock. The Duke? I'd no idea she rubbed shoulders with royalty. Mulberry eyes me with what I can only detect is a little disdain. Maybe he can smell that I'm a normal.

"Would sir like to remove his jacket?" He asks coldly. "There is a fire in the study and it is quite warm." He holds out his free arm, the other holding Ella's coat, and I shrug mine off and hand it to him. I thank him, but he turns on his heel to put the coats away. I'll probably have to let Ella do all the talking here, which these days isn't unusual. When he returns, he leads us up the carpeted stairs. Paintings that look like they belong in a museum line the walls, and every so often there are completely pointless little tables with vases or ornate pots on them. The whole place is warm and opulent but looks like it was decorated in the eighteenth century.

On the first landing, Mulberry directs us to a large set of solid double doors. There's another one of those little tables outside, but this one has a rather elegant looking bowl on it. "Your phone, sir," the Butler addresses me and gestures towards it. I realise he wants me to put my phone in there, I'm guessing as some kind of security measure. I comply a little begrudgingly, but I suppose it makes sense. If something sensitive is going on behind those doors, the last thing they probably need is some hacker getting info through someone's phone. It does make me feel like I'm not trusted though.

He swings the large doors open and announces our arrival as, "Sir, Miss Ella Cooper and her— friend are here to see you."

A rotund man sits behind a large wooden desk cluttered with papers. Behind him from floor to ceiling stands a bookshelf that stretches across and around each wall of the room. A large fireplace in the back of what can only be described as a study roars welcomingly, but it's the only thing in the room that is. Scattered around the room are chairs and sofas, and on every one there sits a person with either a shocked or distasteful look on their face. I feel the heat creeping up my neck. Every man and woman in the room is looking at me.

"Thank you, Mulberry," says the large man that I can only assume is the Duke, and the butler leaves, closing the door behind him. Someone gets up behind me and I hear a bolt slide into place. I try not to gulp at the thought that there's no running now.

"Ella, my dear. We've been expecting you," says the Duke, taking his eyes off me for a moment and giving her a warm smile. "I called an emergency meeting as soon as I heard the news," he says gesturing to the dozen or so other people in the room. "But I must say, I'm surprised you brought an... outsider." The final word is said with a tone that suggests he wanted to say something else, probably a word that shouldn't be heard in the presence of a lady. If I felt like a foreigner in Ella's world before, I feel like a complete alien now.

"Yes, your Grace. I understand and apologise I couldn't give you any advanced warning. We came straight from the restaurant," Ella explains.

"Yes, Gregorio sent a message to me from the hospital. Federico is in a bad way, and the restaurant will have to be closed for several weeks. I did tell Federico not to store such sensitive information somewhere so insecure, but there's just no reasoning with the man sometimes," the Duke sighs and straightens his papers on his desk. "Well, you may as well formally introduce us to your friend," he says, and I immediately feel on the spot. The only light in the room comes from the fireplace and a small lamp on the Duke's desk, which gives the space and everyone in it a slightly eerie glow.

"Yes, sir, of course. This is Curtis Mayes. He's not one of us." This meets a murmur of disapproval from the group, "But, he's promised to help us, and I trust him with my life," Ella says. I've never heard her sound so nervous before, or at least not like this.

"You've taken a great risk bringing him here," says the Duke, once again returning his gaze to me and making me wish the ground would open up to swallow me right now. "The only reason I've condoned it is because of your sister's premonitions," he says, waving to a corner of the room. To my surprise, Agnes sits inconspicuously in an armchair. I wouldn't have recognised her if he hadn't pointed her out. She gives me an almost imperceptible smile and nod before the Duke calls back my attention. "But, whether I agree with your decision or not, the fact is that right now we need all the help we can get. Unfortunately, we've lost contact with Marco and Giovanni. Apparently, they've decided to visit relatives in Italy thanks to that little attack on the restaurant," the Duke sighs.

That explains why they were nowhere to be seen; they ran and hid as quickly as they could. "He will have to undergo some checks, of course, and before we move onto anything else, I'll have to insist that he is probed." I feel a surge of alarm when he says that, and a tall African man rises and steps forward with a hand signal from the Duke.

"Oh, please, Sir, is that really necessary?" Ella sounds a little pleading, and that sets me on edge even more.

"I'm afraid so, my dear, but I promise Mumbe will be gentle with him, won't you, Mumbe?" The man simply nods and takes another step towards me. There's no point in backing down, and there's certainly no good in turning and running away.

"I'm so sorry, Curtis," Ella whispers to me as Mumbe comes even closer. I shake my head in silent resignation and look up at the man. He's at least a foot taller than me, built with muscle and with no hair on his shiny scalp. His large eyes are like black pools set in the whites of his eyes, and I realise that although I'm trying, I can't seem to avert my gaze. I feel like I'm being hypnotised as I stare into them. The black irises seem to be growing first no bigger than coins, then the size of coasters and bigger still until I'm completely consumed in blackness. I don't even protest when I feel his large hands clamp onto each side of my head. At the same time as I feel his grip, I also get a distinct tug from below, and within seconds I'm falling. I realise that of course I can't really be falling, but the sensation is so strong I wonder if the ground actually has decided to swallow me up. Suddenly, I hit the floor and I'm standing in my kitchen at home. Mum and Dad are talking over breakfast and I'm propped up against the counter. Is this an hallucination?

"Wouldn't you agree, son?" Dad says to me.

"Er, sorry, what now?" I say.

"Wouldn't you agree that the Augurs should be segregated?" Dad is thrusting a newspaper at me as he says it and I read the headline: MANDATORY AUGUR REGISTRATION AND SEGREGATION. This isn't a memory, so what is it? I frown, and as I open my mouth to answer, I'm pulled from the strange scene into another. My classroom in Year 4. I'm eight, and standing next to me is the Augur boy that I suddenly thought about only last week. Ethan. The name comes back to me as if it had never been forgotten. Between us, a large papier-mâché volcano spews red soap mixture. Mrs. Page, our teacher, stands there fuming as the classroom floor is being slowly flooded.

"Stop this at once!" She shouts at him. I realise that this one is a memory, not an hallucination, and just like in the original, I stand there uselessly. Ethan looks at me, pleading, but I have no idea what to do. Mrs. Page's voice rises, and I see that she's about to lose it. If she sends for the principle now, he'll surely expel us. I turn to him and say, "You can do this. Just concentrate." I put my hand on his shoulder, and he nods. He takes a deep breath and places his hands into the mess of soap that's soaking us now. The lights in the classroom flicker, and although it takes what feels like forever, the mess finally stops. He smiles with relief as I pat him on the back, and I'm pulled into blackness before I can see the outcome.

The sound of bone crunching draws my attention towards another familiar scene that materialises out of the darkness. A shriek that barely sounds human echoes around the brick walls that tower above me, and it occurs to me that the sound came out of my own mouth. A kick in my ribs makes me call out again and I realise I'm in excruciating pain, my assailants either laughing or cursing as they beat me.

"Augur scum," one spits a glob of mucus on my cheek.

"Freak!" shouts another as he lands a blow to my ear. I'm curled up in a ball on the pavement, my eyes darting around for any sign of help. What did I do to deserve this?

A figure stands stock still, mouth open, across the road from where I'm being attacked. Pain sears through my chest as I'm kicked again, and at that moment I realise that the person across the road is me. I'm the Augur kid that I failed to help all those weeks ago, and I'm being tortured by my own memory. Tears of regret stream down my cheeks, mixing with the spittle and blood.

"Stop," I say feebly.

"You don't get to talk, vermin."

The feeling of energy suddenly courses through my arms and legs, like a nuclear reactor ready to explode. Wait. If I'm the Augur in this scenario, I have powers, right? The anger burns inside me and the street lamps above begin to flicker.

"I said STOP!" I scream. The men that had been attacking me fly backwards, pummelled by waves of ice that seem to be emanating from my body, pinning them to the ground with huge spear-like icicles.

Shakily, I get to my knees and survey my handiwork, but rather than feel satisfied, I feel even worse. The men who had been beating me are skewered in awkward positions. One is clearly dead, the spear of ice having driven right through his throat. The others are either dead or unconscious. I look back across the road to where my Normal self had been standing, but he seems to have scarpered.

A moan goes up from one of the men who is coming round. I crawl over to him and see with shock that one of my icicles has gone through his stomach. He won't be alive for long. His phone fell out of his pocket as he landed and although I don't know why I pick it up. The cracked screen lights up and a picture of a smiling girl, no older than eight, with a pretty woman makes me cry all over again.

"I'm sorry," I whisper to him.

"D-doesn't matter," he replies, "all you Augurs will be dead soon." The final words are slurred as he passes out and the scene around me fades out.

I'm sitting in a black room. The chair is hard and cold beneath me, and all I see is a single lightbulb swinging above my head. It feels like one of those war prisoner interrogation rooms from the movies. I realise I must have been unconscious, and my head snaps up as a figure emerges from the shadows. What is this now? Not a memory. Is my torturing not over yet?

"Curtis Mayes," the voice belongs to a woman, and I glare into the darkness trying to make out her features. "Eighteen. No job, live with your parents, no qualifications, the usual." She sounds bored, like she's reading a fact sheet about me, and I picture her holding one of those card Manila folders, although I can only make out her silhouette. "But in a relationship with Ella Cooper. Now that's an interesting turn of events. How long have you known Ella for?" She asks sharply. I have no desire to answer her and I keep my mouth firmly shut. I don't know if this is some kind of test or premonition, but in either scenario I know I wouldn't say anything.

"Ah, a silent one. I love that. Means I get to play with you a little more. Did you know that your parents have been arrested at the airport? Turns out they'd gone away for just a week and their son was consorting with Augurs before they'd barely left the country. They claim to know nothing of it, but still, we can never be too careful now, can we?" This fills me with alarm, and the thought of my Dad being accused of associating with Augurs isn't great. I picture him shouting, fists up, at anyone who might suggest he'd even knowingly speak to an Augur.

"I don't know what you're talking about," I croak. My throat is dry, and I sound like I haven't spoken in days.

"Oh, I see. And your girlfriend that is currently being tortured downstairs who claims you were the one who drove her to use her powers —she's lying, is she? Never met her before?" A photograph, a Polaroid shot obviously taken recently skids across the floor and stops at my feet. Although the face is bruised and the whole picture is a little bleached out there's no mistaking her; that's Ella, alright. The pain in my chest from seeing her like that is almost overwhelming.

"She didn't do anything," I mutter, the tears stinging my eyes.

"I'm sorry, what was that?"

"She didn't do ANYTHING!" I scream at her. "She's innocent!"

"And how do you explain the one hundred and sixty deaths? Those people were innocent too. What about the families that lost their lives in that fire, Curtis?"

"I don't know what you're talking about." And it's true; I feel like a lost child. I don't know anything about a fire or deaths, yet some part of me feels like I should know.

"Those people would still be alive if you'd stopped her," says the woman. I'm fed up with this. I realise I need to change tack and get in control of whatever this mind game is.

"What's your name?" I croak. She seems taken aback, although I can't see her features in the gloom. I get the impression she's narrowing her eyes.

"Trying to be clever, are we? Well, that won't work with someone as experienced as me—"

"So, you're experienced? You've done this lots of times before?" I ask, feigning curiosity.

"Don't be cute with me, Curtis. You are in serious trouble and your girlfriend's life is on the line—"

"Who do you work for?" I interrupt and aim the question directly at where I'd imagine her face to be.

"You can't do this!" She spits. "I am the one asking the questions here," she says, but she doesn't sound nearly as arrogant as before. I let myself smile, and my dry lips crack with the effort but I don't care. I've managed to get under her skin and that for me is enough to know that I can get out of here if I piss her off enough.

"I can do whatever the hell I like. This is *my* mind."

Just as I finally feel the satisfaction of having won a round of this weird game I feel a tugging sensation in my back and my eyes shoot open. I'm standing back in the Duke's study surrounded by unfriendly faces. I almost wish I was back in the nightmare than here. I blink a few times and

Mumbe's face comes into focus, a hint of a smile on his face.

"He passed. He even got through Miss Banks," he says to the room. A few gasps and whispers escape from the crowd. I hear a sigh of relief from Ella who's standing just a few feet from us. She walks over and throws her arms around my neck, her mouth just a few millimetres from my ear.

"Well done, I knew you could do it," she whispers. It's only now I'm back in the real world I realise I've been sweating. And crying. I wipe the dampness from my cheeks and turn to the Duke, who seems to quickly mask his look of surprise with a well-rehearsed smile.

"Very good, Curtis. You may have a seat," he waves to a small couch near his desk and we sit down. "You've passed one of our toughest tests. Mumbe is an Augur skilled at creating dreams and hallucinations so real that the person feels like they've been transported to another time and place. Miss Banks is one of the hardest, as she is very much a real and formidable enemy for us. I'm pleased to hear you passed with flying colours," he slaps his hand down on the opulent desk.

"I k-killed people," I say numbly, recalling the feeling of being an Augur for just a few moments.

"Ah, very good. If anything, the experience will serve to show you the kind of dilemmas that Augurs must go through every day. I, of course, don't know what memories your mind contains but I can assure you that if you were given the choice between your life or another Normal's, the choice is not so simple."

The Duke was right. Suddenly my respect for the restraint that Augurs could show had gone up a million notches. I sighed heavily, wanting nothing more than to curl up in a ball and go to sleep. Although the pain from the incidents were gone, it was clear that I had been crying as I could feel the salt drying on my cheeks. I probably looked a mess too.

"But I must warn you," the Duke continued, "that everything you hear here today, and every face you see, must be kept in complete confidence.

We can only assume that your... feelings for one of our members is enough to enforce that, but mark my words, if I find out that any information has leaked, you will be the first to be suspected, and you will be severely dealt with." I think the gulp in my throat can be heard throughout the room. It looks like he's expecting me to say something but as my mouth is suddenly very dry I just nod stupidly. That seems to satisfy him, and his attention turns to the papers laid out in front of him. "Well, to business. You found the drive I assume?" The Duke asks Ella. She nods, but doesn't present it, which I find strange.

"Very good," he says, looking relieved. "I'm sure that you have put it somewhere safer than a walk-in refrigerator," he says to her, and she nods. I know for a fact that it's in her pocket, but I keep my mouth shut.

"Ladies and Gentlemen of the Society, we have been attacked as you have probably all gathered by now. The culprit set fire to Gregorio's this afternoon during business hours in an attempt to recover a flash drive. The information on this drive is of an extremely sensitive nature. It contains all of the files that Carlton Munday has accumulated on Augurs over the decades, details of the government experiments that have taken place over the past thirty years, as well as information that would incriminate Munday if ever leaked."

"Sir, does it prove that he's an Augurist?" someone piped up. A wiry woman in her mid twenties with short spiky hair and ripped jeans. She looks just as out of place in this space as I feel, but somehow she manages to appear as relaxed as if she's in her own home.

"No, Lou, it doesn't. Not conclusively anyway, but that is my next order of business for this evening's meeting." There's a suspenseful silence, and I feel the tension in the room rise.

"If we can prove that he is even remotely associated with the horrors of the Facility, then we can discredit him in the press and turn this tidal wave to our advantage. Munday and the Prime Minister are meeting with the Cabinet tomorrow to fully delineate what anti-Augur laws will be passed. We need to expose him before then, firstly to ensure that the meeting doesn't go ahead and secondly to hopefully have him removed from post. The only person who has actually seen the contents of the drive is Federico, but last we spoke he assured me that he had everything he needed on there. Unfortunately, what he did not have was a credible connection to someone who could do anything with the information. It seems we were almost too late and somehow someone found out what we were trying to do, or at least suspected it.

"Ella, I want you to go to the hospital and check on Federico. With Gregorio's closed for several months, it looks like you, Gregorio and Federico, when he's recovered, will have a bit of time on your hands. Without Marco and Giovanni, I'm counting on you right now. You'll be able to do some legwork and help us move things along at a much faster rate now, and I'd like you to report all of your progress directly to me."

"But, sir," Ella pipes up, "shouldn't I be finding a reliable source to give the information to? I want to see that Federico is okay, of course, but it feels like time is of the essence here."

"You are quite right, of course. But rather than put you anywhere near the limelight, I will have to have someone else do that particular dirty work. Lou," he addresses the girl lounging on a sofa again, "I'm going to need you to prepare our contact." She nods as if she knows exactly what he's talking about, though I'm none the wiser. "Before tomorrow is over, we will have Carlton Munday exactly where we want him," the Duke says with an air of finality. Just as much as the other people in the room seem to be tense with excitement, I feel a bag of nerves. A shiver runs down my back, as if something terrible is bound to happen.

An urgent knocking breaks through the quiet. Lou, as I now know her, walks over and slides the bolts out of place and opens the door to a very flustered looking Mulberry.

"Sir, it's the Magic Circle. They've set fire to Downing Street."

CHAPTER 8

At first there's a deep silence as the horrific news sets in. The Duke himself seems to be somewhat stunned but recovers enough to move. Picking up a remote control from his desk, he points it at a wooden panel which promptly slides open to reveal a television screen. It comes on immediately, and a news reporter confirms what Mulberry had said.

"...fear and panic across central London as police work to both evacuate the area and track down those responsible. So far, there are three dead and a further ten who have been taken to hospital in critical condition. It has been confirmed that the Prime Minister is amongst those in intensive care as well as the deputy Prime Minister, leaving many to ask what's next for our country in response to this horrific attack. This is Bill Manford, BBC News." The screen flips back to a shot of the news studio where a clean cut and serious anchorman catches the audience up with the events. He shows images of both before and shortly after the start of the fire, which apparently began with a small explosion in the back of the building. *How do they know it's the Magic Circle?* I wonder to myself right before he answers that question. If the CCTV images of hooded men or women entering the street a few minutes before the explosion, hands glowing with energy, aren't enough, there's a final snapshot of the room interior where the fire started.

The flames have been dowsed, and underneath them on a wall of what looks like the PM's office, a message can be made out. From the way it's been written, the culprits were in a hurry, the letters uneven and plastered across a painting that is all but unrecognisable now:

YOU WILL BE PUNISHED

Underneath, there's the crude symbol of a magician's hat which I already know as the Magic Circle's calling card.

There are mutters from the members of the room, and I know they're saying what I'm thinking: how the hell are we going to stop Augur discrimination now? I silently note that I'm already thinking of myself as 'we' —me and them together rather than it being just their problem. If anything, the Magic Circle have made it worse, causing people to hate Augurs even more.

The Duke, evidently trying to keep his cool but failing to hide his frustration, turns the television off. "It seems we'll have to act faster than I previously thought. Ella, go now. Take Jer with you and let me know what Federico can tell us about the attack. I think I'm going to have to send a healer or two to the hospital in the hopes of drumming up some Augur sympathy, if it's not too late for that already." He sighs, and with a wave of his hand Ella, the young man I can only assume is Jer, and I are motioned out of the room. I grab my phone from the bowl on the way out, and Mulberry, his austere demeanour slightly shaken, retrieves our coats and Jer's jacket.

When we step out of the opulent town house and back onto the London streets, the cold seems to pass right through me. I look at Ella and notice Jer is doing the same; all eyes are on her.

"Well, this is a right pickle," Jer says, his Dublin accent being the first thing I notice. "Ella, I know it's not the best of circumstances, but do you want to introduce me to your boyfriend?" he says to her, smiling at me. I find that in spite of myself I'm smiling back. Maybe this Irish charm thing is doing its magic on me.

"Oh, sorry, of course. Jer, this is Curtis, Curtis, Jer," she gestures, and he holds out a hand for me to shake it.

"Terrific to meet you, so it is," he says, and I get another flash of his white teeth.

"Likewise, mate," I say and give him a grin of my own.

"So, Ells, looks like you're calling the shots in our little party. Want to tell me where we're going?" Jer asks as we turn to walk back towards the tube station.

"Federico is currently in St Guy's hospital, but I imagine he might be under police protection if they've managed to work out that the restaurant fire was an attack in an effort to get to him, which no doubt they have. So, we'll have to be really clever about how we go about visiting, not giving them any reason to be suspicious. I don't have a clue when visiting hours are, and if he's in intensive care we probably won't be able to see him for a while, but let's get over there first and cross that bridge when we come to it." We descend the tube for another thirty-minute ride to St James's Park. It's obvious that after the attack on Downing Street Westminster station will be closed, so we'll have to walk along the river to get to the hospital. Jer mentions that he was planning to come round to mine later and see if he can sniff out anything dodgy as regards my weird nicotine addict neighbour, but under the circumstances we may have to put that on hold. I wave my hand and tell him not to worry about it as there's already enough on everyone's plates, but he promises me that if the evening works out then he'll still come over, which makes me like him even more. He seems to be a genuinely likeable guy and easy to get on with.

"How do you guys get messages to each other if you don't carry phones? News travels faster than expected in the Augur community," I ask him out of curiosity.

"Ah, we're not allergic to phones. Just don't like to keep them in our pockets and whatnot. We just phone each other normally on landlines and get used to the fact that if ya tell someone you're going to be somewhere you actually just turn up. Plus, Agnes always seems to know when I'm home." He talks easily, and his accent is soft like those from the South of Ireland.

St James's underground station is a short walk from the hospital, just over one of the many bridges that spans the River Thames, its huge glass and concrete face overlooking the black water below. I remember reading how French painters used to be allowed up to the roof to paint the

Houses of Parliament some centuries ago, because at the time it was the best view of the place. I always imagine it would be quite a nice view if, heaven forbid, I should ever end up in hospital.

It's a weird thought though, and I shake it out of my head as we step through the revolving doors and into the vast reception area. The smell of disinfectant hits me like a fist in the nostrils, and I recall why I don't generally spend much of my time getting sick: I hate these places and try to avoid them if possible. I recall having to visit my nan on Dad's side before she died, and the whole place made me thoroughly depressed even though I was only twelve at the time.

Ella steps up to the reception desk and asks for the ward Federico is in. To her and our surprise, Federico isn't in intensive care but is sleeping in a ward, and we're lucky enough to have arrived near the tag end of visiting hours. The receptionist warns us, though, that if he's asleep we won't necessarily be allowed to see him, so all the way up in the lift we silently pray that he's awake.

A no-nonsense nurse tells us to wait at the entrance to the ward while she checks on him and leaves us waiting for a few minutes.

"Alright guys, try and let me do all the talking if possible. I need you both to listen carefully in case he says something that I might miss. Federico is a very secretive guy so no doubt he'll want to avoid speaking openly if there are any police or eavesdroppers nearby."

I suddenly realise that of course I'm probably the last person he would want to see on his sickbed. Federico can't stand me.

"Er, Ella, should I just wait here while you guys do your thing? I might be more of a hindrance if I try to play detective around him," I point out. She seems to mull this over for a minute before shaking her head.

"No, I think you should still be there. You might be able to see this from a different angle and find something I've missed. Plus, I'm kind of hoping he'll be a little more taken by you since you were the one that saved his life by finding him." She gives me a smile, but all I can do is return a worried shrug.

"Mr. Caravelli will see you, but as soon as I sense him being overworked I'll be ushering you out," the nurse returns to say curtly. "You have ten minutes of visiting time left, so please try not to wear him out." Ella nods understandingly and that seems to appease her. To our dismay, the most obvious thing we spot when we enter the ward is the policeman stationed near the end of the room.

"Seems a little odd to have a person under police protection in a general ward, don't you think?" Jer whispers to Ella and me. It occurs to me that I had pictured Federico in a little cosy room with someone posted at the door, carefully vetting everyone that went in and out. Evidently this is not the case, and we make our way to the last bed right by the window. It could be because of the cost of keeping him in a private room, or it could be because he's an Augur; no doubt the doctors would know that by now with all the tests and stuff they've been doing. I'm not sure if Augurs have physiological differences to Normals, but if so then no doubt this is looked for as soon as someone comes into emergency care. We shrug the low security off as there's nothing we can do about it now. The curtain around the bed is drawn all the way, except for a small gap on the far side allowing the patient to see the London night skyline, and at the same time for the police officer to see inside the enclosure.

Federico is, surprisingly, sitting up in bed with a newspaper on his lap. He looks tired and pale but otherwise just the same as always, except for a large bandage wrapped around his expansive middle. He smiles sadly at Ella when he sees her and raises a hand to greet Jer, but to me he gives a look that I have difficulty translating. Is that *gratitude*? I smile nervously as he gestures me towards his bed and I'm forced to come right up to him. I can see the bloodshot eyes, the pallid and saggy skin on his face, and I feel some kind of sympathy towards him. To my utter surprise he grabs me in a rough embrace and pulls me down towards the bed. The bear hug is less than three seconds long, but I feel like I'm going to pass out with the shock of it. This huge, stubborn Italian has barely said three words to me since we met ten weeks ago and given me my fair share of dirty looks, but obviously the whole saving-his-life thing has really affected him.

"Grazie," he says hoarsely, and I simply nod, grateful when Ella pushes her way next to me by the bed.

"Fedi, I have some important questions for you from the Duke," she says, her voice almost a whisper. He sighs in acquiescence and gestures her to sit on the bed by him. Jer comes round the other side opposite me and stands in a position where he can see the police officer on duty through the gap in the curtains and nods for them to talk, never taking his eyes away from the man.

"Can you tell me what happened first of all?"

"Si, si. Everything seemed normal enough," he says in his thick Italian accent. "I was at the cooker when suddenly I feel something, some kind of disturbance. I look into the restaurant and the 'ole place is a on fire. Of course, I immediately go to the fridge to see if you-know-what is safe when there's a man in a black 'oodie and black trousers throwing things off my shelves. I have a spatula in my 'and so I try to 'it 'im with it. Well, he is-a surprised to see me, and he throws things at me. After a small struggle he stabs me with a little pocket knife, but I am clever. I know what he is after, and I 'ave 'idden it very well. I think he realizes he isn't going to find it. But there's a blood everywhere and then it all goes black, so I can only 'ope that you 'ave it somewhere safe?" He asks Ella and she nods in reply. This is more English than I've ever heard him speak and it takes me a minute to adjust to the sound of his accent, usually only hearing Italian curse words aimed at something or someone or other.

"Thank God he only had a pocket knife," Jer comments and I agree. At least no permanent damage has been done.

"Did he use, you know?" Ella asks him. Magic is what she means. Did the culprit, other than wearing a dodgy looking black number, show any signs of potentially being a member of the Magic Circle or at least being some kind of Augur?

He shakes his head and sighs with exhaustion. I can just imagine the nurse bursting in and throwing us out for tiring him, and I think Ella has a similar thought. "We'll leave you to rest, Fedi, but just one last thing: is there anything you can think of at all that might point us in the direction of who might have done this? Things are hotting up pretty quickly now, and I'm worried that all these incidents might be somehow related," Ella says, the last bit almost inaudibly.

"I 'eard about Downing Street," he sighs again, sadly this time.

"Don't worry Fed, we'll get through this mess," Jer puts a hand of comfort on the big man's shoulder and it seems to prompt him to say his final piece.

"There was one thing I remember, that I thought was odd. The knife he hit me with was not a normal Swiss Army knife. It 'ad a little peculiar symbol on it," he looks around for something to write with and finds a ballpoint on the nightstand next to his hospital bed. On the corner of his newspaper he draws a symbol which from my viewpoint looks like a large 'W' with an intricate wave on the top and bottom. He tears off the small piece of paper and gives it to me, much to my surprise, and I pocket it just as the busybody nurse draws the curtain aside to announce that visiting hours are over, and just in time too. He gives Ella a hug and both myself and Jer a handshake before letting us go.

"Well that was unexpected. I didn't do anything heroic really, just snooped around where I probably shouldn't have," I say in the lift on the way back down to the ground floor.

"Well, all the same it saved his life. I knew it was a good idea bringing you with us," Ella smiles and gives my hand a little squeeze.

"Alright you lovebirds, I think I've got to take a look at this crime scene meself just in case there is any trace of Augur activity still left around there," Jer says, and we all agree. It would be stupid not to double check, just in case the fire was started by Augur magic and we can tie the attack on the restaurant to the Magic Circle. I kind of understand the need to do that too. It means that if that's the case we're fighting one enemy rather than feeling like they are coming from all over. If the Magic Circle are behind trying to get the data on Carlton Munday as well as the fire in the restaurant, then perhaps the Duke's contact will be able to lead us straight to them. I say as much to Ella and Jer, very quietly of course, whilst we make our way back to the tube station for yet another journey.

"I'm impressed, Curtis," Jer says, genuinely sounding it. "That's a fair bit of deduction you've done there. Sherlock would be proud," he smiles.

"Not just a pretty face," I reply, and we laugh as we get off at Hampstead Heath. Despite all the crap going on, it feels good to have both a beautiful and trusting girlfriend and someone else around who seems like they're a genuinely nice person. I seem to have forgotten what it's like to have close friends since leaving school, and although it's never really bothered me, it's weirdly relieving now.

It takes us ten minutes to get to the horrific site of the fire and what used to be our place of work. Even thinking that it 'used to be' rather than 'is' makes me sad. The blackened hollows that were the front windows seem to gape sadly, like the hollow eyes of a skull. Police tape cordons off any direct access to the front, and there's one officer on duty outside, but we take the back alley knowing that it's unlikely they'll have someone posted back there. To our surprise and dismay, there's a forensic team taking photos in the kitchen and dusting the place for fingerprints. The back door is wide open, so we have a clear view of everything going on inside, and we stealthily walk past as if we are just passersby. At the other end of the alleyway, we stop and Ella turns to us.

"Not good. I didn't expect them to work on it so fast. We're going to have to get Jer in there somehow to do his mojo thing, and there's too many people to stun at one time," she says, as if stunning people is something she does all the time.

"Wait, what? You stun people? How?" I ask, looking at her like I've never seen her before.

"Just a little electric pulse usually knocks a person out when I touch them, that's all. But I could probably only do it one at a time, and obviously someone would figure out what was going on by the time the second person had passed out," she says, as if we're talking about what we had for breakfast and not about causing other human beings temporary unconsciousness. I frown but I realize I can't really judge her. I knew what I signed up for at the beginning.

"So, er, what do you suggest?"

"We need to create a distraction somehow, or at least find a way to put most of their attention somewhere far away enough that I can slip in," Jer says looking at us both.

"I have an idea," Ella says, giving me a sly look which makes my heart rise up in my chest. It's the kind of look that means we're about to get up to no good, and I may just like it in spite of myself.

A minute or so later, we're wandering up to the back door of the kitchen, falling about with laughter and giggling like school kids.

"S'lovely night, isn't it?" She slurs at me as we burst into the room. She throws her arms around me and pulls me into a hard kiss which takes all my willpower to stay in character. There are four people in the kitchen area and only one of them comes towards us to usher us out.

"Excuse me, guys, this is a crime scene. I'm going to have to ask you to leave," says the police woman dressed in a white plastic coverall and plastic shoe covers.

"S'sorry officer," I try and mumble, pretending to pull Ella off me who only pushes towards me harder. We land in a pile on one of the work benches, sending pots and pans flying, laughing all the louder now like the drunken idiots we're pretending to be.

"Linda, come and give me a hand with these two, please," she calls to her colleague, and Ella pretends to collapse even further. Lucky for us, this is enough to bring the whole team on their feet in an attempt to grab our flailing arms and legs.

"Oh, for goodness sake," the woman says, throwing one of my madly waving arms over her shoulder.

"If I hadn't already dusted that area for fingerprints I'd be arresting you for obstruction of justice and tampering with a crime scene, you know," she says to me curtly, and I tense a little at the mention of being arrested.

"S'very kind of you, officerrr. You have a lovely nose, you know that?" I say stupidly, making my eyes glaze over to keep the ploy going longer.

"I'm going to have to call you two a cab," she says, pulling out her police radio.

"Oooh, don't worry Mrs Police Lady, we don't live far away," Ella says, hiccuping exaggeratedly and doing a great job of being a convincing party girl that had a few too many cocktails.

"Whass the way to the nearest Mackie D's?" She asks the police woman, who sighs in response. Out of the corner of my eye I see a movement and hope that it's Jer finishing up whatever it is he does.

"C'mon, baaabe," I say to Ella, trying to pull her away from one of the forensic investigators. He's a tall skinny guy with goggles on top of his glasses, and in the tangle of pretend drunkenness I dive towards Ella for a kiss and deliberately miss, instead kissing his surgical gloved hand.

"Sorry, s-so ssrry," I say on repeat as they practically throw us out the door and into the back alley. We wobble all the way out to the main road until we're sure that no one is watching and then duck behind a telephone box.

"God, I hope that Jer managed to get in and out in time," Ella says, her voice completely normal.

"Bloody hell that was scary," I say. "You're an incredible actress though," I smile at her.

"You're not too bad yourself, mister. If I didn't know any better I would have thought you quite enjoyed kissing that guy's glove," she jokes.

"Ah, I just imagined it was you. All part of my 'method', don't you know?" I say in a mock-Shakespearean actor's voice. I enjoy the sound of her laugh before it is interrupted by the sudden appearance of Jer from around the corner.

"Blimey, guys. That was a close one," he says, rubbing his hands together nervously. From his wide-eyed expression, I'm not sure whether he has good news or bad news, but he looks thoroughly spooked.

"What's the verdict, Jer?" Ella asks him impatiently.

"I think maybe we should go somewhere more private than behind a phone box, don't ya think?" he says looking at me for back up. I nod, realising that talking about Augur business in the middle of the street right next to an active crime scene probably isn't a good idea.

"My house isn't far from here —a fifteen-minute walk if we're fast." They both agree that the comfort of my home would probably be best, particularly as my parents are away and there's no risk of an intrusion, so we make our way along my daily commute from the restaurant to home, Ella's arm threaded through mine on my left and Jer to my right.

At the end of my street I suddenly remember the other reason for Jer coming round and mention it to him, proffering the threatening note that has been crumpled in my pocket all day.

"Oh yeah, your creepy neighbour. I'll get right on it as soon as we've had a cuppa," he smiles, taking it from me and rubbing it slowly between his thumb and forefinger as if he can feel something in the markings on the paper. I let us in to the house and my newest resident, the black cat, is lounging on one of the kitchen chairs when we walk in. If I hadn't already had a bucket load of surprises today I'd probably be shocked to see him, but as it is he's the last of my worries.

"Lovely cat," Jer says, going to give him a stroke. "What's his name?"

"Dunno. He just seems to have adopted me. Not really even sure if it's a 'he'," I say, and the cat gives me a look that suggests I'd be an idiot to think anything otherwise. "Okay, he's a he. But I have no idea how he gets in. Just one of the many mysteries that seem to have appeared in my life lately." I fill the kettle and set out three cups, one for coffee and two for tea. My stomach rumbles violently and I suddenly realise that it's 10pm and none of us have eaten, so I order pizza for delivery from my phone while we wait.

"It's a funny thing," Jer comments, giving the cat a stroke behind the ears, who purrs loudly in response.

"What's that?" I ask as I set a mug down in front of him.

"Well, your cat has an Augur signature," he explains, taking a gulp of tea while he examines my uninvited guest.

"Ella's mentioned it before, but what does that actually mean?" I feel stupid asking because I feel like I should know everything about them by now.

"Well, just like Ella can do stuff that's a bit, you know, different, I've got my unique skill set which allows me to sort of 'read' an Augur from their abilities, what they're like, even who the trace magic belongs to, if I've met them before anyway.

"This little guy either belongs to an Augur or he's been near one lately."

"Well, yeah, Ella," I explain as I sit down and hand her a cup.

"No, not Ella's. She's got a kind of softer feel to her magic. This one's different and familiar to me..." he trails off for a moment. He pulls the note out and rubs his fingers over it again. "Odd though. The cat and this piece of paper don't have a similar feel to them. The note was written by an

Augur I'd reckon, and it'd be easy to say that the cat has had some connection to whomever it was that wrote it, but it doesn't seem that way."

"How could you tell that if it's just a handwritten note though? Wouldn't it need to have been written with magic?" I'm confused how a scrap of paper could have so much information attached to it.

"Well I guess it must have been put in your house using some magic, otherwise I wouldn't get anything from it. It's almost like an aftertaste in my mouth, like a good cup of coffee," and he smacks his lips as if to prove the point. He stares at the cat in curiosity. "Where are you from, eh fella?" he asks it as he strokes behind its ears.

"Well, we could ponder that all day but more pressingly, tell us about the restaurant, Jer," Ella prompts him out of his daydream.

"Right you are. So, like, in the restaurant I didn't get much time to do any deep searching while you two where messing around — nice acting, by the way," he winks, "I did manage to find an Augur signature — that bit of trace magic I mean — near where the fire started."

Ella nods enthusiastically at this news. "Did you recognise it?" She asks.

"Sort of. It was vaguely familiar, but I couldn't tell you exactly who it was, only that it's someone I've encountered before. I'd be willing to bet good money that it's a Magic Circle member, particularly as you saw him in the tell-tale black hoodie," he nods to me. I had mentioned the whole thing on the train en route to Federico, so between us we were already convinced that it was Magic Circle related, but hearing him confirm it is still surprising.

Taking his hand away from the cat for a moment, who has decided to sit on his lap, he pulls out a small notebook from his jacket pocket. It's a small black thing with smart binding, like an artist's sketchbook. He flips each page enthusiastically for a moment.

"Let's see, let's see... oh yeah, here we go," he slaps the open page and flings it down on the table.

Ella and I lean closer to get a better look. There's a date and time from only a week ago, plus a list of random words like 'earthy', 'dust', 'metallic' and a little squiggle that I can't decipher.

"That's great, Jer, but what does it mean?" Ella asks, and I feel relieved it's not me asking this time.

"It means that I have definitely encountered this Augur before. This particular guy has a unique little, er, call it a flourish, to his magic. So, I can confirm that the guy who set fire to the restaurant is the same guy that set fire to the Prime Minister's car last week," he nods smugly. So Jer must have been sent round to the scene of the crime by the Duke after that incident too, to see what he could find. I don't know why, but I feel shocked by this revelation and my heart begins to thud in my chest. It's like up until now I kind of kept everything separate and compartmentalised in my head. The incidents happening to other people didn't feel like they could really be related to ours. But now that I know the same Augur is responsible for these two attacks it almost feels like it's on top of me and pressing down hard. I don't even hear them talking after that as I try to digest the information.

There's an Augur sending threatening notes to me and jeopardising my relationship with Ella. The currently content-looking cat has also had some run-in with said Augur, leaving it with some magic signature on the cat.

Another one has both set fire to the Prime Minister's car almost harming--or worse--her husband and child, but the same Augur has also set fire to my place of work, a place which consists 99% of Augurs and one Normal: me. And we now know that *that* Augur is a member of the Magic Circle. We also know that the Magic Circle set off an explosion in Downing Street, although why I'm not entirely sure. It feels like there's no escape from the madness now.

"You okay?" Ella asks, and I realise I've been quiet for a while.

"Er, yeah. As good as can be. I guess I just wasn't prepared to have a small terrorist group on our tails trying to get to us, or more accurately trying to get the one thing you have..." I stop myself before giving too much away. I know Ella trusts Jer, but she didn't even tell the Duke where the flash drive was.

She smiles and nods. "No one's going to find it, don't worry," she looks between me and Jer confidently.

The doorbell rings and I jump out of my seat, happy to realise that it's actually the delivery guy with the pizza and nothing more serious. I eat like it's my first meal of the day, which it isn't but might as well have been. You get used to controlling your appetite when you work in a restaurant and have to look at other people's food all day, but at least usually you have something in your stomach beforehand.

As we eat, I can't help but ask something that's been bugging me for a while.

"I know that Ella's an exception to the rule, but how do your powers work? I mean, it's not like you suck in some electricity right before you go and investigate a particular place, is it?"

Jer smiles as he breaks off a slice and holds it poised in his hand. "Nah, I think it's a bit like with Agnes and people like that. Until Normals got all clever and started sending digital signals around everywhere, filling the Earth with moving energy of some form or another, we probably wouldn't have been able to use much of our abilities at all. I know because in remote parts of Ireland I've not been able to tap into me magic very much. Maybe on a sunny day, though we don't get many of those. In some places there's only trees and grass for miles and miles around, and although I could still do something it wasn't as intense as when I'm in a building full electricity and that. My girlfriend can't really use her powers at all without touching something that has at least a battery in it though, so I think there are different degrees of it all. A bit like Ella doesn't need anything to channel off of."

I think about that for a moment. It kind of fits with what that Connelly guy was saying about Augurs not being a problem until people developed technology.

"So, you two met at Gregorio's?" Jer changes the subject. I nod while trying to catch a bit of dripping mozzarella on my tongue.

"You managed to bag your Normal, then?" he says to Ella as if I'm not here. "I mean, I'm assuming this is the guy you were going on about?"

I shoot her a look, and she seems to be smiling embarrassedly.

"Seriously? Jer knew you liked me too? Was I the only person in the universe that thought you didn't?"

They almost fall off their chairs laughing at the look on my face, and in the end I can't help but chuckle, even though the irony of it is almost unbelievable.

"You know she spent two months pretending she had no interest in me at all?" I say to Jer.

"Ah the old hard-to-get game eh? Very clever. I'd say it worked though, wouldn't you?"

"Yeah, I guess it did," I say and give Ella a smile. There's a silence while we finish up our pizza, and Jer clears his throat loudly.

"I guess I better get back to the Duke and give him the news. He'll be waiting up for it and I don't want to keep him." He washes his hands at the sink and throws his jacket on, giving me a friendly slap on the shoulder and Ella a quick hug before letting himself out.

"Damn," I say a few minutes after he's gone.

"What's up?" Ella's asks as she throws the pizza boxes into the recycling bin.

"I meant to ask him if he had any notes that would help me out about the guy next door. I feel like he's tied into this somehow." *Could he be the person who left the note?* I wonder. But the cat isn't his, I don't think, and I get the feeling that he and the feline aren't friends.

"Ah, don't worry. We'll probably be seeing plenty more of Jer now that you've been properly inaugurated," and she laughs at her own joke. Inaugurated. It's a completely different word, but I get the feeling that in some way I have been accepted into this terrifying group of strange and wonderful individuals.

We clean up the cups and head upstairs, at which point it hits me that Ella is going to probably be sleeping in my room. Not probably, but definitely. I can't lie, I've been thinking about it a lot. Who wouldn't? But I've pushed it out of my mind each time at the thought of Agnes's premonitions. Even before I knew what outcomes Agnes had predicted for us I'd been trying not to think about it in case Ella could somehow read my mind.

Ella goes to the bathroom and I sit at the edge of my bed, suddenly hot and nervous.

When she finally comes out, she gives me an expectant look and sits next to me on the bed and I'm both excited and terrified at the same time.

"Ella, is this really happening?" I ask somewhat stupidly. She smiles, and the room practically lights up.

"Yes, Curtis, this is definitely really happening," and she leans towards me. We kiss, but it's not like the strong electrifying kind. Everything about her is softer. Her expression, her lips, even the way she tugs at my shirt is gentle and coaxing.

My t-shirt ends up on the floor, and she runs her warm hands over my chest. This is about the time that I wish I had visited the gym at any point in my life. I've still got the muscles of a footballer, but they're mostly on my legs.

I slide her top over her shoulders, and she pushes her bare skin against my torso. I can't help my sharp intake of breath, and she stifles a giggle, but I'm laughing too so it's okay. As she moves her hands up my back I draw her into another kiss and enjoy the feeling of warmth that spreads from my face through the points where she's touching me.

The thought of Ella's overbearing sister probes its way into my head, and I freeze. Can she see us right now in one of her visions?

"Agnes—" I try to interrupt, pulling away and looking into her eyes.

"Shh, forget about Agnes. This is about you and me and nothing else. Just trust me. Can you do that?" I do, more than anyone I've trusted in my whole life. No question.

"Absolutely," I say and there's nothing more to discuss.

CHAPTER 9

I wake up to the sound of birds chirping outside my window and an unfamiliar weight on my leg. As I open my eyes I see Ella's blonde hair across my pillow, her head turned away from me. I almost want to pinch myself at the sight of her next to me. I can just make out the sound of her gentle breathing, still fast asleep, as the sun leaks through a gap in the curtains and falls across her bare shoulder. It's freezing in the house, and I can make out little goosebumps across the surface of her skin.

My eyes travel down the bed to find the cat purring softly at the foot of it, which would explain why my leg has gone to sleep. If it's light outside it must be some time after eight, I calculate, what with it being December. And although that's normally early for me to get up on a weekday, it seems I'm not getting back to sleep now. My bed is small and cramped for two, and I resolve to invest in a double when I next get paid. Hell, I might even ask Ella if she wants to move in with me somewhere away from the threat of my parents where it's just her and me. Too soon?

But then I realise that with the restaurant shut down for the time being I have no idea where the pay is going to come from, so I'll probably have to endure the watchful eye of my Mum and Dad for a while longer. Or I could move in with her? But the thought of living under the same roof as Agnes gives me a little bit of the creeps.

So, I have to add finding a new job as well as a new place to live to my worries. I don't want to be away from Ella for any minute of any hour of any day if I can help it. Last night was amazing and I could relive it every night for the rest of my life quite happily.

Cramped up against the wall, I have the sudden desperate need to move, but it doesn't look like I'll be able to do that without waking her.

I attempt to pull my arms and legs out of the duvet and slide to the end of the bed, but as the cat doesn't seem to want to move either, and I end up falling off all together with an audible, "Oof," sound.

She stirs and her eyes open. "Morning," she says, stretching.

"Sorry, I was trying not to wake you up," I say, clumsily pulling on a jumper and trousers. "Coffee?"

"That would be amazing," she yawns and the cat, giving up its spot at the end of the bed, decides to follow me.

"Oh, now you want to move," I tell him. He gives me his usual differential look and a swish of his tail before pushing past me down the stairs. The kitchen is as we left it last night, empty pizza boxes on the counter top and mugs on the draining board. I rinse them out to warm them up and put the kettle on before donning a pair of trainers I left by the back door to take the empty boxes out to the recycling bin outside. I unlock the door and the cold winter air hits me like a sledgehammer. My breath appears in front of my face like a cloud of smoke. Trying not to slip on the icy path, I shuffle down to the wheelie bin at the side of the house, which is almost frozen shut with the cold, yanking it open and sending particles of ice flying up towards me.

I wrestle with it for a moment, shoving the rubbish down inside and slapping the lid shut, only to shuffle back to the house. I can't have taken me more than two minutes in total to do all that, but I hear noises coming from upstairs and assume that Ella's already up and having a shower.

"That's odd," I say to myself as I notice the kettle didn't come on after all. I flick the useless switch a few times, then try a different plug socket to no avail. "Another power cut," I mutter to the cat, but when I turn around he's nowhere to be seen. There's a loud thump from upstairs and in a sudden paranoid panic I race up the stairs to check if everything is okay. Did Ella fall over in the shower, or is it something worse? There's no one in the bathroom, and I rush straight past the open door into my bedroom, thinking maybe she's fallen out of the bed, but the sight that greets me is worse than I expected. Ella is standing in the middle of my room, duvet held tightly to her body with one hand and a ball of glowing energy in the other, but to my horror it's what she's facing that scares me even more. A man in a black hoodie is standing in the corner, a lighter in one hand and his fingers aflame in the other. I try not to have a heart attack as I realise that one of the Magic Circle's members is currently standing in my bedroom in a face-off with my girlfriend. The cat is standing on my desk, back arched and practically spitting at him in fury.

"So, it's true, you're the Augur that doesn't need electricity to use their power?" he says, and his voice is hoarse, like someone who has inhaled too much smoke.

"Cigarette guy?" I say in shock, suddenly then realising how stupid I sound. "I mean, you're my bloody neighbour! What the hell are you doing in my house?" I shout at him.

"Curtis, stay out of this," Ella says quietly to me and I feel almost hurt by that.

"How do you know I'm not channeling electricity through the floor?" she asks him, her voice angrier than I've ever heard before.

"Because I caused a power cut about ten minutes ago. So, either you're Ella Chisholm or you're someone else who has that same ability. Which would be just as good as far as I'm concerned." He seems almost casual as he talks, as if his life isn't being threatened by another powerful Augur. My eyes watch the dancing ball of flame in his hand and a thought occurs to me. If he can manipulate fire using just a little cigarette lighter, then it could be possible he caused the fires in both the restaurant and Downing Street. But no, the world couldn't surely be so small that a pyromaniac Magic Circle member happens to be living on my street.

"Ha, well this isn't Ella Chisholm, so you've got that wrong," I say defiantly, sounding braver than I feel. Ella's eyes don't leave him, but I see her pull a face and realise I've probably said something stupid.

"Oh, right, of course. She changed her name, didn't she?" he says rhetorically. I spend a moment feeling confused until I realise that he's probably right. Ella could have easily changed her name after her parents died if she knew there were people looking for her, and no doubt Agnes made the whole thing happen. I feel slightly irritated by the fact that she didn't tell me, but now isn't the time to start having a domestic about it.

"What do you want?" Ella asks him through gritted teeth.

"To find one of the most powerful Augurs who's been hiding in plain sight," he smirks. "Which, thanks to your not-so-special boyfriend, wasn't that hard to do, actually."

"Hey!" I protest, feeling insulted.

"Listen, I'm not here to argue with you about your taste in men," he says to her, ignoring me, "but I am here to tell you about a proposition."

"You have nothing that would be of interest to me," Ella says cooly, and as she clicks her fingers a small spark of electricity flies off and hits him in the hand. He drops his lighter and swears, his power extinguished while he fumbles to pick it back up.

"Wait, wait!" he holds up placating hands as she makes to move towards him, her hand glowing even brighter. "I'm honestly not going to do anything to hurt you, I just need to talk to you, okay?"

"Curtis, grab the lighter," she says to me, and I do so trying not to look petrified.

"Just a minute of your time is all I need. If you don't like what I have to say I'll leave, but I think you need to hear this," he says sounding much less confident now his fingers aren't on fire and his source of energy has been taken away from him.

"I don't want to talk to you, whoever you really are," she says angrily.

"If I told you my name is Edward Clarence, would that change your mind?" he says hurriedly, the words almost tumbling over each other to get out of his mouth. Although that in itself doesn't mean anything to me, this obviously affects Ella in a way I didn't expect. Her jaw practically hangs open with surprise, before she checks herself and gives him an even fiercer look.

"You're lying," she says and takes another step towards him, small sparks flying from her fingers as she rubs them together.

I have no idea who Edward Clarence might be or what he might want with us, but if he knows something about the Magic Circle and what they're planning, or if there's even the slightest chance he might be able to help us get the information out about Carlton Munday, I feel we need to take it, even if Ella doesn't see it immediately.

"Ella," I try to say quietly, but there's no other noise in the room to obscure the sound of my voice, so I might as well be shouting. "I think we should hear him out. He might know something useful about, well, you know," I say, giving her a wide-eyed look and hoping she can somehow read my mind. She considers this for a second whilst not for a moment looking less annoyed, but eventually nods and lowers her hand. "You could at least have had the decency to knock on the door rather than barging in here like a criminal," she narrows her eyes at him, unimpressed. She's kind of scary when she's angry, and if I didn't find it so terrifying I'd probably enjoy it.

"Look, I needed to prove that it was really you before I said my piece, hence the power cut and the breaking and entering. I've been trying to find a way to get to you for a while now and couldn't believe my luck when you started going out with my neighbour," he nods sideways at me.

"You mean to say that you living next door to me was a coincidence?" I ask in disbelief.

"Kind of. I knew she was in the area. I've been looking for Ella Chisholm for the best part of five years, after I found out what had happened at the facility," he says and the look of shock on both of our faces is hard to hide. "I know about the facility for reasons that I can't go in to right now, but the important thing is that you, Ella, are in incredible danger."

"Tell me something I don't know," she says, sounding almost bored. I notice that the glowing in her fist has stopped too, so she's obviously not feeling like she's about to attack a defenceless Augur. "If you're really not here to hurt us then you can wait downstairs while I put some clothes on and start from the beginning." I realise that she's still clutching the duvet around her middle and apart from it being like a fridge in the house it's not the best circumstance to have a meeting. "And put the power back on, will you? It's bloody freezing," she says and waves us both out the door.

Five minutes later, our uninvited guest is in our kitchen, the kettle has boiled and despite wanting to smash him over the head with it, I'm handing him a mug of hot coffee. The cat decides to accompany me rather than stay with Ella, and as we sit in the kitchen with an air of awkwardness around us, he stares at the intruder from a spot on the kitchen counter with a look more disdainful than he's ever given me. It makes me feel quietly smug to know the cat is on my side.

"So," I say, breaking the silence, "do they call you 'Edward' or just 'Ed' for short?"

"Honestly, mate, no offence, but I have zero intention in being friendly with you," he says and sips his coffee loudly. That annoys me almost more than the fact that he broke into my house. Luckily, before I can make a nasty remark in return, Ella walks through the door in jeans and a thick jumper, her hair tied up in a loose knot.

"So, 'Edward Clarence'," she says, making inverted commas with her fingers, "why would the Duke's son, of all people, be hunting me down?" she throws herself into a kitchen chair like a sulky teenager and pulls the cup of coffee I set down towards her.

"What? The Duke as in *the Duke*?" I ask.

Edward sighs and barely acknowledges the question at first, but a look of daggers from Ella seems to prompt him to open his mouth.

"Yes. The Duke. Secretly an Augur and head of the Society, as you guys like to call yourselves. The ones who think they're saving all of Augur kind by stealing sensitive information from the government in order to prevent the exposure and registration of Augurs everywhere. AKA my father," he explains grimly.

"But you ran off and joined the Magic Circle, didn't you, Ed?" Ella says rather than asks. I had guessed as much, what with the black hoodie and criminal disposition, but knowing that he's also the Duke's son makes it a hell of a lot more disturbing.

"I'm not here to talk about me," he replies, his jaw tensing and his hand tightening around the grip of his coffee cup.

"So, what are you here to say?" she says impatiently.

"Listen, I know you don't like me and you don't have to, but the Magic Circle know everything, I mean *everything* that the Society, and my father, are planning. From his plan to leak the information about Carlton Munday to the press today, to him planning to use your boyfriend for the dirty work," he nods at me, again acting as though I'm not able to hear him. That's news to me and I try hard to mask my surprise.

"Even if that was true, and I'm not saying that it is, how could they possibly know that?" Ella asks him.

"Because your little group isn't as tight as he would like it to be, just like the Magic Circle is made up of a few people wanting to fight for Augurs' freedom and the rest are just lunatics and idiots who like to blow stuff up." I scoff at that statement.

"How could anything the Magic Circle does actually result in freedom for Augurs?" I ask him incredulously. He shoots me a look that only confirms his dislike for me.

"I wouldn't expect you to understand, Normal. Honestly, you people think you're so much better than us, but Normals are worse than Augurs. You're more violent, vindictive and ready to attack anything that comes near you. Like wild animals almost, but less intelligent." The insult is so childish, I know I shouldn't rise to the bait, but I stand up abruptly, ready to punch him right in the nose. I've never been much of a fighter, but his whole bravado makes me want to smash his perfect teeth down his throat. He rises slowly, like someone trying to calm an angry puppy, breaking into a smirk as he does so.

"What are you going to do? Scowl at me to death?" his smile has no warmth to it at all.

"You can get the hell out of my house, for a start," I realise my voice is rising.

"Or what?" He steps towards me, and as he does I can see the resemblance now between him and his father. Cold and calculating eyes, thin lips and although Edward's pallor probably isn't helped by his nicotine habit, he has the pale skin of someone that could only be descended from a long line of British ancestors. His accent is that of someone who has been well-educated rather than my slightly more softened Londoner.

"Or I'll call the bloody police, for a start," I say indignantly.

"What, and have them arrest your girlfriend too? I don't think so, 'mate'." He has me there and he knows it. We don't need the extra attention, and even if I told them he'd broken in he could probably say he saw suspicious Augur activity from outside the window. Ella would be arrested and tested or worse, because even if it wasn't public use of magic the police probably wouldn't hesitate to find a way to make it seem worse than it was. Whilst I try and think of a clever retort, Ella has pushed her way between us, both hands giving off a subtle glow that everyone can see.

"When you two have stopped with the 'who can be most irrational' contest, I'd like to get to the bottom of your reason for breaking and entering so that we can get on with our lives," she chides us like small children. Edward stares at me with all the disgust he can muster before sitting down in a huff. To my credit, I hold my own until he looks away, feeling like this is in some way a small victory for me, as juvenile as it sounds.

"As I was saying," Edward continues almost as if he was never interrupted, "there's a leak in your little group and someone is telling all your plans to a member of the Magic Circle. The reason I know this is because, despite what you guys may think, we're actually not all just a disorganised bunch of criminals."

"Why are you telling us all this?" Ella asks the question that I've been thinking.

"Because, as much as I might resent my father's efforts to control people, when I heard what happened to you all those years ago and how you lost your parents, I did vow to myself that I would do what it took to take down Augurism. It's been the only thing that made sense to me over the years."

I try not to scoff at his suggestion that he has any kind of moral compass.

"So why did you leave and join the Magic Circle?" I ask, trying not to sound as critical as I feel. Edward glances at me and narrows his eyes, as if sizing up whether or not to say anything more.

"Because, at the time, they were doing something about the problem. And because of my girlfriend..." he trails off and studies his cup for a moment. I feel like laughing at him for leaving his family, and probably a hefty inheritance, for the sake of a girl. But how is that any different to me getting involved with Ella and the Augurs, really? The answer is that it isn't really different at all, and I almost —almost —pity him.

"Look, five years ago the Magic Circle was a fairly organised group of intelligent Augurs who had members in key political positions. They were genuinely trying to make situations better for the rest of us and wanted to help Augurs everywhere. They levied for the prohibition of magic to be lifted, and although it's still illegal in London and other major cities, it's not anywhere else. That was them, although they weren't calling themselves the Magic Circle at that point, or not publicly. I joined off the back of a bad argument with my father about how, no matter how good his intentions were, he was more interested in PR than people.

"But then we lost our leader and things got out of hand. The executives appointed to hold the group together end up disagreeing and arguing, and everyone wound up going in different directions. That's when the attacks started happening and, rather than making peace between Normals and Augurs possible, they are making things worse, without a doubt."

"You say 'we' and 'they' like you haven't quite figured out whether you're in or out," Ella observes.

Edward pauses again before answering. He's like a pot that is ready to boil over at any moment, the slightest change of temperature and he could explode. But to my surprise, instead of blowing up and telling her to keep her nose out, he replies sadly. "To tell the truth I haven't. Cassie — my girlfriend — well she left a couple of months ago and I've been on the fence ever since."

Ella gives him a sympathetic look, but I'm not convinced.

"So, is your being on the fence the reason that you're here?" I say, trying to take the irritation out of my voice.

"Pretty much," he shrugs. "Look, thanks to someone in the Society, everyone in the Magic Circle knows that the Duke is planning to use you to expose Carlton Munday's connections to Augurs, " he says nodding at me. This time I can't hide my expression. "Yes, that's right. The fact that you're on board and have been accepted, at least tentatively, into their group isn't out of the goodness of their hearts. It's because from the moment my father found out about your existence, he planned a way to use you." He leans back in his

267

chair and crosses his arms while I digest that information. I look at Ella for answers, but she frowns and gives me a look that says, 'news to me' so is no help.

"You think that the Duke wants to use me, a Normal, to expose Carlton Munday to the press?" I ask incredulously.

"That's right. I would go and tell you to see him just to prove my point, except that's exactly what I'm here to tell you not to do," he says matter-of-factly.

"But that's crazy. He didn't even know I existed until yesterday," I retort.

"I don't think so. He knew that there was a Normal starting to get involved with Ella from the moment it happened. I told you, the Society is full of holes, and someone is keeping a very close eye on you both."

Ella keeps silent for quite a while, obviously working through his argument in her head. She inspects the inside of her coffee cup whilst chewing her bottom lip — something I've seen her do several times when she's thinking hard.

"Whether I believe you or not — and I'm not saying that I do — the only way to really prove it is to actually go and see the Duke ourselves," she says finally.

"Don't do that! That's the whole reason for me coming here!" Edward bursts out.

"Ed, listen, we appreciate that efforts you have gone to to track me down, but I don't really see what choice we have. We can't just up and disappear just because Curtis may or may not be sent on an errand for the Duke. It's illogical and there's much more at stake," she tries to reason.

"But you'll be doing exactly what he wants you to! I know that if Curtis carries out even the simplest part of his plan it will end up in disaster," he bangs his fist on the table and it makes the cups rattle.

"How can you possibly be sure of that?" Ella argues.

"Because I know him! His end game always has been and always will be for Augurs to end up not just equals with Normals but in charge of them, 'like in the old days' he always said to me as child. My entire life I've had it drummed into me that Augurs are the superior race and therefore should be running the world. But because we've always been the minority, we've been squashed by our sheer lack of numbers and the fear and hate that Normals have created against us. It's not Carlton Munday I'm worried about, it's *you*," he points fiercely at her. I can't read Ella's expression to tell whether she's worried, scared or angry. A mix of emotions seems to cross her face as if she's internally wrestling with herself. I notice that her fingertips are glowing faintly again and I'm not sure if this is because she feels threatened or just can't control it.

"Look, you don't owe me anything," he says, trying to calm his voice down, "but — God, they're going to kill me for saying this — at the last Magic

Circle meeting I heard that they needed you for the next step of their plan."

"Did they actually say her name?" I ask him.

"Well, no, they said, 'the power-source,' but there's only one of those that I've ever heard of, and that's Ella," he replies defensively.

"Doesn't prove anything," I point out, although it's not sounding good and even I can see that it would be stupid not to be more careful right about now.

"Arguing about it isn't going to make a difference," Ella says abruptly, getting up and putting the cups in the sink. "I appreciate your time, Edward, and your consideration. I can imagine that tracking me down and coming here was a big risk for you and I don't want you think that it was a waste, because it wasn't."

"So, you guys will get out of town?" he asks hopefully.

"I don't know what we're going to do yet," she admits and looks at me, but I'm no help at all right now.

"Let me put it this way: if you don't, then bad things are going to happen, that much I know. If you were just to disappear one day and cut all your ties to the Society they'd be stuck. Although they haven't directly asked you to do anything yet, I could bet my life that whatever they're planning will require your powers." He makes a move to leave, through the front door this time, and barely says goodbye as he walks down the path, lighting up a cigarette when he gets to the front gate. I close the door and turn to look at Ella, who looks tired and serious now.

"What do you want to do?" I ask her.

"Have a shower and breakfast. Then we'll have to figure out what our next move is," she says, climbing the stairs. I make a bowl of cereal and sit in the kitchen while I wait for her, pushing thoughts around in my mind like an intricate pattern of marbles. The Duke and his prodigal son are the first thing I think of. Their poor relationship isn't actually that different to mine and Dad's. He's heavily opinionated and thinks only of himself. The Duke seems to be similar in so many ways, but with a lot more power, money and influence.

If the Duke really wants Augurs to take over, how on Earth could he do that? Carlton Munday, the politician that has rattled all of the Augurs and is threatening their security, is the obvious target for both the Magic Circle and for the Society. And here we are, Ella and I, stuck in the middle of all of it without knowing what to do. The thought of running away somewhere suddenly becomes the most appealing option, particularly when it's her they're after. I know that no matter what happened, she would never use her powers to hurt people, but she could be put in a position whereby she didn't have a choice.

"Do you think it was him who set fire to Downing Street and Gregorio's?" I ask her as she comes back downstairs, hair damp from the shower.

"I doubt it. If he's half in and half out, I doubt he'd do something as risky as that. Bear in mind they have more than a hundred members."

I think about the Society, no more than about twenty members from what I could see if you include Mulberry and the Duke. How the hell do they stand a chance?

"Wow, some deep thoughts going on there," she comes in and taps her index finger on my temple. I take her hand and kiss it and she slides her other arm round my shoulders from behind in a hug.

"I love you, Curtis," she says quietly, her face resting next to mine.

"I love you too," I say, but I can't push out a feeling of dread that is starting to form in the pit of my stomach.

"We're going to be okay, you know that, right?" she says, pulling away and coming round to perch on the side of the kitchen table so she can see my face.

"I hope so," I sigh, and get up to go shower. "Help yourself to cereal or whatever you want," I say as I walk upstairs. I wish I could believe her, but I can't shake the feeling that something bad is about to happen.

CHAPTER 10

An hour later we're standing outside the Duke's townhouse, and I feel like I'm going to be sick.

"Are you sure about this?" I ask, searching her face for any sign of doubt.

"Positive. Despite what Edward said, this really is the only way that we can be sure of the Duke's intentions. I don't like the secrets and the hiding, and he's been kind to me since I ended up here, so I think this is the right thing to do." She looks confident and resolute, so despite my feelings I know I'm going to have to go along with it, unable to convince her otherwise.

Mulberry opens the door with his usual sharpness and lets us in. He isn't as dismissive of me this time as he was before; he actually asks me for my coat rather than asking Ella, and I think maybe I'm coming up in his estimation somehow.

We're shown up the stairs to the Duke's study, and my phone goes in the bowl just as before, right before we enter the room. The Duke isn't at his desk but is instead sitting in an armchair with a book by the fireplace which is roaring away, making the whole space warm and cosy.

"Ah, Ella, my dear. Come in, come in and have a seat," he snaps the book shut and places it on a table, standing up to greet her and giving her a kiss on each cheek. "Curtis, good to see you again, lad," he shakes my hand and gestures for me to sit down also, and we each sit in a large armchair. "Well, I did hear most of the account of yesterday from Jeremy. That dear boy came over late last night to tell me what you had discovered at the hospital and the restaurant, but I assume you want to give me your own account of things?" he looks at Ella expectantly and I realise that I am once again relegated to letting her do all the talking. She doesn't give away any of the real reason that we're here in her account of yesterday's events, nor does she leave any details out. I'm slightly embarrassed and horrified to hear her description of how we managed to distract the police at the scene of the fire, but she makes me come off well in it, as if I was the sole reason for them getting the all-important information they were looking for.

When she finishes, the Duke leans back in his armchair and steeples his fingers for a moment, inspecting us both from his chair. Eventually he nods. "Very good, both of you. That is the information we really needed. Once Jeremy came to see me last night, I asked him to visit Downing Street to see what he could pick up on the attack there. He telephoned me from there and, although briefly, confirmed my suspicions. As it transpires, the same Augur who is responsible for the attack on Gregorio's was also present at the scene of the explosion, and he thinks he has found another connection between one of the girls that was there with an attack in a small village a few weeks ago. So, there's no doubt about it, stopping the Magic

Circle, along with exposing Carlton Munday for the fraud he is, are now our top priorities." He speaks with authority, like a player who knows exactly what their next ten moves in chess are going to be with certainty. I can see why Edward and he don't get along; it would be impossible to change his mind on anything.

"What did you have in mind, your Grace?" Ella asks, using his formal address.

"Well, initially I had planned to have Lou visit our Augur sympathiser at the papers, but with the PM and her deputy in hospital I worry that either the Magic Circle have done us an inadvertent favour by delaying the talks or, more likely, have created a catalyst for having new Augur laws passed. At such a delicate time it might be better, and faster, if a Normal does that particular duty for us. It also means that I can ask Lou to do something else equally important," he says, without elaborating on what that thing might be. He looks at me, and I feel compelled to say something, but on Ella's strict instruction I keep my mouth shut. "Curtis, what would you say to potentially running an errand for the good of all mankind?" he asks me, trying to sound casual. But his cold eyes are steadily fixed on me, as if trying to pin me to the backrest of the chair I'm sitting in. I can't look at Ella because I know that would probably make things worse somehow. I nod slowly, meeting his stare. "O-of c-course, your Grace," I stutter, mentally kicking myself for sounding so uncertain.

"Very good," he gives me an unfriendly smile. "Very good, indeed. I will require you to take the drive that I know Ella has so safely stashed away somewhere to a friend of the Society's. I shall write down two addresses for you, but you'll need to memorise them and then we shall throw the paper in the fireplace. These people have agreed to help our cause, and the first is my best kept secret," the Duke's voice drops to a whisper, as if the bookshelves might overhear him, "and I don't want him falling into the wrong hands. Visit my friend here and tell him I sent you. He will take the drive and put the information we need for the press onto one drive, and the information that we *don't* want given to the press on another. Ella, you are to look after the second, and Curtis, you will be custodian of the first. He will securely erase the data from the drive you give him so that we don't have that information in too many places, and once you have done that you will need to take it directly to the second address I give you.

"This person is absolutely hell-bent on exposing Munday as much as we are and will do exactly what we need to make sure that any laws Munday tries to pass are disregarded due to his bias in the situation."

"Your Grace, do you know what's actually on the stick?" Ella asks, feigning curiosity.

"My girl, I know that the Augur that obtained that information ended up dying for it. I don't personally know, oh no. To be in my position and have sensitive information such as this would no doubt compromise my status. You know as well as anybody in the Society that I take a risk on a daily basis just by hiding my true identity. But I have been told that it would bring down the empire that Munday has tried to create with such ferocity that no one would be willing to believe a word the man then says.

"It's difficult to know when you aren't always on the front lines how much pain he has caused for Augurs. True, initially he was given the position of Civil Defence Minister because he showed himself to be capable of making unbiased decisions for the protection of all citizens, both Augurs and Normals. But it has become clear over the years that this is nothing but a front and a ploy to raise him in power.

"I've never revealed this to anyone," he says, leaning forward and looking at us conspiratorially, his beady eyes darting between myself and Ella as if to make sure he has our undivided attention, "but I discovered that the reason for Munday's success was because he had direct involvement with the Facility."

Ella can't disguise her shock, although I'm sure she tries. The Duke nods in affirmation, "Yes, I'm sure of it now. The brutal experiments that so many of us were subjected to were instigated by him," he sighs and clenches his fists as if wrestling with the thought of all those Augurs being tortured. But I doubt that he, in his fancy office with his Royal connections and title, was ever subjected to any pain at the hands of Munday or the facility. Not like Ella and certainly not like her parents, who would probably still be alive if the place had never existed.

I realise what kind of a position this puts Ella in. She can't *not* help now, no matter what Edward thinks about his father or how much danger it might put us in. If Munday is connected in some way to her parents' death, then I'm sure she'll stop at nothing to put him away.

"But, your Grace," she finally manages to say, "I thought everyone connected with all that was arrested at the time?"

"Not everyone, my dear. It took me years to figure out who Munday was really, and if the information on that drive is what I've been told it is, then we have the proof to put him behind bars for a very, very long time." In the silence that follows, the only sounds are the ticking of a large clock on one of the shelves and the crackle of the fire. It would be a peaceful sort of a sound if things weren't currently so awful, and it brings me no comfort as I sit contemplating the rock and the hard place that we seem to have gotten ourselves stuck in the middle of.

"But now, the best cure for this particular malady is going to be a good dose of action," the Duke says, slapping his knees. He stands, and we follow suit, taking it as our cue to be prepared to leave. Walking over to the desk that is still littered with papers, he takes an expensive-looking pen and writes several lines on a small thick card. He hands it to me and I read the two addresses, showing them to Ella as I do so. She nods when she feels she can remember them and I try desperately to commit them to my own memory before tossing the card into the fireplace. The whole thing feels like a strange ritual, and watching the card brown and curl up at the edges until it disappears is almost like an omen in itself.

"Ella, I would ask that you accompany Curtis for the first meeting. My contact is not the trusting type, and he'll want some proof that you are an Augur before doing anything for you.

"However, I insist that you keep well clear for the second meeting. I don't want you within a square mile of that building when Curtis is handing the information over. Do you understand?" he asks, his expression serious.

"Of course, your Grace. I understand," she says quietly, "but how will your first contact know that we are representing you and aren't some people from the Magic Circle?"

"Ah, of course. Show him this," the Duke fishes out an object from his desk drawer. It's a pocket knife with a delicately carved handle set with mother of pearl, and Ella barely looks at it as she passes it to me for safe keeping.

With another kiss on each cheek for her and a hearty handshake for me, we leave the magnificent study, me with a pit in my stomach that only feels like it's getting deeper with each step.

"Well," I say when we are far out of sight of the Duke's house and marching through the throngs of London shoppers on Regent Street, "now I really don't know what to think."

"I do," says Ella, keeping her eyes firmly ahead of her and speaking with a low voice. She threads her arm through mine so that we don't separate in the crowds, and I welcome the feeling. She's like an anchor keeping me firmly fixed to the ground, and I never seem to feel like it's all getting too much, even when it obviously should be. Any sane person would have gone completely mad by now with the pressure, the surprises and the constant threats to our survival. But, I muse to myself, that just goes to show that I can't have been completely sane to start off with. What's that line from *Alice in Wonderland*? *We're all mad here… All the best people are.*

"So, he tells us to do exactly what Edward warned us against, but we're going to do it anyway?" I ask, already knowing the answer.

"I don't see what choice we have, Curtis," she replies sadly. We veer around a group of tourists taking selfies outside Hamleys, and I think how nice it must be to go somewhere completely different, a total change of environment, not just for a holiday but for good. We could go to France or Spain or even to Africa. I hear that Augurs are actually respected over there, and although in most of Europe magic is restricted, I'm sure they must be more lenient than here.

"Okay, this may sound crazy," I blurt out, pulling her to one side and stopping for a moment in a closed doorway, allowing the strangers to pass us by. "Why don't we just take off? Go somewhere that no one knows us and start over? Where you can, you know, be yourself," I say quietly. Ella gives me a sympathetic look and then to my surprise she kisses me hard on the mouth. I welcome the feeling that it brings, a warmth inside me as I kiss her back, my hands finding their place around her waist. When she pulls away, she keeps her face just inches from mine.

"Curtis, I'm sorry about all of this, I really am. But I can't run away. Apart from the fact that it would be letting all of my friends down, I can't leave the country. I mean physically I can't leave the country. I've no passport, and it's been the law for decades that if you are an Augur you have to have it printed on your ID. I've never left England because it would mean that there would be some record of my existence on the government database. My parents almost didn't bother with birth certificates for Agnes and me, that's how mad it was.

"Look, if you don't want to do this, it's not a problem to me. I'll tell the Duke that we've broken up and that you won't be helping us any more—"

"Oh my God, Ella, please don't say things like that," I say and hold her all the more tightly. "I told you that I'm here for good, whether you like it or not. If you told the Duke that we weren't together, no matter whether that was true or not, he'd probably send Mumbe to come and finish the job he started on me yesterday. I want to help you, all of the Augurs, but I just can't stand seeing your life being taken away from you by the constant fight for other people!" I sigh irritably and place my forehead against hers. "I just think that we've gotten ourselves into something and I don't see a way out."

"I know, I know," she says, placing her hands on each side of my face, "I can't say I'm sorry enough, alright?"

"Ella, I don't want an apology from you — it's not even your fault, I just wish that there was some way to get out of doing their dirty work without endangering your life," I say, feeling an anger rise in my chest that isn't aimed at her, but at the stupidity of it all. "I may not like where we're going, but I'm not giving up. For as long as you're willing to put up with the danger, I'm willing to stick it out with you. But please, please promise me that if at any point you genuinely see a way out, you'll take it, alright?"

"I promise. And you promise *me* that if at any point you feel like you can't handle this life anymore you'll run as fast as you can away from us and never look back, okay?" The vow she's asking me to make is impossible for me to keep. I'd never leave her now, and I know it. I run my hands nervously through my hair and she gives me a look that stops me half way through the motion. I can't help but laugh. "Sorry, sorry. Look, I can't promise you that I'll ever run away but I can promise you that I'll never get to the point where I can't handle it, so help me God." She gives me another kiss as if to seal the deal and we head toward Piccadilly Circus where we can take the Underground to our first stop.

The Duke no doubt expects us to go to wherever the drive is stashed and retrieve it before visiting his 'contact', but he doesn't realise that Ella has been keeping it on her the entire time, so there's no need to make any extra stops.

The first address I memorised is in Golders Green which is straight up North from where we are by about half an hour. Although Ella advises against it, I use the map on my phone to at least find the general area of the postcode, as I'd be lost otherwise. I can't imagine that any spies will be checking out my browsing history any time soon and I doubt that my phone is on MI5's most wanted list, so I figure that it's fairly harmless.

The map takes us from the tube station down the main road and into a network of terraced houses, cramped together and in need of repair. The area itself is generally quite nice, so I'm surprised to find the house in question looks dilapidated. The windows evidently haven't been cleaned in at least a decade and ancient net curtains that hang in the front are grey with age. There are three buzzers at the front door, which means that the house has been split into apartments, which isn't uncommon in most of London, but the outside of the house almost looks two small to house three separate flats. The paint on the front door is peeled off, although it looks like at some point it was painted blue, maybe in the 80's. There are scratches around the front door keyhole and there are round dents which look like someone has tried to bash it in a few times.

"Which bell is it?" I say, looking at the three buzzers, none of which have names on them. Ella peers at them for a few moments before taking a calculated guess and trying the top one. There's no intercom so if it's not right we'll find out soon enough. After a moment we hear a door open and a scrape of feet on carpeted floor. The door is unlocked and opens just a crack, the chain still in place as a precaution.

"Hello?" comes a quavering, elderly voice.

"Sorry to trouble you, Madam, but a friend told us this was the house of Marvin. Did we get the right address?" Ella asks with such sincerity you'd have to be mad not to want to trust her.

"Oh, that boy," the lady says crossly. "Yes, yes, his flat is upstairs, but I don't know if he's in. It's the second buzzer if you want to try," she offers. I can see a milky green eye examining us through the space between the door, and although it's an old voice with cataract vision there's an alertness there, as if she's used to having to fend people off.

Ella pushes the middle buzzer and we can hear it ring somewhere above our heads. The bay window above us looks down onto the doorstep and there's a twitch of a net curtain, although I don't actually catch a glimpse of anyone.

"Hmm. Sounds like he might not be in, sorry my dear," the lady says, closing the door and locking it behind her before we can protest.

"Well that didn't go so well," Ella says to me.

"But he's there —I saw something in the upstairs window so he's probably just hiding from us. Want to, you know, do your thing?" I suggest, not wanting to get her into trouble but not seeing any other way.

"You think that's really a good idea out in the open like this?"

"Well, the Duke did say that he'd want some proof that you were, you know."

"There's a lot of 'you knows' in there, Curtis. We're going to have to figure out some kind of code," she jokes, but I can see she's working out the best way to proceed. We listen in silence for a moment to check that there's no one waiting on the other side of the door and when we're confident the old lady has returned to her flat Ella places her hands flat against the door, top and bottom of where the locks should be. Within seconds I hear the chain sliding back in its place and the latch lifting up, and all it takes is a gentle nudge from me for the door to open. The stale smell of old cooking that has ingrained itself into the wallpaper and carpets hits us as we enter, and I let Ella take the lead as I close the door silently behind me.

We tiptoe past the door to the ground floor flat and step lightly on each step on the staircase, keeping to the sides where the wood is less worn and therefore unlikely to creak as much. On the first landing, which is where I assume Marvin is living based on where his window was, is a door that was painted white some decades ago but is now an off yellow colour. The locks look brand-new though, and I wonder if he has to get them changed often.

"What now?" Ella asks me, whispering.

"You're asking me?" I say, taken aback.

"This is technically your mission, so I'm going to let you take the lead."

"Bloody hell. Okay, I would say best to use your mojo again, but we have no idea what this guy is like. He could be standing on the other side of the door with a gun in his hand or he could be about to dive out the window at the first sign of trouble."

"So? What's the plan?"

"Argh. Okay, open it, but be ready for trouble," I sigh, not sure if I'm making the right call at all. I'm not really used to being put into the position where I have to call the shots. Ella places her hands on the door like before but this time she frowns with the effort.

"There's at least eight separate locks I'd reckon," she says. "Not impossible but not great either —as I've no idea where they are I could just as easily take the door off its hinges by accident."

"Blimey, this guy is tough on security. Do you want to give it a go or should we try knocking?"

"Let's give him the benefit of the doubt," she says, and gives the door a light rap with her knuckles.

To our astonishment the bolts start sliding back. There are indeed eight locks of various types, some that require keys from inside and others that appear to need passwords, as we can hear the pushing of buttons from behind the door. Eventually the door opens to reveal a pasty-faced man with greasy blonde hair and an impressive beard.

"Come in, quickly!" he hisses and opens the door wide enough for us to pass through, closing it definitively behind us and re-locking it, which takes nearly a minute in itself. The flat smells like unwashed body, and although there isn't much more to see than a corridor with two doorways branching off it, I suspect that if we were to go into them we would find more dirty laundry than a launderette.

"So?" the man I presume can only be Marvin says to us, his hands placed on his wide hips.

"So, er, hello," I say holding my hand out for him to shake. He looks at it but doesn't take it.

"Names first," he says, ignoring my proffered hand.

"I'm Curtis, Curtis Mayes," I say, dropping my hand to my side.

"Ella Cooper," Ella says not bothering to put out a hand but instead folding her arms and looking at him impatiently. She's not yet given up using her alias, it seems.

"Marvin, no last name. You have something to show me?" he says abruptly. He's not the most likeable guy, I observe, lacking some of the social niceties we've become accustomed to. Evidently, he doesn't get out that much.

I fish into my pocket and pull out the switchblade that the Duke gave us and hand it to him, although I feel unsure as to whether handing a knife to him is a good idea or not. He grabs it from me and flicks it open, inspecting it for a few moments before closing it up and handing it back to me. "And the drive?"

This time Ella fishes around in her pocket and pulls out the small silver oblong, handing it to him with a similar amount of reservation.

He squeezes past us to a doorway through which he can just fit, without inviting us to follow him, but we do anyway. The room, which would otherwise be considered a living room to any normal person, looks like the inside of a dilapidated space ship. A large desk runs along each wall with several computers on, under and above each. There are no less than ten different screens, some on, some off and one playing cartoons with the volume on low. Marvin sits on a chair which looks far too small to accommodate his weight and wheels from one machine to another, eventually settling on one that he taps furiously at before plugging the USB drive into the computer. He rolls over to a drawer on the other side of the room and scoops out two more USB sticks, one in the shape of a teddy bear and the other a plain red plastic item. Whisking back over to the computer he started at, he plugs the drives into a little box with dozens of ports in it and hits the keyboard several times with enthusiasm. He doesn't bother to give us a running commentary of what he's doing, but he does murmur a little while he's working. I get the general gist that he's trying to use an isolated and un-networked computer to do the job of transferring the data onto two separate drives. As far as my basic knowledge of computers goes, I take this to mean that the data can't be accidentally hacked or retrieved if it isn't connected to anything else. It takes him all of about five minutes, and it would have taken less, he tells us, if he hadn't had to decrypt his own encryption.

"You encrypted it originally? So, you supplied the information in the first place?" I ask, realising that this is the mysterious source of the data that the Duke was so unwilling to share.

"Yeah, well sort of. Me and one of you," he says, meaning an Augur I'm guessing. "Interesting girl, but she was killed." That was what the Duke had said, yet Marvin says it as if it was just another day at the office. I'm sad for her, whoever she was. "I told him at the time that it made no sense to put all his eggs in one basket, but he didn't listen. So, I made it virtually unhackable, even by me," he boasts. I make a noise that sounds like I'm impressed although I'm only vaguely listening, my mind still on the Augur that lost her life.

"This one's for the papers," he says, pulling out the teddy shaped USB stick and handing it over his shoulder without looking at who is going to relieve him of it. I take it begrudgingly, wishing that he'd given me the slightly better looking one for my errand, particularly as it's designed so that the silver flash-drive section sticks out of the bear's bottom. "This one's for whoever he's decided to give it to," he pulls out the red one and Ella takes it over his shoulder. He scratches at a pockmark on his cheek absentmindedly, a gesture he's probably done several times by the looks of the scars on his face, and spins around to look at us.

"Whatever happens, the red one doesn't go back to him. And nothing is traced back to me," Marvin says to us. We both nod emphatically. I've got no reason to grass on him and neither does Ella, so I don't see any problem with keeping that particular promise. I don't know why anyone would be worried about a geeky normal helping out a bunch of Augurs really, but then I think about myself. It's no different to what I'm doing when you look at it. Fighting a fight that anyone would say isn't really mine but so obviously is. Ultimately, we're not fighting for Augurs against Normals, but for fundamental human rights. That feels a little deep, even for me, but it gives me an appreciation for Marvin who is evidently doing just the same: doing what people may think is wrong, but for all the right reasons.

"One last thing," he says as he gestures to the door, a signal I take to mean that he wants us to go, "don't trust anyone. Really. Not even each other." Ella and I nod with something less than enthusiasm and he goes back to the business of unlocking every bolt and passcode until we're finally out. Without even a grunt by way of goodbye, the door shuts behind us and we hear everything sliding back into place with a sense of finality.

CHAPTER 11

"Well," Ella says, inhaling a deep breath of fresh air, "that went off surprisingly without a hitch."

"Don't speak too soon," I say, eyeing a police car that has come around the corner. We try to look inconspicuous, her hand in mine in deep conversation like a couple that have nothing to hide. The car cruises by without incident, but it doesn't stop me from exhaling when it's out of sight, and I realise I've been clutching the teddy bear USB drive in my fist tightly. The last thing we need at this point is to draw any unwanted attention, and if Marvin is the kind of guy I think he is then he might have already been on a few of the 'most wanted' lists for some cyber crime or another. If he supplied the data to the Duke in the first place, then no doubt he ended up in a few databases that he shouldn't have.

"Hey, Earth to Curtis," Ella says, squeezing my other hand.

"Sorry, just wondering how he managed to get the data in the first place," I say, nodding at my pocket.

"I can make a calculated guess," she says, looking equally unhappy about it. "No time to worry about that now. It's show time," she says as we walk back to the underground station. I feel like I've spent more of the past few days on the Tube than I have in the past few years. At least there's something constantly homely and familiar about the London transport system, and as we gently sway back and forward on our way to our next station I feel grateful for the anonymity that living in the city can bring. No one else on our crowded train cares who we are, where we're going or what we've done. They're just trying to get to one place or another, usually reading something, texting or sleeping.

Our next stop is High Street Kensington, and after two changes we decide to grab some lunch just outside the busy station. I welcome the feeling of food in my stomach, even if it's just a sandwich and a cup of coffee.

"Where are you going to go while I make the drop?" I ask, trying to sound cool. I have to admit, saying 'make the drop' alone adds some kind of credibility to what I'm doing.

"What do you mean, silly? I'll be keeping a very close eye on you," she says, taking a mouthful of her own sandwich.

"But the Duke said—"

"I know what he said, Curtis, but you don't think for a second I'm going to let you out of my sight, do you?"

"Well, I admit that I'll feel better if I know you're nearby. But I don't want anyone to catch a glimpse of you in case anything goes wrong."

"No problem. We'll find a good spot that I can spy on you from, but don't say things like that — nothing is going to go wrong," she gives me a smile, and that simple gesture alone makes me believe her totally. We finish our late lunch and wander in the direction of the newspaper offices which are located down a side street next to one of the large department stores. It looks like over the years all the bigger stores have been split up into smaller units, and lucky for us there's a cafe that almost looks directly into the main reception where I'll have to wait. I watch her go in, grab a magazine from the news rack and order herself a tea, positioning her body so that she can look over the top of the page without seeming suspicious.

For some reason my palms are sweaty as I walk through the revolving door and into the main lobby. It's modern but slightly shabby, like it was designed with the future in mind but actually decorated in the nineties. There are two uncomfortable looking armchairs, all metal and grey leather. The walls are black marble and the floor is cream marble, with a few potted plants dotted about the place. On the left wall there hangs a huge montage of various headlines from the past century, on the right is a wide half-desk that comes up to my chest. A disinterested receptionist is on the phone, typing at her computer and chewing gum simultaneously. Her eyes flick up from her screen for a second, and she nods briefly to signify that she's seen me.

"…I understand, Mr. Barker, but you're just going to have to send an email. No, I'm sorry, he's not available to speak to on the phone. I understand you don't know how to use a computer, but I'm afraid that's not really my— okay, yes, a letter will do the trick. To the regular address, yes. I'll make sure he sees it, Mr. Barker. Okay, thank you, take care, goodbye." She finally hangs up and looks up at me whilst still typing on her computer.

"How can I help?" she asks without sounding like she actually wants to help at all.

"Er, I'm supposed to see Mr. Avers here?"

"I'm not sure if he's in the building, but I'll try his desk for you. Do you have an appointment?"

Do I? Somehow the Duke failed to mention it if I did, and so I take a wild guess.

"Yes, he's expecting me," I try to lie smoothly, forcing myself not to run my hand through my hair.

Avers, of course, has no idea who I am, and the thought occurs to me that he'll easily turn me away if I tell them my real name.

The receptionist picks up the handset and seems to get through.

"Matthew? Your afternoon appointment is here," she says, tapping her pen impatiently on her desk. She listens to something and glances up at me, covering the mouthpiece and whispering, "Edward Clarence, right?"

I try to hide my surprise by nodding eagerly. Why does Edward have an appointment to see Avers? And, more importantly, how the hell am I going to pull off being a white, blonde noble-born bastard?

If she's suspicious in any way, she doesn't show it.

"Great, I'll send him up," she says, sounding as bored as possible as she replaces the receiver in its cradle.

"Sign the log please," she says to me without further explanation. A crude visitor's log lays open on the counter and I fill it in and sign it as E. Clarence to keep the charade going, but she doesn't even look at it. "Into the lift, third floor, third right, Mr. Clarence," she says, pointing to the end of the lobby. I thank her and follow her instructions, stepping out of the lift onto the third floor and finding myself in a long corridor with grey carpets and magnolia walls. If no expense was spared on the lobby, it certainly was here. I walk past each one slowly, examining the names. Why did Edward have an appointment with a reporter? Was he supposed to be doing this dirty work for the Duke rather than me? My thoughts are a jumble and I try to reconcile them before I put on the biggest charade of my life.

There are seven doors leading off from the corridor, three on each side and one at the end, but

I do as I'm told and knock on the third. A voice tells me to come in and I find the small space occupied mostly by papers, files and coffee cups. There's a decent sized computer on the desk and a thin black man sitting behind it. He stands up to greet me and I shake his hand, already liking his warm greeting a million times over Marvin's cold one earlier.

"Nice to meet you, Mr. Clarence. Please, have a seat," he gestures to a solitary visitor's chair that faces his desk. He walks around me to close the door, but not before checking the corridor to see if there was anyone behind me.

"I must say, I was surprised to hear that you decided to visit me in person," he says, assuming, I suppose, that I am indeed Edward Clarence.

"Oh, I'm sorry—" I begin to say, but then I catch myself. Visit him in person? How else was this supposed to go down? I don't look anything like him. For starters I'm half West-Indian and Edward comes from a pure line of British ancestry. I guess in the winter months you could say I just look like a tanned white person, but even that's stretching it a bit.

"No need to apologise, I'm excited to hear what you have to tell me about the Magic Circle and the Society, as you said it was called. It's certainly better to discuss these things face to face rather than over the phone, and far more secure, I'd say," he goes on, oblivious to my hesitation.

"Yes, of course," I say, not sure where to take the conversation. This meeting evidently *wasn't* an errand for the Duke. It was obvious this morning that Edward wasn't happy with the Magic Circle and was equally pissed at his father, so it shouldn't be any surprise that he wants someone to publish a story about it. But why would he pick this particular reporter, this particular paper? The same one his father has chosen to expose Carlton Munday for whatever crimes he may be guilty of?

"Matthew, can I call you Matthew?" I ask, to which he nods and smiles, "I think I have access to some very, very interesting information. The problem is I need to know that if I give it to you

you're going to do what's needed with it to make it known," I lean forward and lower my voice a little. I push my accent to the limits of how posh I can get it, imitating Edward's clipped Chelsea-boy inflection.

"Well, that's what I'm here for. You know, for years I've been wondering if there was more to the Magic Circle than the general public knew, but now that you've as good as confirmed it to me, I'm sure that they're connected to the Society, although I'm still waiting for proof that that particular group exists. Did you bring the list of members you were mentioning?" he asks me excitedly.

I have to think fast. Edward told him about the existence of the Society, which means that he was going to supply him with a list of names of members to prove it. That includes, no doubt, Ella's name, as well as Agnes and Jer, which is not good at all.

"I'm still trying to get my hands on that info, Matthew. But I do have something that might be of even more interest to you," I say, fingering the teddy bear USB stick in my pocket.

"I hope you are going to deliver on that promise, though, as it would make an amazing story: SECRET AUGUR SOCIETY COLLIDES WITH MAGIC CIRCLE," he says, reading an invisible headline in front of his face and gesticulating dramatically. He seems like a nice guy, but I can see that his primary concern is getting a good story, and somehow I need to turn that to my advantage.

"Yes, absolutely, of course. But what if I could get you proof that an even bigger conspiracy exists?" I ask, trying to catch his attention. He arches an eyebrow and wakes up his computer, I imagine to open up a document and take notes.

"What kind of conspiracy?"

"Well, I've come across some information that implicates the Civil Defence Minister in a number of inhumane Augur experiments, amongst other things," I say, wracking my brains for something better to say. Of course, I don't really know what's on the USB drive, but I've gathered bits and pieces from the Duke and Ella which all sounded pretty alarming to me. Maybe something will make this curious reporter bite.

"You mean Carlton Munday? He's actually acting Prime Minister now," Matthew says casually, fingers poised above the keyboard waiting for me to say something worth him writing down.

"What?"

"Yes, well, with the attack on Downing Street yesterday and both the PM and deputy PM in hospital, he's acting in their stead right now. Probably not the best time to publish dirt on him, to be honest, what with things so sensitive right now."

"Oh God," I say, running my hands through my hair nervously. With no other option, I have to revert to the initial plan of dropping the USB drive and leaving it in his hands. "Look, I have information on this stick," I pull it out of my pocket and place it between us on the desk, "I can't say exactly what it is or where it came from, but I know people who are relying on you to publish it. Can you manage that?"

Matthew Avers narrows his eyes and studies it for a moment, looking up at me.

"You're not Edward Clarence, are you?"

"No, look, I'm sorry. I couldn't think of any other name that would make you see me, but you promised a certain person that you would help publish data on Munday and I was given the task to give it to you. I have no idea what it is, honestly I don't, but I do know that he's bad news, and if he's currently holding the reins, that means a lot of trouble for some very good people," I say placatingly.

"So, who are you really?" he asks, picking up the drive and studying it.

"I don't think it's worth saying. I'm just a completely ordinary guy who got roped into helping because I care what happens to these people," I say sincerely.

"So, you're a Normal that fell for an Augur, is that it?" he gets straight to the point. I'm slightly shocked and don't hide the fact very well.

"I don't see what that's got to do with anything," I say defensively.

"Well, stranger, it has a lot to do with a lot of things, but I hear what you're saying. Augurs are people like you and I but different. I'll look at the data on the stick and see what I can do with it for you and your friends." He plugs the stick into the side of his computer and taps away for a few minutes. I would have imagined Marvin to put some sort of low level security on it, but Matthew doesn't seem to be stopped and gets right into it.

He taps and clicks and scrolls for several minutes and I sit there, not sure if I should leave him to it.

"Don't you want to know what's on it?" he asks me.

"Er, okay," I say, even though I don't really want to know at all. I'm starting to find that the more I know the worse it gets, but curiosity gets the better of me and I come round to his side of the messy desk to read over his shoulder.

He's flicking through documents, some with pictures of a very young-looking Munday with a group of doctors, a group of politicians, shaking hands with various people that I'm clueless about. There's a scan of his ID for something called 'FADE'.

"What's FADE?" I ask aloud. Matthew clicks on it and zooms into the image of a keycard, the kind you would swipe to open a security door. Facility for Augur Detention & Experimentation: Head of Research, Carlton Munday MD.

"Looks like you were right, Munday was connected to something strange," Matthew says, closing the image and opening up a folder entitled *Experiments*. There are several hand written and typed reports of various procedures carried out on Augurs of all ages and abilities. Some of the experiments are as simple as drugging the subject and seeing how it effects their abilities, but others include bathing the person in electrical impulses and determining whether it dampens or enhances their powers. Although at first none of the names are familiar, I can see that the ages of the Augurs tested ranged from the age of four or five up to their eighties.

He flicks through each one, clicking, scrolling and then closing each report. Towards the end I notice names which shock me. *Louise Partridge, age fifteen.* The girl in the photograph is wiry, wide eyed and looks like she has an attitude problem. I immediately recognise her as a much younger Lou, the girl that was in the Duke's study last night.

Jeremy O'Donnelly, age sixteen. The file is eight years old but there's no mistaking Jer's young face, ready to take on the world with one look. I don't want to see any more, to know any more about their history, but I can't tear my eyes away.

The last report makes my heart stop. *Name of subject: Ella Chisholm, age eleven.* The report comes on full-screen and I can see everything that was done to her. *Method: zero power. Subject capable of self-contained energy. Drugs administered: Peyote, benzodiazepine, barbiturates. Effect: None. Subject still capable of power.*

I can only imagine that the report was written before Ella broke out of the facility but it makes my eyes sting to read that they did those things to her. She was eleven years old, taken against her will and drugged. I feel like I'm going to be sick and I have to look away.

"I think I've seen enough," I say to Matthew and make to leave.

"Wait! Just a few more minutes of your time, please," he says and gestures back to the chair. Although I want nothing more than to get out of there and get some oxygen into my lungs, I do as he asks and sit back down.

"This is some barbaric stuff, that's for sure. You know, being a reporter, you have to have a certain willingness to confront the evil that men can do," he says, picking up a pen from his desk and examining it absentmindedly.

"Rather you than me," I say, rubbing my eyes. I feel mentally exhausted.

"Although I'll have to do a bit more digging, I would imagine that if Carlton Munday has signed even one of these reports he can be implicated in an investigation and removed from post," he says, almost talking to himself. That gives me a surge of hope at least.

"That would be amazing. I think it would save a lot of people in the long run," I say, relieved to be speaking to someone who may actually be able to do something more effective than myself. "If it's alright with you, I'll leave you to it," I say, getting up to leave again.

"Sure, sure," he says, staring at his screen once more. "Oh, but hang on. How can I reach you if I have any questions or need to get more info from you?"

I deliberate about whether or not to tell him my name and just hand over my phone number. Could there be any harm in it?

"Curtis," I eventually say and grab the pen from him to write my number down. "But I don't want anyone else getting that number," I warn. He nods and gives me a warm smile, his perfect white teeth showing.

"Of course, Curtis. Thanks for bringing this to me," he stands and gives my hand a final shake, and I see myself out.

Mission accomplished, as far as I'm concerned. I look forward to letting things run their course and hopefully just spending a few days with Ella alone at home.

I step out of the lift to find the reception empty, which seems odd but could just mean that the receptionist has gone to the bathroom. I sign out of the visitors log and step through the revolving door onto the street outside. The sky is blue, and I breathe in the cold December air in great deep breaths. My hands instinctively go to my pockets as I scan the cafe windows for a sign of Ella, but the winter sun is bright and reflecting off the glass, making it difficult for me to see anything inside.

I look up and down the street and notice a black car in the middle of the road. I dismiss it at first, but it revs its engine as I cross the road and I speed up instinctively. It stops a few feet from me and a tall man steps out of the passenger side. Am I getting paranoid in my old age, or is he walking towards me?

I look to the cafe again, but Ella is nowhere to be seen. Has someone taken her? I go right up the the window and peer in, shielding my eyes from the reflection by cupping my hands around my face, but as I do a hand clamps down on my shoulder.

"What the—" I spin around and find the tallish man with sunglasses on standing behind me. I find it odd that he'd be wearing them in the middle of December, but I don't get a chance to make any enquiries because before any formal introduction, he pulls his arm back and hits me. I don't see the fist coming, so when it hits me on the jaw it sends me flying to the ground. I never was much of a fighter, so it takes me a moment to get my bearings as I scramble up. I push myself back on my feet and scan my surroundings for some kind of escape route, but I'm at a complete dead end. He comes towards me again, and the second blow is aimed at my stomach, which winds me and sends me back to the concrete, desperately trying to get some air into my lungs. He doesn't let up, but instead grabs my arm and drags me to one of the black cars, opening the back door and throwing me into the back. I kick out just as I lay on the back seat, hoping that he'll be thrown off by my sudden act of retaliation. My foot catches him on the shoulder, but rather than be knocked off his feet as I'd hoped, it seems to just annoy him. He slams the door on my leg and I scream out in pain, but it's enough to stop me fighting back for now. Stuffing me into the car completely, he closes the back door. He climbs into the passenger seat at the front and I notice a man at the wheel I hadn't spotted before.

In total agony from head to toe I attempt to sit up and at least try to catch sight of Ella out the window as the car begins to pull away. I instantly regret it as the sudden movement causes my head to feel like it's going to explode.

I get what I think is a glimpse of her coming out of the cafe, a look of confusion across her face, and I bang on the window trying to get her attention. Maybe she saw me being beaten up? I can only hope, because it doesn't take me long to realise that the windows must be blacked out and she can't see into the car at all. If she heard me she doesn't show it, because she seems to be looking up and down the street frowning, her blonde hair whipping round as she turns her head this way and that. I bang louder, but the car pulls round the corner and within seconds she's lost to sight and we're threading our way through the traffic on Kensington High Street. I grab the door release, but of course it does nothing, the locks evidently managed by the driver.

"Knock it off or I'll stick you in the boot," Sunglasses, as I've decided to call him, says to me gruffly. He removes something from his fingers and pockets it. Knuckle dusters, I realise. No wonder it all hurt so much. I lean back on the cool black leather, my stomach feeling tender from where he punched me and my jaw feeling worse. I don't even want to think about my leg right now, which I can picture is probably going purple under my jeans. I wouldn't be surprised if it's broken, but I daren't move it now.

"Who are you?" I ask, wincing with the pain that speaking causes me. I touch my cheek furtively and find that the corner of my mouth is split and bleeding.

"Shut up," he says, and doesn't bother to make any further comment. Realising that saying anything else will probably only make him more angry, I shove my hands deep into my pockets and stare out the window, trying to get a sense for where we're going. I recognise one or two landmarks at first: the Royal Albert Hall, Marble Arch, Hyde Park. But then we're in parts of town that I've never been before, and I soon become confused. Are we going North? We haven't crossed the River Thames from what I can tell, and neither of the other occupants seem to want to give me a guided tour. I try and memorise anything and everything that looks like it would help to find my way back home, but then I realise that would imply that I'm going to escape these people, whoever they are.

With my hands back in my jacket pocket, my fingers curl back around the Duke's switchblade and a surge of hope runs into my chest. I could flick it open and stab sunglasses in the neck and then the driver in the eye, one-two, like they do it in the movies. But who am I kidding? I've never used a knife for anything more than cutting sandwiches and the likelihood of my success is minimal. I feel like a coward and an idiot, childish for thinking that I could defend myself and foolish for getting captured, even though I have no idea yet even why. Some sensible part of me is trying to reason with the irrational and tell me that I should hide the knife and use it when I'm not in a locked car with no actual escape route.

Twenty minutes, forty, and then what feels like over an hour passes us by. I think about Ella and what she will have made of my sudden disappearance. I don't even know if she saw me leaving the building before I was caught so she might still be wandering up and down the street waiting for me to come out. My heart sinks at the thought of her waiting there for me for hours. She's smart, I tell myself. Smarter than me, that's for sure. She wouldn't have walked right into some kind of weird trap and gotten captured, and even if she did she would have been able to magic her way out of it. I did nothing more than act as an effective punching bag.

We seem to be driving through the docks somewhere, although along the River Thames that could mean we are in one of many places. There are low concrete warehouses, cranes, areas that are surrounded by scaffolding and large lorries everywhere.

"Put this on," Sunglasses says to me, throwing a black piece of cloth over his shoulder. It's some kind of linen bag and I realise he means for me to put it over my head, I'm guessing so that I don't see exactly which building we're in.

"Is this really necessary?" I ask, stupidly.

"Put it on or I'll knock you out and drag you in," he threatens, although he says it in boredom as if he's said a similar thing many times before.

"Blimey, alright. Keep your hair on," I say, imitating a sense of humour that I currently don't have. I pull the bag over my head, trying not to touch my tender face as I do so, and leave myself in darkness. Wherever we were headed, it seems that we've finally arrived.

CHAPTER 12

My head stuffed inside the sack leaves me with nothing but a few pinpricks of light through the cloth. It smells like sweat and bad breath and I try to breathe through my mouth, although it doesn't really help.

The car slows, and I can hear a low hum coming from outside, which I figure is the sound of an electric door opening, like the kind you get in garages. The car inches forward and eventually comes to a complete stop, but no one gets out until the electric doors are fully closed and there's nothing but silence.

I hear both Sunglasses and the driver open their doors at the same time, and then the door on my left opens shortly afterward.

"Out," he says, and I picture him holding the door open for me. I shuffle along but as soon as I put weight on my bad leg I cry out and fall on the floor. He tuts and pulls me up but I realise I can't walk on it at all without feeling like I want to throw up. Not a good sign. Sunglasses is evidently not the compassionate type as he swears and curses at me, throwing my arm around his shoulder and dragging me to wherever we're going whilst I try to hop on one leg. Every bounce makes me wince and I can feel my hands shaking, a feeling I vaguely remember having when I tore a ligament back in secondary school during a football game. I insisted to my Mum at the time that my leg was broken, but after a trip to A&E, an X-Ray and a visit to an unsympathetic doctor's office, it turned out that it was just muscle damage and that I would need to "stop whining and man up," as my Dad said at the time. This feels the same, but worse, and I wonder if it's at all possible to 'man up' when being kidnapped and beaten up by total strangers.

I hear doors open and close and we climb into what must be a lift, because I hear the impatient push of a button and the familiar feeling of being pulled against gravity as it descends. The whole thing seems to be taking an age thanks to my slightly invalid state and Sunglasses only grumbles and scoffs at my slow progress. I wonder to myself if he's still wearing shades indoors, but then worry that maybe I have concussion because thinking thoughts like that in a near-death situation are not at all logical or sane.

Eventually I'm dumped in a chair, cold and hard, like the uncomfortable type you get in classrooms. My hands are tied behind my back but at least my leg has been left alone; they probably realise that I'm not about to go running anywhere in a hurry. There's a shuffle as Sunglasses leaves and slams the door behind him. The air is damp and cold and ever-so-slightly salty, which makes me realise we must be close to the sea somehow. I guess at some point the estuaries of the Thames do meet the ocean, so it's possible we've driven all the way across London to one of those ports.

"Mr. Clarence, it is an honour," says a cool voice, female and vaguely familiar. I laugh, and the sound is alien to my own ears: slightly manic, like a man from a lunatic asylum.

"You think I'm Edward Clarence? Give me a break," I choke as the pain in my jaw throbs through my head. With the hood over my head, she probably can't see, but I'm way darker than he could be even if he'd gone on holiday to a hot country for a month.

"Well, if you're not Edward Clarence, as you supposedly said you were only a few hours ago, then who exactly are you?" says the woman not missing a beat.

"I'm nobody. Nothing of interest to you, so can you do me a favour and get me to a hospital?" I croak.

"Oh, nobody. I see, I see," she says as if thinking to herself. I'm wracking my brains to figure out where I know the voice from but what I'm sure to be slight concussion is now clouding my thoughts. "That's a shame, because I thought you might possibly be able to tell us about Curtis Mayes." The sound of my own name on her lips gives me the creeps. It sounds unnatural, like it doesn't belong here, in this place.

"Never heard of him," I lie.

"Really? Oh, that's a shame. Because we have his girlfriend and would very much like to ask him a few questions about her." I freeze. They have Ella? But how? *Think, Curtis!* She's trying to play me, I'm sure of it. She can't have Ella —I saw her on the street with my own eyes. She knew I wasn't Edward Clarence too. How could she? So, she knows I'm Curtis Mayes, but wants me to say it, so that she has a reason to keep me detained maybe.

"I demand a lawyer and my phone call," I say lamely.

"Oh dear, Curtis. You've been watching too many movies. There will be no lawyers and no phone calls, oh no. Did you not hear that the Acting Prime Minister passed an emergency law as his first act on post that anyone associated with Augur terrorism can be detained and questioned at the discretion of the government agencies in charge of civil defence?" She's trying to sound cute, with her soft sing-song voice and clipped British accent. Not a trace of common in her, like Edward Clarence, I think to myself. But the sound is getting on my nerves. If I had Augur powers I'd be ripping the place apart right now with her in it. A small part of me realises that it's the first time since being with Ella that I've actually imagined myself with powers and wonder why.

"I'm not associated with Augur terrorism," I say.

"Nice try, but I have footage of you entering a known cyber criminal's house, a newspaper's offices where you claimed to be a known member of the Magic Circle, as well as entering the Duke's London home on no less than two occasions. If you were Edward Clarence that wouldn't seem so odd, but as you claim you're not him I can only assume that you're up to something. As it happens, that's enough for me to detain you for up to ninety days without any further evidence. It's true what they say: you can't even pick your nose in London without CCTV catching it," she says in a failed attempt at humour. I don't laugh and I'm dying to take this claustrophobic sack off my head.

"If you want to talk to me you can at least remove the hood," I say feigning cooperation.

"Promise you won't bite?" she jokes as there's a rough tug from behind me and the hood comes off. I blink in the bright light but there's nothing really to see. I'm sitting in a pool of phosphorescent light that comes from a lamp overhead, and the rest of the room is pitch black. I'm unable to snap my head back in time to see her behind me before she retreats into the darkness at the edge of my vision.

If I could reach my pocket I could grab the knife that's still sitting there, but my arms are threaded through the back of the chair and there's just no way. What a waste, I think to myself angrily.

"There, now. Tell me what you've been doing at Jonathan Clarence's house, Curtis," she says smoothly, her heels clicking on the concrete floor just out of sight.

"I think my leg is broken," I say, ignoring her.

"I'll be sure to have a medic look at it when we're done here. But you need to answer my questions first. What can you tell me about Clarence, or the Duke, as he likes to be known?"

Silence. I ponder it for a moment as she waits for my answer. I sigh and hang my head, as if searching the ground for answer. What can I tell her that will keep her happy but won't hurt any of the people that I know will be affected by anything I reveal here and now?

"You don't owe them anything, Curtis, so don't make this difficult for both of us. Just tell me what you know, and we can get you cleaned up and that leg looked at. They haven't done anything to help you at all, you know?" she says sounding a little more sincere than before. "I mean, don't you think it's odd that I got the phone call of where you would be at exactly what time in order to pick you up? Does that not indicate to you that perhaps someone is pulling strings that you're unaware of, and you're nothing more than a piece of their intricate game?"

I don't want to go down that line of thought but immediately can't help it. The Duke is the only person who knew what our mission was and where I would be. Admittedly, he probably didn't realise that we'd be putting the plan into action so soon, but he knew that at some point I'd be visiting the papers. Christ, he even warned Ella to keep well away. He can't be trusted, I know that for sure, but she wouldn't be asking questions about him if she already knew the answers. I'm wracking my brain desperately for some out, something that I can tell her to keep her happy without doing more damage. But what can I possibly say?

"Curtis, tell me what I need to know, and I can make sure that you and Ella are safe. I know that you two are an item, and that you'll do anything to protect her." I would smirk if my face didn't hurt so much.

"How could you possibly keep her safe?" I ask incredulously.

"Well, it doesn't take much to get someone a change of ID, a passport and some kind of witness protection plan. That's got to be a better option than being at the beck and call of someone who probably doesn't care whether you live or die in the attempt to get what they want." She makes a good point. Isn't this the solution that I've been looking for? Trying to get Ella to leave the Society and run somewhere, anywhere with me?

"Yes, that's right," the woman says smoothly, filling the silence, "you two could get away from all this if you would just tell me anything you can about what the Duke is doing."

"You know," I say suddenly, "the problem is, I can't really tell you anything because I don't know what's going on. I was asked to give a USB stick to someone. I went along with it because, well, why not?"

Telling her the truth of what I do know can't hurt, I realise. "The reporter I gave the information to opened it up and there was evidence that Carlton Munday had been the Head of Research in a place called 'FADE'. They used to do experiments on Augurs. Drug them, electrocute them and then see if it would affect their powers. Kids, old people, you name it. It was barbaric, and Munday was in charge of it all," I say monotonously. I don't know whether it's the head injury or something else, but abruptly, like a flash of lightning, it hits me as to where I know this woman from. "But then, you probably already knew that, didn't you, Miss Banks?"

It was like an itch I couldn't scratch —the voice, the setting, the clicking of heels —but the vision I had when Mumbe seemed to be testing me, what feels like a lifetime ago but was only yesterday evening, came back to me. Now I don't know whether what he showed me was part of his own memory or some kind of distorted vision of the future, but the Duke clearly said that Miss Banks was a threat.

There's what I hope is a stunned silence. It goes on for quite some time and I can't tell, in the darkness what her actual reaction is.

"I suppose," she finally says, "that you won't tell me where you got that name from?"

"You wouldn't believe me even if I did," I sneer.

"Curtis, I need you to work with me here. The fact that you know about FADE helps massively because you'll understand why I'm actually trying to stop it from happening again, but so much worse," she sounds sincere, almost pleading.

"That makes no sense at all. I thought you were part of the government?" I ask.

"Yes, but I'm part of the government that is actually trying to create equality for Augurs, despite the many attempts at various groups to make sure that doesn't happen."

"I still don't get it. You said you thought I was a terrorist. How can you be trying to create equality for Augurs by holding me here?"

She sighs deeply and steps into the light, almost dead in front of me. Her dark hair is tied tightly into a bun, and she wears a skirt suit with a black blouse underneath. The only bit of colour on her is her shoes, which are high, shiny red things that look as lethal as she does. "I can't tell you everything. I shouldn't even really be revealing myself to you, but I'm going to give you the benefit of the doubt. You seem like a good kid, caught up in things that you don't really understand."

"You got that right," I snort.

"I work for a part of the British government that includes anti-terrorism, something that the Magic Circle fall into. We call ourselves ATU —the Anti-Terror Unit. In order to give Augurs a chance at equality we need to put a stop to the idiots who are making it worse for themselves. But my job also includes an ongoing investigation about FADE that was never closed. A lot of people died when that facility went down, but it was never, ever part of the government. The funding came from outside sources, as did the personnel and everything they did." She walks towards me so that I can clearly see her face. Although I'm in the light and she's still in the shadow I can see her dark irises. Her eyes are plaintive and earnest.

"So, if you had a stick which contained information on FADE, which somehow exposes Carlton Munday, well that's going to make a lot of people ask a lot of questions, and I need to know the answers before they do."

"Why? Surely the investigation should be public, if there's going to be one?" I ask, thinking clearly for once.

"Because right now there are a lot of people higher than me on the food chain who are proposing something that closely resembles FADE, but this time government funded. They don't think it's inhumane if it's criminal Augurs being locked up, and they would be the perfect candidate for mental health 'testing'," she makes inverted commas with her fingers. "Which, when you look at it is basically exactly what FADE were doing, except the drugs have different names and the electroshock therapy is considered treatment instead of experimentation."

I have no idea if what she is saying is true but despite myself I'm starting to feel like there's a tiny chance she could be telling the truth.

"What would you do with the information if I told you where I got it from?"

"It depends on what it is you tell me. At worst it's not going to help at all and I'll be right where I started, stumbling in the dark and searching for the person who's pulling all the strings. Between you and me, I think that it's all connected. So, if you can tell me something that I don't know that can point me in the direction of where to look, I'm going to investigate."

"I've got friends who are trusting me with their identities. If somehow they're connected to this, I don't want anything to happen to them," I say, trying to bargain with a chip I don't really have.

"Curtis, it depends entirely on how deeply connected they are to FADE, or people that know about it. But I can promise that if they are innocent bystanders, like yourself, I'll do what I can to keep them out of it."

"Weird way to treat an innocent bystander," I say nodding towards my leg, which feels worryingly numb. She sighs again, something that she sounds well-practised in.

"I'm sorry about Steve. Unfortunately, he was not my choice for bringing you in, but I had to work with what I had."

I should not trust her, I tell myself, but so much of what she's saying rings true that I feel like I want to.

"Fine. Look, I got the data from the cyber criminal you mentioned, or at least I'm guessing that's what he is. He seemed dodgy enough," I half shrug. She seems to look a little relieved to hear me say something that she actually wants to hear.

"Unfortunately, I don't know his name, but it sounds like you already knew where he lived if you had people watching his house." The white lie can't hurt. She nods once, a simple gesture that speaks volumes. The police coming round the corner right after we left was not a coincidence.

"And as for the Duke, well, I don't really know what's up with him. He told me to give the data to the reporter but the only reason I did it was because there was the promise that Carlton Munday might be exposed, and his determination to implement Anti-Magic and Anti-Augur laws everywhere seemed good enough reason to have him removed from his position. The man is trouble, and now he's basically running the country it seems like all the more reason to get rid of him.

"I'm no rebel, but all the Augurs I know are good people, trying to live their lives and not be interfered with." Although all the Augurs I know are also mixed up with the Duke in some way or another, I think to myself. "Besides, if I could do anything to make my girlfriend's life easier and stop her from hiding all the time, I'm prepared to do it."

The words tumble out of me, like an open tap, and I feel relieved to finally be able to tell someone something about it all. She seems to think about it for a moment, I imagine wondering what to do with me now that I've told her everything I know. Eventually she nods again and crosses her arms.

"Thank you, Curtis. That has been incredibly valuable. Now, let me get someone to look at your leg and you can be on your way," she turns around and makes to leave.

"Wait! That's it? But what about Munday? And the Duke? What are you going to do about them?"

"That's for me to know, Curtis. I'm just going to add our little interview here to my files and see if any of the information I have from you is now actionable. Believe me, I'm dying to be able to put someone behind bars, and if you've helped me to do that, well, all the better for your girlfriend." She leaves it at that and turns on her heel. Somewhere in the darkness I hear the electronic buzz of a security door opening and her heels clicking away.

As I sit there, alone in the damp room, I wonder to myself what the hell has happened. How did I get into this mess? Have I completely screwed it up for everyone by admitting that the Duke is involved? I can't even remember if I mentioned him. I shake my head and swear under my breath, just as I hear the door open again.

"Do you kiss your mother with that mouth, laddie?" a Scotswoman says to me. She walks out of the darkness with a white lab coat on, a holdall in her right hand.

"Sorry, I didn't realise anyone was listening," I mutter miserably.

"Och, dinnae fash, lad, I'll have you out of here in no time, okay?" the singsong voice comforts me, although I know I'm becoming altogether too trusting of strangers. Particularly ones that cause me injury and then come to patch it up later. Her auburn hair falls to just below her shoulders and her green eyes sparkle even in the dinginess of this place. I age her somewhere in her forties, but she could easily be older with a very good complexion. She opens her medical bag wide open, and I see an array tools, bandages and concoctions as well as syringes. She selects various items with efficiency and lifts my trouser leg to inspect the damage done, tutting under her breath a little. She orders me to do various things with it, which I find difficult but not impossible, and she cuts my wrists free so that I can stand and try and walk. I yelp out in pain when I do, but she tells me it's a good thing I can still feel anything, which I should be encouraged by apparently.

"Well, I'll bandage it up and give you some meds for the pain, but you'll have to rest a few days," she says tersely.

"Really? Can I get that in writing?" I ask, dying for a few days of rest now. She laughs, a musical sound not unlike Ella's but deeper and more mature.

"What's your name, Doctor?" I ask as she goes about her business.

"You can call me Dr. Lingham, laddie, but I doubt you'll be seeing me again any time soon, so don't worry about remembering it," she replies. Once she finishes with my leg she gives me an injection, for the pain, just below the knee, which hurts almost as much as the leg does, then gives my cheek a full appraisal. By now I can feel that it's swollen and bruised, but the blood has dried where the skin broke.

"That's going to leave a mark for a few days," she says as she applies some clear, cold liquid to it, "but it looks worse than it is, so just be sure not to lie on it when you sleep, and the body will heal itself."

"Thanks, Doc. How'd you get mixed up with a bunch like this?" I venture to ask.

"What? The government? Well, I'm good at my job and they pay me well, so I'd consider it a natural progression, really," she shrugs. I suppose that's what it is really —just another job to these people. And 'the government', the giant, unthinking machine that it is, isn't always filled with bad people, I reason to myself. Just like all Augurs aren't bad. Or good. My mind flickers back to Edward Clarence, who was ready to out all the members of the Society, and probably the Magic Circle too, just for some kind of revenge. I shake my head and then realise that she can see me doing it.

"What's the internal debate about?" she says as she puts a plaster over the cut on my cheek.

"Ah, just trying to understand something is all," I sigh.

"Well, I say the best thing is to talk about it. Not to me, mind, but just to someone. No good bottling things up inside that wee head of yours," she says, offering me an arm so that she can escort me out of the room.

"Thanks," I say again, and she presses a button that was nearly invisible on the wall in order to let us out. Limping and leaning on her the whole way, she walks me down a corridor that the lift sits at the end of. I can't help but feel excited to see it, knowing that I'm going to be out of here in a matter of minutes and then reunited with Ella once I've figured out how to get back home. I silently pray that she's okay and hasn't done something stupid, like call the police or the army or sent out a search party.

The corridor is a long thing with big glass windows on each side, most of which are completely pitch black, although there's a light coming from one near the end. I realise it must be one-way glass where you can see in, but the subject can't see out, probably a similar affair to the one that I was in only moments ago.

There's another poor sod tied to a chair in the room and the sight gives me the chills. How can they possibly justify treating people like this? Oh, yeah. Affiliation with Augur Terrorism is all they currently need. I imagine with the dampness of the place that this operation has been out of business for a while, but thanks to Munday's new law they've been bringing people in left, right and centre.

As we pass the window, I try and resist the urge to peer in, even though I'm sure I'm not supposed to be seeing anything. Hell, Dr. Lingham will probably get in heaps of trouble for not putting the sack back over my head before leaving the interview room. The unfortunately familiar figure of Miss Banks is inside, staring down her victim, evidently waiting for an answer.

But then I see who the prisoner is, and my heart stops dead in my chest.

Tied to the chair, head hanging limply but face still visible beneath his dark hair, is Jer.

CHAPTER 13

I stand right in the middle of the corridor and stare in horror through the glass. Dr. Lingham takes a moment to realise what has made me stop so abruptly.

"Oh, sorry, laddie but I can't have you interfering with interviews and government business. I'll already be in trouble for breaking protocol and allowing you to see the examination rooms," she flusters about me, trying to pull me towards the lift.

"That's my friend in there!" I say, trying not to shout and alert anyone more deadly than the doctor that I've seen something I shouldn't have.

"Oh, gosh, well I'm sure they've got good reason to be holding him or he wouldn't be here. Listen now, I need you to go home and rest your leg, remember? If you try and stop an official investigation you'll be arrested and then there's nothing I can do for you," she's practically pleading with me to let it go, although she does it in as serious a voice as she can muster. I try to think quickly. What weapon do I have? Only the switch blade in my pocket, which honestly isn't going to do much against the likes of Miss Banks and Sunglasses Steve, if he decides to show up suddenly. But Jer is an Augur so maybe he can do something I don't know about and help get us out without losing our or anyone else's lives.

The only Augur power I've known him to use is that 'magic reading' thing he can do, which isn't going to help us here at all, plus he looks in a bad way.

Do I screw up the chance to grab Ella and run now that I've been freed, or do I leave Jer here at the mercy of these people? I only give myself a second to contemplate the second option, but really there's no question. I have to help him.

Obviously, Miss Banks inside doesn't know what is going on behind her as it's a one-way window, which gives me the element of surprise. Thinking on my feet I grab the doctor's kit bag out of her hand before she has a chance to react and fling it open. I quickly scan the contents to see if there's anything I can use and settle on a couple of syringes full of what I'm guessing is some kind of anaesthetic, praying that it's not just a flu shot that will end up doing little more than annoying someone.

I hear a sound that I've only ever heard in shows on the TV: the click of a safety catch coming off and a gun being cocked. I look up to find the barrel of a Glock 17, standard-issue police and military weapon, pointing right at me in the steady hands of the Doctor. I remember reading that was what police were armed with somewhere, and the useless piece of information seems to surface now for no good reason at all.

"Doctor, please," I put my hands up, although they're full of syringes that are primed and ready for use, "I honestly don't want any trouble. I just want to help my friend. He's a good guy and would be of no use to you here."

"I want you to leave before you get any more hurt, laddie." Her voice is certain and unwavering, but something in her eyes tells me she isn't honestly going to shoot me. I could be wrong, but I'm sure that doctors swear an oath or something that must include that they can't shoot people. The gun is just a couple of inches in front of my face, and I guess that if one of these syringes has something useful in it the best place to put it would be in an arm. That's where they take blood samples from, so there must be an easy-access artery there, but her lab coat is going to be too thick to pierce through. I quickly judge the distance between myself and her body. I'm not drilled in close combat, and my reaction time isn't the best, but impulsively I push her gun arm out of my face with as much power I can muster and stick a syringe into her neck, pushing the plunger. I hear the gun clatter across the corridor and the doctor looks at me furiously, hitting me on the face that she's only recently patched up. It hurts, but I'm too determined to do anything other than grunt in pain. "You're going to regret thissss, laddie," she says faintly. Apparently, the neck was a good place to aim, as she slumps in my arms a moment later.

What was in that thing, horse tranquilliser? I only give myself a moment to wonder before dropping the syringes and dragging her limp body, my leg screaming with the effort, to one of the empty examination rooms. They are simple things that only need a keycard to open them, and the Doctor's ID dangles from her neck. I unclip it from its lanyard and scan myself in, hearing the electrical buzz of the lock being released.

"Sorry, Doc," I whisper as I lay her down in the darkness. I head back to the corridor and then realise that I've left her equipment bag wide open which looks incredibly suspicious to anyone who might walk past. I decide to put that in the room with her out of some kind of respect for her belongings, which feels idiotic but strangely necessary.

I scoop up the syringes and the Doctor's gun which had skidded over to the side and try not to think too much about what I'm about to do. The element of surprise is the only thing that's going to help me here. I scan the keycard and push the door as soon as I hear the sound of the release. I know I have little choice but to hope I'm as lucky with a second syringe as I was with the first, so I hold the gun awkwardly in my left hand, its weight uncomfortable and alien in my grasp. The syringe I used on the Doctor had clear liquid in it. All of the others had a slight tinge to the contents, so the likelihood that they will have the same effect is slim at best.

The sound of the door opening makes Miss Banks turn, but very slowly, as if she's reluctant to take her eyes from her subject. It works to my advantage as I stick the syringe in the back of her neck, and she makes a small sound as it pricks her skin. But rather than fall to the ground like the

Doctor she hits my hand away in anger as she spins around. I hold the gun up but take a step back, my hands shaking despite myself.

"Oh, for goodness' sake," she says flustered and pulls her own small gun out, pointing it at me with a far steadier hand.

"Curtis Mayes, you are more trouble than you are worth," she says bitterly.

"How rude. That's not what you were saying to me half an hour ago. What happened to me helping you to protect everyone? Augurs included?" I ask with a bravado I don't actually feel.

"This is so much bigger than you or me, Curtis. You need to think about what you're doing right now and realise that you are stopping me from doing my job," she says, sounding not unreasonable.

"I don't doubt that for a second, Miss Banks, but *you* have to realise that you can't go around hurting people that I care about if you want me to cooperate," I say, the truth of my words hitting home to me as I speak. I feel like I've inadvertently become some kind of Augur freedom fighter.

"You are such a child," she says exasperated. "This young man was found snooping around an active crime scene. The scene of an Augur explosion, no less," she says tilting her head towards Jer without taking her eyes off me. I look at Jer, who I think is conscious but barely.

"He could help you, you know, if you would just untie him from the chair and treat him like a normal human being instead of some kind of criminal," I point out.

"We tried asking nicely, but he insisted on causing trouble. What choice did I have?" she asks rhetorically.

Jer is murmuring something that I can't make out and I worry that maybe he's been drugged or worse.

"What have you done to him?" I ask, trying to edge my way towards him without her noticing. I know we're at an impasse, guns trained on each other. I couldn't even bring myself to pull the trigger if I had to, and I know it. She, on the other hand, would probably have no problem with it at all.

"Just a bit of sodium thiopental and an encounter with Steve," she says dismissively. "Have you ever fired a gun before, Curtis?" she asks, narrowing her eyes at me. I haven't, and I'm sure she knows it. I know there are all kinds of things involved, like recoil and aim and the sound being so loud in an enclosed space that it can make you temporarily deaf.

"I used to go shooting," I lie. It comes easily, but she doesn't look convinced. Whatever half-arsed plan I might have had when I came into the room has gone completely out of the window, and I'm desperately trying to figure out an alternative. If Jer would just wake up enough to use some of his power right about now that would help massively. But why hasn't anyone come to Miss Banks' rescue? Surely there are security cameras everywhere and back up just waiting for things to go sideways when interrogating an Augur?

"Where's Sunglasses Steve now?" I ask her, stalling.

"Just upstairs by the car, waiting for you so that he can drive you back to your girlfriend. I imagine he'll be getting pretty impatient by now and will come down to see what's taking you so long," she says cooly. I don't look forward to another encounter with him any time soon and wish that I had something other than a gun that I'm unskilled enough to fire and a pocketful of syringes that may or may not be of any use.

"I'm sorry, Curtis, but your time is up," she says, cocking the gun and aiming it steadily at my head. Our outstretched arms are only a meter apart and I'm sure that if she shoots from this distance she will not only hit her target, but that target will splatter against the dark walls like a burst watermelon. The thought of imminent death should terrify me, and in some ways it does, but equally I feel like there's no use in giving up when

I've gotten this stupidly far. Plus, there's Ella, who sweeps across my mind at that moment like a cool cloth on a fevered forehead. She's the entire reason that I'm here and why it's worth not giving up. As if in silent answer to my prayers, Miss Banks suddenly crumples to the floor, knocked in a lightening-fast impact from a chair. The blow sends her gun flying across the room into the shadows and her thin shape is sprawled out on the ground, unconscious. I look up in shock as Jer stands, haggard and panting with effort, and places the chair neatly back where it was.

"Bitch," he spits at her limp body and rubs his wrists, which he somehow managed to untie while I was stalling.

"Mate, thank God you did that," I say, hugging him in relief despite the pain it sends through my body. He pats me roughly on the shoulder, then drags himself over to the corner where the gun fell and scoops it up. Somehow it seems to suit him more than me. He has an eye that is slowly turning black and swollen, and he looks like he hasn't seen daylight in a while. "You look bloody awful," I say, almost apologetically.

"You don't look too grand yourself," he says in his gentle Dublin accent, and I realise it must be true. "Any plan of action from here, boy wonder?" he asks me as I gently tread around Miss Banks' body and buzz us out of the room. "Honestly, no. But I have a keycard that will get us through doors and we have two loaded guns, so I'm kind of hoping we can wing it." He attempts to roll his eyes, but I think it hurts too much so he motions me to lead the way.

Out in the corridor there's no sign of life. The interrogation room I left the Doctor in is still locked and dark, and there are no other rooms with the telltale glow coming from inside which would indicate that someone is inside, so I tell Jer we should make our way to the lift. I'm limping, but I refuse his offer to lean on him as, honestly, he doesn't look up to taking any extra weight right now.

"What is this place?" I ask as we step inside and I assess the rows of buttons. I can only assume that floor zero is the ground and that all the minus numbers are the various basement layers of this place. There are five of them, and it looks like we're on minus three.

"Some kind of counter terrorism unit of the government is all I could gather," Jer says whilst I hit the 'zero' button.

"That nasty piece of work that did this to me, and probably that to you," I say motioning to his black eye, "is probably waiting right outside the door."

"So, shoot now and ask questions later, is it?" he asks.

"Sort of. I've never fired a gun before to be honest, so I'd rather not shoot anyone if I can help it," I confess. He feigns surprise but then gives me a smile.

"I thought you 'used to go shooting', was it?" he jokes.

"And I thought you were helpless and unconscious," I retort. The levity of the moment passes as the lift stops and the doors open slowly. There's no welcoming 'ding' as it reaches its destination, or comforting recorded voice telling us that we've reached the ground floor. It's a big space, like a large metal box with enough room for five people to stand abreast in the middle. With a signal from Jer, he and I plaster ourselves to the walls on each side so that anyone looking in will, upon first inspection, think it's empty. To my satisfaction, Steve, still wearing his sunglasses, steps into the lift, evidently thinking that now would be a good time to check out what's going on downstairs. Jer doesn't hesitate for a second and hits him over the head with the barrel of his gun.

Unfortunately, Steve is mostly fat and muscle, trained to do the heavy lifting and people-beating when necessary, so all it does is mildly annoy him. With a roar that you could only expect to come from such a big man, he swings round to hit Jer, but as his body moves I see an opening. I grab a syringe in a panic and plunge it into his thick neck, knowing that it will only act as a brief distraction but hoping that it might do more. Like an angry bear being attacked by bees, his attention immediately turns to me and I see his fists, the size of hams, clench and aim towards my already tender face. My body automatically crouches down, and my hands go up in supplication, like a reflex action. His first fist lands in my solar plexus, near enough to the spot he hit me earlier and with just as much force. His second fist never finds its home as a huge impact, like a compressed hurricane, throws him off his feet and plasters him against the back wall. Slightly winded but also astounded I get up and peer out of the lift to see my saviour.

Standing just a few meters away, legs apart and hands glowing, is the short, spiky-haired girl I remember as Lou. Her fingers crackle with energy, and she throws a small object on the ground angrily, which I realise is a mobile phone. She dusts her hands off and a few remaining sparks fly off her fingers before they return to normal.

"Lou?" Jer asks, as shocked as I am to see her here. He steps out of the lift towards her and she tugs his collar to pull him down into a rough kiss. He groans from the pain but seems to get over it pretty quickly. Obviously, this is the girlfriend he mentioned. The fact that it's a feisty, wiry girl like Lou shouldn't be surprising at all. I clear my throat as I hobble out of the lift, and she lets him go, right before she punches him on the arm.

"You bloody idiot!" she says to him before turning towards me. "And you! Ella's going to bloody kill you," she fumes, grabbing me by the arm and half dragging me to the black Mercedes that I was escorted in. She opens the back door and motions for me to get in, and Jer climbs into the front passenger seat. Lou gets behind the wheel, and I ask where the driver got to.

"I took care of him first," she says, turning the key that was already in the ignition and starting the car. I guess that's where the phone came from that she so ruthlessly threw on the floor. There's a panel of buttons by the handbrake, and she presses one of them, which causes the metal grill at the far end of the warehouse to open. It's dark outside so it must be some time after five in the afternoon. Could be later. How long was I gone for?

I sigh and lean back in the seat, grateful that I've got people who know what they're doing around me. Despite the slight madness of the situation, Lou is happy enough to talk as she drives.

"As soon as I knew you'd been taken," she says to Jer, "I pulled in all the favours I could. Marvin accessed the CCTV that showed the car you'd been grabbed in and, thanks to your mobile phone, he was able to figure out where he'd stopped. That was the third warehouse I had to break into before I found you," she says almost bitterly, making me feel like we should be apologising for the inconvenience. I suddenly pat my pockets and feel the familiar rectangle inside my jacket.

"Can they track me now?" I ask, pulling it out.

"Probably. Best to dump it," she says with zero emotion. I'm not sure how I feel about that. Not because it was expensive, but because it's my one line to my parents, if I get to speak to them again. Gone are the days when I'd memorise phone numbers and without it I wouldn't have a way of getting hold of them. I settle for switching it off although I don't know if that will help.

"That's why they have such a hard time tracking Augurs down," Lou continues, oblivious to my dilemma, "we're digitally invisible. You might as well be too, considering how much time you spend with us now," she points out.

"Have you spoken to Ella?" I ask her, tiredness washing over me now that the adrenaline has stopped pumping through my body.

"Yes, and I told her to stay as far away from these people as possible. She wanted to come with me, but I told her it would be too much of a risk. She can be stupidly stubborn sometimes," she says, almost like a big sister that's been trying to keep her out of trouble and has been failing. "I told her to stay at your house, although I don't know how sensible that is with Edward Clarence as your next door neighbour," she points out.

"Whoa! He's your neighbour? Was he the creepy person sending you death threats?" Jer says to me. I realise a lot has happened since I saw Jer last night, including that particular revelation.

"Yeah. I don't think he's interested in harming Ella though," I say. "He's a hothead but he's not actually a nasty guy. Just a bit volatile."

"You've spoken to him then?" Jer asks.

"He paid us a visit this morning, and it wasn't to bring us a pie and welcome Ella to the neighbourhood," I say wearily. The landscape around us is building up from low warehouses to taller buildings as we drive back into the busier part of town. We're hitting the evening rush hour, so progress is slow, and Lou is getting antsy.

"We need to dump this car as soon as we can," she says, looking for somewhere safe to stop.

"I won't be able to make it on public transport with my leg," I say, and it throbs as if to affirm it. I can see the grim expression she pulls from the rearview mirror, as if she was hoping I wouldn't say that.

"We'd look dodgy as hell on the tube anyway, what with our faces in the states that they are," Jer points out. His eye is still swollen, and I can tell that my cheek is too from the way my mouth feels when I talk.

"Okay, so we need to change vehicles and get out of town as quickly as possible," Lou says, as if she's talking about planning picnic to the park and not running for our lives. "First, we'll go to yours to scoop up Ella, and then we'll hit the road. I just need to get off the main road," she says, navigating a traffic jam and driving down a side street. She drives competently, like she does it all the time. I passed my driving test last year and haven't gotten back into a car since. Dad doesn't let me drive his, and I haven't exactly needed to own my own car. The thought of my Dad suddenly hits me, and I realise that I'm not even going to be able to say goodbye to them. How long will Ella and I be gone for? A month? A year? Maybe longer.

We're going to have to see what Matthew Avers does with the data I gave him on Carlton Munday, and if we're lucky there could be some major changes to the system in a matter of days. But we'll have to do it from a safe distance, particularly now MI-dodgy-as-hell are on our tails.

"Do you know what that place was?" I ask Jer now that we've got a moment to talk.

"Some kind of government facility, but for what, I'm not sure."

"Miss Banks told me she was part of the Anti-Terrorism Unit, ATU she called it. So, basically, now that Munday is Acting Prime Minister and has issued some kind of state of emergency, she can pretty much arrest anyone who even smells like they might be connected to Augurs," I tell him.

"I figured as much," he nods. "She said something similar to me. But what was odd was the lack of security and the kind of low-budget feel of it all."

"It looked to me like they opened shop recently," Lou pointed out, winding her way through the residential streets of what I assumed was South East London. "Everything was either very new, like the security doors and this car, or very old, like it had been out of use for a long time."

That gets me to thinking. She's right, of course. The interrogation rooms were old and damp, like they'd just been pulled out of mothballs from some forgotten time. And the fact that there were several basement floors was another telltale sign. The lack of security cameras, or at least ones that were being manned. Even Dr. Lingham seemed kind of new to it all, like she'd just been hired to help out. There was no teamwork or unity between the few members of this unit that we had encountered.

"This'll do," Lou says, interrupting my train of thought. She's pulled into a narrow avenue and parked in the only available spot. Jer helps me out of the car and we follow her lead to a small old

Nissan Micra that looks like it was bought in the nineties. A layer of grime covers the back window, and there are patches of rust here and there; a sure sign that it hasn't had much love lately.

"No car alarm, no GPS, and it probably won't be missed," she explains. "I just need to reach over here," she places a hand on a lamppost and another hand by the lock on the car door. There's an imperceptible flicker of the light, more like a slight dimming, and the door unlocks itself. She climbs in and unlocks the other doors from inside.

"Why couldn't you just channel energy from the car battery?" I ask.

"Because I don't want to drain it before we've even gotten it started," she explains. That makes sense I guess. Car batteries charge themselves as the car is running, so with an old model like this it could take a tiny sap of energy to drain it before we've gotten it on the road. Plus, Lou has to then steal a bit of energy from it just to kick it into action, as the key is nowhere to be found.

The old car isn't nearly as comfortable as the plush leather of the Mercedes, but I do feel like we're invisible, just three young friends on the road in their old battered car driving across town. The suspension doesn't handle the potholes and bumps in the road as well though, and every jerky movement makes me feel like my leg is going to fall off.

The fact that we just stole someone's car does play on my mind though. "Don't worry, Curtis," Lou says, as if reading my mind. "We've probably done them a favour, as now they can get a nice new car on their insurance." She's got it all figured out, I think to myself. All neatly justified for the greater good.

It takes an hour and twenty in the little Nissan to my house, and I feel an odd excitement to be reunited with Ella. We've only been apart for a few hours, but it feels like it's been longer.

Lou wisely drives past the end of my road so that we can keep an eye out for any trouble before we park up outside, and my heart sinks when I spot two police cars parked outside my house.

"Dammit. We're going to have to go with Plan B," Lou says, continuing on past the turning, not daring to get any closer.

"What if Ella's in there with the police outside?" I ask, distraught.

"Curtis, you forget that Ella has been an Augur all of her life. You've been with us just a week. She knows exactly how to run," she explains. It doesn't make me feel any better, but I see her point.

"What do the Augurs do that decide not to run?" I ask.

"Depends. Some of them hide in plain sight, like the Gregorios and Federicos of the world. Most keep to themselves. Some become addicts and just try to drown out the world around them. We're all just trying to get on with our lives, just some of us manage better than others," she says.

"And some of us want to change the fact that we need to run and hide," Jer points out, putting his hand on Lou's knee as she drives. It's a simple gesture but one that means a lot even to me. People like them, the other members of the Society, even Ella and Agnes, a small group of what could loosely be called rebels trying to make things better for everyone. Maybe not the Duke though, I think to myself.

"Does the Duke know what happened?" I ask, trying not to reveal any emotion in the question.

"I'm not sure, why?" Lou asks.

"Just curious, I guess," I reply and look out of the window. She seems to know her way around town, as within fifteen minutes we're off the main road again and in the back streets that look familiar to me. Ella's neighbourhood, I realise. Lou does the same trick she did with my street, driving down the bottom and looking upwards so that she can continue on past if there's any sign of trouble, but the road looks clear. She turns right and into it and drives slowly past the neat houses. The lights are on in most of the windows. Tuesday night, everyone safely at home probably making dinner or putting the kids to bed. Lou pulls up outside

Ella's house and motions Jer to get out, as I'm not going to get very far without help. The house is dark except for one light in the front, and I wonder if it's Agnes's room.

"Shouldn't I be getting out too?" I ask, as if for permission.

"Best you stay here, Curtis, just in case there's any trouble," she advises. What kind of trouble could there be in picking my girlfriend up from her house, I wonder? Plenty, when it comes to Ella, I remind myself.

Jer unfolds himself from the cramped passenger side and I watch him intently through the window from my seat at the back, striding up the path to the front door. He rings the doorbell and waits patiently. I don't know why, but my palms are sweating again despite the cold, and I feel oddly nervous, worrying about things that haven't happened yet. No one comes to the door, but he tries the door handle and it opens, which surprises me.

"That can't be good," I mutter.

"It is odd," Lou admits, as Jer turns around to us to give us a signal that he's going in. The few minutes he's gone I count in my head, like a timer waiting to go off. When he finally does reappear, I exhale and realise that I've been holding my breath. He climbs back into the car and shrugs.

"Weird. The TV's on in Agnes's room as usual, but there's no one there. It's like they nipped out for a pint of milk and were planning to come right back. Ella's room is empty and there's no Augur signature to speak of, so there hasn't been any magic in that house for at least a day or two."

"What do we do now?" I ask, the fear in my chest threatening to rise up and make me hysterical at any moment.

"Ultimately we need to stick to the plan," Lou replies.

"And before that," Jer interjects, "we need to get fixed up. Curtis is no good to anyone hobbling around like that, and I look a right mess with only one eye in action." He makes a good point.

"What hospital is going to take us in without asking questions though?" I ask. Lou laughs, a sort of cackle but it suits her.

"We ain't going to a hospital, dummy. They'd be on to us in a second. We're going to a healer."

I heard the Duke mention healers before but didn't think anything of it. Now I realise that these are probably Augurs capable of fixing people up, mending broken legs and so on. I imagine they're hard to come by, otherwise we'd have them in every doctor's surgery and emergency room in the country.

"Honestly, guys, I want to find Ella before we do anything else. My leg can wait," I plead. If this is what I feel like when I know full well that she can look after herself, imagine what's been going through her head the whole time I've been missing.

"We're going to fix you up first, Curtis. Ella's fine, wherever she is. Especially if she's with Agnes," Lou says and pulls the car out and back onto the road.

"They're a formidable team, those sisters," Jer explains, trying to ease my concern. "Really, she'd be more mad at us for not sorting you out before going to find her."

"Fine, fine," I say, leaning back on the seat and trying not to sulk. "How long will it take to get to a healer?"

"Mumbe will be able to help us with that," Lou says, looking at me from her rear-view mirror, "and I know exactly where to find him."

CHAPTER 14

The building we pull up at forty-five minutes later is a tall red brick town house shrouded in darkness.

"Looks like no one's home," I whisper, leaning forward in my seat, although I'm not sure why I'm whispering.

"Ah, looks can be deceiving," Jer says, hopping out of the car and helping me out of the back. The Nissan is one of those two-door cars where the front passenger seat has to fold down to let the backseat passengers out, which is awkward when your leg has expanded to the size of a balloon. He throws my arm around his neck, and I hobble up to the solid front door, all polished brass and varnished oak.

There are several apartments in this building, and there are five names to choose from on the panel of doorbells. Lou presses one confidently, and I listen to hear it ring inside, but there's nothing. Must be somewhere upstairs, I think to myself and grimace at the thought of having to climb what could be four floors. The doorbell panel serves as an intercom, and I notice a small CCTV camera set into the top of it, and I imagine that somewhere upstairs Mumbe is looking at a small grey screen with our three faces in it, wondering whether or not to let us up. Rather than talk to us through the speaker though, I hear a quiet buzz as the door catch releases. Evidently, he's made his decision. Lou pushes it open and hurries us inside, making sure it shuts firmly behind Jer as he helps me through.

The interior is smart; dark wooden panels along the walls, clean carpets in the hall and up the staircase that is almost dead in front of us when we come in. There is one door on the ground floor that has a brass number one nailed to it, recently cleaned.

"This way," Lou whispers, and guides us up the stairs. I guess that Jer has been here before, so she's saying it for my benefit. The walk upstairs is awkward to say the least, and I hang onto the banister on my right whilst Jer helps support me on my left. Despite the cleanliness of the place I can't help but notice how impersonal it all feels. Like none of the neighbours probably speak to each other if they can help it other than perhaps a polite nod in passing.

We make it all the way up to the top floor, passing another three doors; just my luck that we need the apartment in the attic. The door is opened as we arrive, and the concerned face of Mumbe appears, looking quickly from Lou to Jer to myself.

"Is David here?" Lou asks without so much as a 'hello'. He nods and gives us a gesture that indicates we can come in. A man of few words, I've noticed.

A loft apartment with probably only three or four rooms opens out before us. We walk directly into a tidy living room space which would be dark except for the candles lit everywhere. A hatch in the wall leads to a kitchen and I can see the shine of worktops and kitchen appliances from where I stand. There are two doors, one at the far end of the room and another to the right, plus a glass wall to the left that opens out onto a balcony. Everything is cosy and feels right where it should be, the kind of home I'd like to have with Ella one day if things ever get back to normal, although I realise I'm not sure what normal is anymore. The thought of Ella pulls at me, and I must pull a face because Jer gives me a concerned look.

"You alright?" he asks looking down at my leg.

"Yeah, sorry. It's not the leg, it's Ella. I don't think I've been away from her for more than a few minutes at a time this past week," I sigh. It sounds stupid even to me, but I can't help it.

Lou seems to be comfortable no matter where she is, whether at the Duke's house, in a secret government facility or here, in another person's flat. She sits herself down in an armchair like she owns the place and Jer sets me down on a long sofa carefully.

"I'll get David," Mumbe says, and leaves through the door in the back of the room.

"We'll find her, Curtis. I'm like a human bloodhound when it comes to Augurs, so as long as you stick with me we'll be fine," Jer says, and pats me on the shoulder gently. I smile and try to push the thought of her out of my head for the time being.

"He doesn't say much," I nod towards the door that Mumbe has just left through.

"Comes from being all the wrong kinds of minority in the eyes of everyone else, I guess," Jer shrugs. I'm not sure what he means, but Mumbe comes back in with a man that I can only assume is David. He's as tidy and well-kept as the apartment is. Nothing is out of place, and his straw coloured hair is combed into a perfect parting. A good-looking guy. He and Mumbe make a nice couple, and I realise that's what Jer means.

"God, you are a mess," David says to Jer, who gives him a lopsided grin.

"Ah, barely a scratch, Dave. Can you mend my friend here first?" he says, gesturing to me.

"Nice to meet you. I'm David, never 'Dave'," he says, holding out a hand which I shake whilst he gives Jer a harmless eye roll.

"Curtis. Thanks for helping us out," I say.

"All in a day's work," he says and asks me to hitch up the leg of my jeans whilst he inspects what's under the Doctor's bandage. I think of Lingham suddenly and feel a little sorry for her. I hope that whatever I injected her with doesn't have lasting effects. She was a nice lady when you take all the working-for-the-evil-government out of the situation.

David unwraps the bandage and I wince when I see the black and blue splotches on my leg, which has clearly swollen. "This is going to feel a little unusual," he warns as his hands put the lightest of pressure on the bruises. At first it feels like a gradual heat running up and down my leg, then like the worst case of pins and needles I've ever felt. I make a strange noise, somewhere between a yelp and a cough as I try to hide the sudden outburst. It doesn't break his concentration, but the corner of his mouth turns up as he attempts to conceal a smile.

"Don't move the leg for at least ten minutes," he says and then inspects my cheek, turning my chin so that the light catches it. He tuts and then does a similar thing; a gentle pressure right on the swelling, the heat rising in my face, the feeling of pins and needles as the tissue must be healing itself.

"Any other ailments?" he asks once finished.

"He punched me in the stomach, but honestly other than a bit of bruising it's not worth bothering about," I say, patting my abdomen. It's still a bit tender, but there are no broken ribs. He nods and turns to Jer, whose eye is almost closed with the swelling that the black eye has brought on.

"Walk into another lamppost?" David jokes, and Jer laughs.

"Hey, you should see the other guy," he replies.

"To be fair, the other guy suffered more at the hands of Lou than you, Jer," I point out. Lou gives her devilish cackle and winks at us. David works his magic, quite literally, on Jer's face, and a finger that had apparently been broken but that he'd not complained about or even mentioned. The fact that he'd been wandering around all afternoon with a broken finger and hadn't said anything makes me feel bad for making such a big deal about my leg.

"It's going to take a little while for the body to finish repairing itself, so I suggest you stay right where you are for now. Is that everything?" David stands up, hands on hips to assess his work.

"Would have been a whole lot worse if Lou hadn't turned up," Jer admits.

"Typical luck of the Irish," Mumbe adds, speaking for the first time since David came into the room.

"You can say that again, mate. But now for another matter. If Curtis and I were picked up by these ATU people, then I imagine they're going to start pointing fingers and arresting anyone who even looks like they might know an Augur."

"Miss Banks said she arrested me because I was seen going into the Duke's property," I say.

"So, London isn't exactly the safest place for us to be right now," Lou chimes in.

"We're not going anywhere," David says, and stands next to Mumbe as if asking for back up.

"You don't have to, but I would say it's the smart move. Our problem is we can't find Ella or Agnes and we can't go running around town looking high and low for them either," Lou explains.

"The last time I saw her she was looking for me outside the press offices in Kensington, just as I was being kidnapped," I say. All four pairs of eyes turn to me inquisitively, and I realise that they have no idea why I would be at a press office in the first place. Is it really my place to even tell them?

"The Duke asked you to go to the papers?" Lou asks. She tries to make it sound non-threatening but it's difficult for her to control her voice, I can tell. I didn't think she of all people would have a problem with it, but maybe the simple action of being asked to do something with that level of responsibility has caught her off guard.

I run my hand through my hair nervously. Why would the Duke not tell them?

"He asked me to leak the info on Carlton Munday to try and have him removed from his position. But that was before he was made Acting Prime Minister."

"That's pretty big. Why would the Duke ask you to do that?" Jer asks me and I shrug in reply.

"More importantly, why wouldn't he get one of *us* to do that?" Lou asks.

"All I can say is that when Ella and I went to see him he said that a Normal needed to drop off the stick and Ella was to stay as far away from the office of the newspaper as possible. Of course, she didn't, she stayed across the road and waited for me, but just as I stepped out I was picked up by that thug, and the rest is history." They look troubled, and I understand why. They don't want to hear that the Duke wouldn't trust them with something as simple as dropping off a USB stick, but now that I know what's on it I can see his logic. The Duke was effectively giving away their private lives, their identities. I doubt he intended for me to even see what was on it, more like a dump and run, and I feel bad for not telling them what I know but I only think it will upset them if I get into it. Besides, I don't think they were all lucky enough to get a new identity after the facility went under. They simply picked up where they left off and tried to piece their lives back together.

"There's something up with that," says David.

"Too bloody right," Lou says, crossing her arms and looking away.

"Look, I'm sure that just like with Ella he was trying to protect you guys, to stop you from getting too close to the action," I try to reason. I'm not sure why I'm trying to defend him really, but I don't like the feeling that I've acted as some kind of exterior influence that is secretly pitting them against each other.

"None of that really matters now," Jer, the voice of reason, comes to my rescue. "The point is we need to find the girls and get the hell out of here as soon as we can." Everyone nods in agreement.

"Well, we can get some feelers out," David says looking at Mumbe, who nods in reply.

"I'll make some calls," he says in answer to my perplexed look that comes from wondering what 'feelers' he could possibly put out at this hour. Without another word, Mumbe leaves the room through one of the doors. The one on the left must lead to other rooms, whereas I'm guessing the one on the right is a bathroom or utility room.

"Hungry?" David asks us, and we all nod emphatically, making noises that reflect the fact that none of us have eaten in hours. "You stay right there, I'm sure I can throw something together," he says and goes through the same door.

The room is warm and cosy, and if there wasn't a constant feeling of panic threatening to consume me I'd probably fall asleep on the leather armchair quite happily. Instead I realise I'm still in some kind of fight-or-flight mode.

"You alright?" Jer asks, his head leaning back against the headrest. I'd think he were asleep except I can just see the slits of his eyes. A guy used to relaxing when he can between running, fighting and the general mayhem of being an Augur.

"Yeah, kind of," I say, rubbing my hands over my face. I appreciate how my cheek no longer feels like I was hit by a golf ball and doesn't hurt to touch.

Lou snorts, "Don't lie. You're completely freaked out."

"Okay, yes. I'm terrified and freaked out and worried all at the same time. I'm not sure what to do with myself, and I expect some kind of government agents to come bursting through the door any minute," I blurt, angry with myself for being incapable of keeping it together.

"We'll get Ella. She can't be more than a few hours ahead of us, wherever she is. The government won't be able to find us just yet. No one will be missing that battered little car that we've nicked, and by the time anyone realises it's gone we'll be somewhere else. Different car, different city. No need to panic, okay?" Lou says calmly.

"You've done this before."

"When you're different you get used to thinking differently. No sane person would know where all the exits are in a room at any time. No Normal is going to be worrying about being hunted or chased just because they can't do what I can do," she shrugs. "But that doesn't bother me. It's a way of life and I deal with it better than some."

"What do other people do?"

"Oh, I don't know. They pretend they're normal, I suppose. Some of them numb it all out —junkies, addicts, bums and homeless. I'm sure a lot of the guys living on the street are Augurs. I was in secondary school with a girl who took pills every day because she said it made her forget that she even had powers. But God knows where she is now. No rehab is going to have her, that's for sure. Drugs make Augurs unpredictable."

"I've also heard of the Augurs consuming so much energy it practically kills them," Jer comments. I raise an eyebrow at him.

"What do you mean?"

"Well, just like Lou needs to absorb energy to use her powers, right? There are some that get addicted to that feeling and take so much that if they don't use it they can die." I wonder what happened to the Magic Circle members that stopped the Underground that day. Maybe they weren't Magic Circle at all but some Augurs that were chasing a high.

My thoughts wander to all those Augurs who were experimented on with medical drugs, electroshocks and whatever else the scientists decided would be good to do with them. I find myself amazed at their resilience, but it also makes me feel sad.

"Then you've got the Duke," Jer says, interrupting my thoughts. "Someone trying to possibly make a difference and make things better for us."

It occurs to me that I haven't managed to tell them anything about what happened before I was kidnapped.

"I think Edward Clarence was trying to expose the Society," I say suddenly.

"What? How?"

I explain my temporary ploy to get into the news office and how Avers was so excited to see me when he thought I was the son of the Duke.

"I knew he left home at the first opportunity to go and run off with the Magic Circle," Jer says with a hint of distaste.

"Well, that was partly down to his girlfriend. That and the fact that his relationship with his father is tenuous at best. When he broke into my house this morning he was pretty passionate about the fact that the Duke was up to no good and he was determined to get us away from it all. Well, Ella actually. He couldn't care less about me," I say.

"So, the son turns on the father and tries to get rid of the Society. Why, though? I don't know that the Society has done anything to the Magic Circle, has it?" Jer asks.

"Edward Clarence isn't really working for the Magic Circle any more, or so he says. He said that his girlfriend left and there was something wrong with the management of it which has left him on the fence ever since. I feel like there's something about the Duke he's not telling me, but I don't know what."

"He's a very secretive man," Lou says, "I mean, I've been working with him for five years and I never met his son. He picked me up when I fell off the rails a few years back, homeless, stealing cars. It was just a messed-up time after…" she trails off. A memory that's better left untouched, I think to myself. The picture of the girl, fifteen, in an encrypted computer file on Avers' computer springs to mind. Captured, imprisoned and probably experimented on before eventually being released. Jer leans over to her and puts a hand on her arm briefly as if to say, 'it's okay'. She gives him a half-smile and shakes her head.

"Same here. Not breaking into anything but drinking way more than I should and getting into more fights than I could handle. He picked me up, cleaned me up and gave me a purpose."

I look between the two of them. If one good thing came of FADE I guess it's that it brought two people, unlikely to have met otherwise, together. An odd match, but a good one all the same.

"What you grinning at?" Lou asks, and I wipe the smile off my face.

"Nothing, nothing. Just glad that you guys have each other," I say, trying not to sound too sentimental. Truth is that not having Ella here is like being a ship without an anchor. I feel like everything I've done lately has oriented around her, and now she's not here I'm not sure where I fit in. My self-pity is quickly pushed from my mind when David throws the back door open. I panic momentarily until I see him carrying plates with food on them. Stuff I'm familiar with — sandwiches with cold meats, crudités and dips. He places them down on the low coffee table and heads back to get three bowls of soup.

"You had all this in your kitchen? Were you planning a dinner party?" Jer asks what I'm thinking.

"Always be prepared for guests. That's what my mother says anyway." He smiles and sits down on the floor, helping himself to one of his sandwiches whilst we tuck in.

"How long have you guys lived here?" I ask between mouthfuls. The soup is like some kind of elixir for my body, its warmth spreading through me and the colour coming back into my face. I had no idea I was so hungry.

"Three years now in this apartment. But we met when we were twenty," he smiles again. I hadn't really aged him, but he could be somewhere in his mid-thirties. Mumbe has another ageless face but I'd peg them both at 35 to be safe.

"And you? Are you originally from London?"

"Born and raised. My mum's a West Indian brought up near York. She'd like all of you very much," I look around the room at the people that have become my friends, probably closer than anyone has been in a long time. Unlike my Dad, who would probably go completely mental if he knew I was sitting in a room full of Augurs.

"Did Ella meet your parents?" Lou asks.

"No, thank God they're away right now. I don't know how I'm going to explain all this to them when they get back. Or if I'll even see them again," I say a little sadly. Not because of Dad, but really because Mum won't know what happened, and Dad will be no consolation at all.

"The war's not lost yet, Curtis," David says kindly.

"I know, but I feel like us running away almost means that it is. I did everything I was supposed to," I say frustratedly. "Down to giving the stick to the reporter. But now it's all a waiting game to see if he'll do anything with it. Then there's the Anti-Terror Unit – we're defenceless against them."

"It's easy to get overwhelmed when you're losing more than winning," David says calmly. "But the thing to remember is that as long as you can do something about it, anything at all, it hasn't beaten you yet."

I can't argue with that voice of reason.

"So, what now?" I ask Lou, who seems to know what we're doing more than anyone.

"Now you try and get some rest whilst Mumbe finds Ella, or at least some trace of her. With any luck we'll be hearing how Carlton Munday has been removed from post in the morning papers and any Anti Terror Unit won't be able to touch us. We'll be gone before they know what's going on."

She makes it sound so blissfully simple, and although I wouldn't call her the optimistic type, her certainty puts me at ease. I lean back into the comfortable sofa and allow myself to close my eyes for a moment, blocking out the sounds around me and trying to concentrate on the sound of my breathing.

"Curtis, wake up!" Lou's urgent voice breaks the silence and I realise that I've been asleep.

"Wha— what's going on?" I panic as I see the look on her face.

"Two black cars have just pulled up outside the flat," she says pulling me to my feet.

"Lou, we've got to go!" I hear Jer calling from one of the other rooms.

"Is it…?" I daren't complete the question, but I think I already know the answer.

"Yes, Curtis. It's the ATU. They've found us."

CHAPTER 15

I follow Lou through the door and find Mumbe and David in a bedroom that must face the front of the building. The room is completely dark other than the light coming through from outside. Jer is there with them, peering through the blinds from an angle so as not to be seen, and a shaft of light spills across the wall.

"Are we sure it's them?" I ask, trying to keep the fear out of my voice.

"It's them. I just saw Steve get out of one of the cars, though he's moving much slower than he was earlier thanks to Lou," Jer replies. I angle myself next to him to take a look myself and see four figures on the ground far below. Although it's quite a distance and dark out, I can see the figure of Miss Banks in a long winter coat. Their breath is visible as they breathe in the cold night air and they huddle in their scarves, looking up at the buildings and completely dismissing the stolen Nissan that's parked outside.

I look around the bedroom and see an alarm clock on a tidy nightstand. The glowing numbers tell me that it's 1:00am, so it's taken them a few hours to find us.

"How long was I asleep for?" I ask surprised.

"We all slept for a couple of hours. Seemed like the right thing to do," Jer shrugs as if to say it couldn't be helped. I feel frustrated that we didn't just leave and give ourselves a head start.

David swears and pulls Jer back from the window. "I think they just figured out which floor we might be on, or at least it looked like they were going to try. We need to get you out of here now."

"Us? What about you?" Lou asks.

"Like I said before, we're not going anywhere," he says, and Mumbe nods as if to affirm it. She exhales in exasperation and gives them each a rough hug.

"I hope you know what you're doing," she says gravely. They hand us all hats, scarves and gloves, and I put them on followed by my coat which Mumbe hands me.

"They aren't disguises, but at least they'll let you get onto a bus without being spotted for a while," Mumbe says. He hands Lou a piece of paper with something on it that I can't make out in the darkness.

"Get to this address and then the rest should be straightforward."

We let them lead the way out of the bedroom and into the narrow kitchen. Along the left wall is a long worktop in marble with various appliances on it, but at the far end of the kitchen is a glass door, and I can see the balcony from the living room runs along that whole side of the house.

"Take the fire escape ladder to the roof and do what you can to get yourselves to Acton. Stay out of sight until the first train's out and then make your way to this address. Beryl will help you from there," he explains.

"I'll give Mum some advanced warning," David says, which answers my unvoiced question about who Beryl might be.

"Thank you, both of you," I say and give them both a handshake, which seems insufficient for everything they've done and probably still will before the night is out, but it will have to do.

"You're a good kid, Curtis," David says and pats me on the arm fondly. I wonder why people insist on referring to me as a child when I feel like I've aged about twenty years in the past few days.

"Curtis, get your arse up here!" Lou whispers, half way up the safety ladder that leads to the roof. Jer has gone up already, and I'm relieved to find that my leg is working perfectly as I follow behind. I catch Mumbe locking the balcony door from inside and disappearing into the dark of their apartment, which makes me feel sad and I'm not sure why. I push thoughts of how the two of them are going to face up against the likes of the Anti-Terror Unit, but I have hopes that they can hold their own.

At the top of the ladder is a gutter running along the building which I clamber over and pull myself up onto the roof on my stomach. Jer helps me to my feet, and I take in the view.

"Wow," I say as the sight of London at night glitters before me. We're surrounded by rooftops of all shapes and sizes, huge chimney stacks and the combination of old and new tile work everywhere.

"How's your parkour?" Jer jokes, and laughs when he sees my face fall.

"Come on, you two!" Lou says in the darkness, her voice quiet but being carried over the silence around us. London is like a different city up here, beautifully lit up but at the same time almost peaceful. I'd like to dawdle a while longer and enjoy the view, but Lou has already picked her way to the far end of the roof we're on. She gestures for us to follow and we do so, trying to be as light on our feet as possible. The buildings are terraced here, so there are very few gaps in the row of apartment blocks, but some of the buildings rise up to more than four floors and in order to get to the other side we have to press our bodies against the bricks and shuffle sideways on a large window sill to reach the other side.

Being in the middle of town, the houses are all connected for whole blocks before they break off into roads below, so we have to cover as much distance as we can above before reentering the streets. There's the occasional alleyway but nothing more than a single file affair that is easily jumped over, even for a novice like myself.

"Where exactly are we?" I ask Jer, walking lightly behind him across a long flat rooftop that feels like it must house some kind of office complex below.

"Near Soho," he says, his breath steaming in the cold night air in front of his face.

"And we have to get to Acton? Bloody hell, that's a long way," I say. Lou is a few feet in front of us, her thin frame dealing with the exertion well. I reckon she's the kind of person who would work out at least a few times a week. Other than my walk to work, I haven't done any exercise in a while and it's taking its toll now. The roofs here slope downwards, but there are wide flat spaces on either side, so there's plenty of space to walk. Some have balconies and extensions built out onto them, but considering the lateness of the hour we're fairly safe from being spotted.

"Do you think they'll be okay?" I ask.

"They're made of tougher stuff than us, that's for sure," Jer replies.

"They won't have given us away, but we have to realise that the ATU aren't stupid. Let's just hope they aren't right behind us," Lou looks over her shoulder as if trying to see if we're being followed and I instinctively do the same. We're already two houses away from where we started but unfortunately still in sight. I should be looking ahead but something catches my eye from behind the glass. There's someone there, I'm sure of it, and as I peer into the darkness I think I see the balcony door open. "Oh my God," I say and pull both Jer and Lou down to the floor instinctively without explanation.

"What the hell?" Lou asks me angrily.

"Stay down, I think someone is out on the balcony," I whisper. As long as we're still we should be safe, I hope.

After a few minutes, Lou decides to look.

"Nothing coming," she whispers. "But let's keep low just in case they're right below us." We nod in agreement, and she picks out a route that involves minimal noise making but a hell of a lot of climbing under things. Gutters, pipes, people's skylights all get in the way of a straight route to the end. We have to spend most of our time on all fours, partly because standing up would get us spotted faster but also because it feels almost safer to move that way when there's so much distance between us and the ground below.

When we finally reach the last building on the block, my body is aching with the cold despite the winter gear David and Mumbe gave us. The only part of me that still feels warm is my recently repaired leg, which I figure is some part of the healing process.

"This is it," Lou says as the three of us peer over the edge of the rooftop. There's a low wall preventing us from falling straight off and I sit down, leaning my back against it for a moment to catch my breath.

"Do ya see a way down?" Jer asks. I look briefly to my left and right as Lou examines the walls below for some sign of another escape ladder.

"Nothing down there," she says, sitting down next to me and leaning her head back against the wall. Jer crawls over to us and sits next to her so that we end up in a neat line of exhausted bodies.

"If it weren't so freezing I'd opt to stay here until we're sure the coast is clear," I admit.

"I think we should keep moving. We'll be better off on the ground at some point. I'm just hoping that by the time we get there the ATU are long gone," Lou replies.

"Same here," Jer adds.

"But it's not like we can just climb through someone's window and walk through their house," I point out.

They consider this for a moment.

"We could find a fire escape. There's got to be one around here if one of these buildings is an office or something," Lou says, getting on her feet again and walking hunched over to the other side of the roof. She disappears out of sight behind a large pipe but comes back within moments shaking her head. "Nothing. I hate to say it, but we're at a dead end. We either need to backtrack or climb down somehow."

"So, there aren't any Augurs that can fly, then?" I joke, and they both laugh at that.

"No but I knew a guy back in Dublin who thought he could whenever he'd had too much to drink. He wasn't even an Augur!" I chuckle at the thought of it, followed by a shiver that threatens to rattle my teeth inside my mouth.

"Damn, it's cold."

"Too right. Let's get the hell off this roof, eh? We're all smart cookies, we should be able to figure it out between the three of us."

I was enjoying a moment's rest, but now I peer over the edge of the wall and down to the street below. As I expected, we're at least twenty metres from the ground so jumping isn't an option. Soho is busy even for a late Tuesday night, or early Wednesday morning depending on how you look at it, and there are the occasional passing cars and pedestrians beneath us. I skirt round to the left side of the building and see an alleyway only three metres wide, the office block opposite being about a metre lower than the one we're on. My eye catches something on the roof over there. A door, probably a fire escape, small and bolted from the outside, but with any luck Lou might be able to get us in.

"I can't believe I'm going to say this, but I think we should somehow jump over to the next building," I say pointing at it.

"Why the hell would you want to do that?"

"Because I think I can see a fire escape there that we could use to get down and out. Don't get me wrong, I'm not sure I could do it myself, but it's my only suggestion so far."

Lou puts her hand on her chin thoughtfully.

"I think it's a terrible idea, but I actually don't see another option. I might be able to help you be a little more aerodynamic though," she says eyeing me up.

"So, you *can* make me fly?"

She laughs drily. "No, dumb arse. I can probably help give you a little push though if there's any electricity running through some wires or something up here." I recall the way she knocked Steve off his feet in the warehouse, as if an invisible ball of wind hand hit him in the stomach. She did that by channeling energy from a mobile phone. I hope she isn't thinking of the same treatment for me, but she's already looking for a power line to use.

"Ah, here we go," she says spotting a cable that is neatly tacked to the wall. It runs all the way up to the TV aerial, so hopefully no one is up watching night time telly to notice the sudden power outage we're about to cause.

She kneels and puts a hand on it, the other pointed palm forwards in my general direction.

"Ready?" she asks as I edge my way backwards in preparation for a run up. *Try not to think about it*, I tell myself. Like doing the long jump at school, but with a concrete landing and certain death if you don't make it.

I nod and take a run, covering the distance to the ledge within a couple of seconds. I leap as high as I can, hoping that with Lou's help I might be on the right trajectory. An impact in my back, like being hit with a bowling ball made of air, throws me forward at an alarming speed. It happens almost too fast, and the hard surface of the adjacent roof comes to meet me as I smack into it, hard.

"Ouch," I manage, lifting myself up slowly. I don't know what hurts more, my front or my back. A few moments later Jer lands next to me, but slightly more prepared than I am, he manages to stay on his feet rather than face-palming like I did.

"You should've gone first," I say bitterly as I rub my forehead. There's a gravelly imprint on it and my nose smarts a bit, as do my knees, but I don't think anything is broken.

Lou lands deftly next to us and I look at her like she's some kind of super human.

"What? That was nothing," she shrugs off the attention and makes her way to the fire escape door that sits amongst the air vents and chimneys around us. This is certainly an office block from the shape of it.

She rattles the door handle impatiently but as expected it's locked from the inside. She pushes her hands against the door, and I think she's trying to see if she's got anything left in her to unlock the door, but after a few moments she makes an exasperated sound.

"Ah, bloody hell," she says as she kicks it impatiently. "I need something to power off of," she says, holding her hand out as if I'm going to suddenly produce a large battery or something.

"Isn't there a wire or cable around here somewhere?" I say, searching the ground.

Unlike the houses, there are no aerials on the roof of this building, and I figure probably not that many people watch TV whilst they're at work. "Can't we just bust it open?"

"What, and set off an alarm? Not one of your brightest ideas."

I nod, momentarily defeated when I realise that I've got a power source right in my pocket.

"Er, will this do?" I say pulling out my phone.

"You still have your phone? Curtis!" she chides, "That could be how they found us at David and Mumbe's!"

"But it was off!" I protest, not wanting to have been the cause of any trouble.

"They might have been clever enough to figure it out anyway," Jer says sounding at least a little calmer than his girlfriend, but still unimpressed.

"Crap, I'm sorry guys. I just didn't want to lose the only way to contact my Mum if I'm honest," I apologise. Lou grabs it off me and turns the power on without speaking. The screen lights up and with it a bunch of notifications appear to my surprise.

"Someone's popular," she says, and I take it back from her protectively to look at the messages.

Two voicemails, a load of missed calls from an unknown number plus two texts. I read them quickly, feeling like my phone is going to be snatched out of my hand at any second.

Curtis, this is Matthew Avers. I'm trying to reach you. It's important. Call me!

That surprises me. The message was sent about 11pm, so long after our lunch time meeting, and I wonder what it is he wants.

Hello love, hope you're doing fine. Are you eating okay? Dad and I having a great time — weather lovely. See you on Saturday, Mum x

That one pulls at my conscience and I feel a moment of sadness. Jer hands me a pen and offers a page from his precious notebook, the one that accounts for all the different investigations of different Augur signatures he's done in the past. I jot down Mum's number and Matthew's and then as an afterthought I take Dad's as well, just in case. I don't think I've phoned him more than once in my life, but you never know.

"Can I listen to the voicemails?" I ask, feeling like I need permission. Lou gives a surly nod and decides to stand watch over the edge of the building to give me some privacy.

I press the buttons and hear the familiar voice of Matthew Avers again.

"Curtis, it's Matthew Avers. Listen, I really need to speak to you. A girl came in here all guns blazing. Unfortunately, I couldn't help her as I've no idea where you went, but she seemed desperate to find you. I could only tell her what we'd found on the drive that you gave me, although I don't think that will help her. But look, that's not why I called. There was something on that stick that I think you need to see before you go back to the person you got it from. There's half a file on there

and it seems like the other half has been kept separate, but I'm hoping you might be able to tell me where it is. I've spent all day trying to piece together some kind of coherent article, but this missing piece is all I need. Curtis, it'll take down a whole empire!" He says enthusiastically. *"Look, just call me back, quickly. Please. Okay, thanks. Bye."*

I get a sinking feeling in my stomach. Ella must have marched into the building as soon as she couldn't find me, and worse, he's found something out and I bet the other half of it is on Ella's USB stick. Marvin was too clever, telling us not to trust each other. Now, rather than get her involved, I'll need to be the one willing to get him the rest of that information and point the finger as a witness or whatever. But it's more than that. It's the fact that Carlton Munday probably won't be removed from post unless there's someone to accuse him, and a newspaper reporter isn't going to be allowed to do that. I shake my head in frustration and hit the screen to hear the next message, but I nearly choke with shock as I hear Ella's terrified voice.

"Curtis! Oh my God, what have they done with you? I'm so worried," she chokes back a sob which is like some form of torture to me, *"I'm going to see Munday. Or the Duke. Christ, I don't know, but I have to do something and I can't just stand around while someone tortures you or… or worse."* She doesn't sound rational at all and I wish I had some way to tell her that I'm fine. That she needs to get as far away from Munday as she possibly can.

I search for any sign of a number that goes with the missed calls, but it looks like she called from a payphone. The fact that she phoned me means that there's a chance she could call me again at any time. I have to keep it with me now, regardless of the ATU or anyone else using it to track me.

"What's up? You look like you saw a ghost," Jer asks. I tell him about both messages, trying to keep my voice steady and not sound hysterical at the thought of Ella walking straight into some kind of danger.

"We can't help her if we stay here," Lou points out. I hand it back to her, and as she holds it she places her other hand on the door handle. I hear a faint click from behind the door. "There. Now be prepared for the possibility of an alarm going off and us having to run."

"Er, we have another problem," Jer interjects. "We have some seriously dodgy looking company below," he peers over the edge of the roof and onto the street below and I join him to find two familiar black cars pulled up below.

"Oh my God."

"Can't we just catch a break?" Lou asks rhetorically, throwing her arms up in the air. "There's nothing to be done boys, we're going to have to keep going. Curtis, dump your phone now. Throw it as far as you can over there somewhere," she says waving off to the distance from where we came. My heart sinks, but I do as I'm told, doing my best to give it my hardest throw. It lands on the street below some way away and I see some of the figures on the street below look around at the sound of it landing, but luckily they look in the wrong direction.

"Did it work? Are they distracted?" she asks, hand poised on the fire escape door handle waiting for the all-clear.

Something has sparked their attention, that's for sure, because I can see them sticking their fingers in their ears. Like spies with intercoms that are on all the time. They seem to be conferring with each other before climbing back into their cars and driving away at breakneck speed.

"That was weird," Jer says, watching the cars go until they're out of sight.

"I didn't throw it that far," I point out.

"I don't think that's why they left," Lou says, sounding distracted. I look up at her to see her staring somewhere in the middle distance. I follow her line of sight all the way to the South where the river will be. The familiar sight of the Houses of Parliament and the London Eye just by it are just visible from here. But what makes my heart stop is not the breathtaking view, but rather what's happening to it. One by one, block by block, all the lights are going out. Not just in the tower blocks or on the streets, but everywhere. Within a few moments every building, every house and every street lamp is off, and we're plunged into total darkness. It's a blackout.

CHAPTER 16

"That can't be good," I say. In the darkness around us, sounds are almost amplified; dogs bark, sirens wail and car tyres screech. But there isn't the mass chaos one would expect because at least half of the city is asleep. It takes a moment for my eyes to adjust, but with a little light from the moon I can just make out Jer and Lou's surprised faces. The wind ruffles our hair and coats, and at the same time Jer exhales loudly.

"What is it?"

"I don't know quite how to say this, but I'm picking up some heavy Augur activity from somewhere over there," he points somewhere in the distance.

"You can do that?"

"I'm as surprised as you. I guess I can when it's this big. It feels like someone is setting off a nuclear bomb with their powers."

"Do you recognise who it might be?" Lou asks.

"No, too far away," he shakes his head. "But I have a feeling, and you're not going to like it, Curtis."

I think I know what he's going to say. Big Augur activity? A lot of power coming from one place? Based on what everyone's been telling me, that sounds like something Ella could manage.

"It's her, isn't it?"

He nods, but I feel the motion rather than see it, thanks to the darkness.

"What do we do now?" Jer asks and I realise he's looking at me. So is Lou.

"What? How should I know?"

"Mate, it's your call. Do we use this opportunity to get the hell out of here and to safety, or do we go and get Ella? We're with you either way."

I don't even consider the first option. Getting Ella to safety is the only thing that makes sense to me, and I feel a resoluteness in knowing what I have to do.

"Where did the power cut start from, do you think?" I ask Lou, who points somewhere off to the South.

"Houses of Parliament area."

"Or Downing Street?" I ask. She nods. "Yeah could be. That's a bit of a giveaway isn't it?"

"Well, then that's where we're going," I say decisively. It feels oddly exhilarating to be calling the shots for once.

Lou yanks open the fire escape door to reveal a pitch-black stairwell. I immediately regret throwing my phone away. "I can't see a thing."

"I don't exactly have night vision meself," Jer points out.

"We're just going to have to go slow and steady," Lou says in front of me. We tread carefully and in a line, listening for each other's footfalls and making sure we don't end up in a pile at the bottom, wherever that might be.

After several minutes of descending Lou stops and whispers, "I think I hear something." There's a sound of shuffling coming from somewhere, possibly behind one of the walls. We seem to have come to the bottom of the stairwell as I feel the walls open out. Running my hand along them slowly, I eventually find another door and say as much. "Shall we risk it?"

"Not much we can do otherwise. Bear in mind I don't have anything to juice off of if we get in trouble," Lou reminds me.

"We'll just have to use our wits and charm," Jer jokes.

"I've got a knife," I suddenly remember.

"Whoa, that's a bit unlike you, isn't it?"

"It's not mine. The Duke gave it to me," I explain. There's a loaded silence from both of them. I guess it sounds like there's some weird favouritism going on. "It's not like that. I needed to prove I was with him—" I try to say.

"Doesn't matter, Curtis. It's good that he trusts you, really. We're just surprised because he only met you a couple of days ago, that's all," Jer says soothingly.

"None of it matters right now, okay? Let's just get out of here." Lou finds a door handle in the darkness and opens it onto a large foyer that we can just about make out in the dimness. I can just see the street through the huge glass panes, illuminated by the moonlight. But looking around it doesn't seem like there's anyone here.

"Who's there?" A nervous voice comes out of the darkness. Male, possibly some kind of security guard. There's a fumbling noise and the sound of someone swearing, then the click of a torch that gets us right in the eyes.

"Bloody hell," Lou says, holding her hand up to shield her face from the light.

"I'm afraid I'm going to have to detain you here for being on private property," the guard says, recovering when he sees we aren't monsters or armed robbers.

"Sorry mate, we got stuck out on our balcony and because of the blackout we couldn't get any help. We found your stairwell open and we're just trying to get home," Jer says easily, his hands up and spread out, the look of innocence on his face.

"But the alarm should have gone off," the guard says, reaching over to a phone on his desk and picking up the handset. "Nothing. Must be an all-out power cut," he says.

"Right, and we couldn't even get to a phone to call for our neighbours to let us back in," Jer explains.

"Oh, right," the security guard says and comes over to us from his hiding place, which I can see is a large desk in the middle of the space. "Fair enough. What a weird thing to happen," he says, coming round with keys in his hand, walking to the massive glass door at the front of the building.

"Tell me about it, gave us quite the surprise," Jer laughs naturally. I'm in awe of his ability to get along with pretty much anyone if he wants to. That and bending the truth seem to come easy to him when the need arises. "Listen, you wouldn't have a spare torch, would you? It's just that we might need it tonight if they don't fix the power quickly."

"Oh, yeah sure," the guard goes back over to his desk and reaches behind it, pulling out a heavy-duty object that resembles a weapon more than a torch. He hands it to Jer, our self-proclaimed spokesperson for this particular interaction, and unlocks the glass door to let us out.

"Keep safe, kids," the guard says to us as he waves us off and locks the door behind us.

"Smart thinking," Lou says and takes the torch off him, switching it on and illuminating the pavement in front of us.

"Hey! Look what I found!" I exclaim as I spot a mangled object on the floor. My sad, cracked phone that I threw off the roof is laying in the middle of the pavement in pieces. Luckily it's just the screen that's messed up, the rest of it still together. I hurry to scoop it up and try to turn it back on. It flickers to life, but half of the LCD is black so it isn't much good to me.

"I guess the ATU aren't interested in tracking us now if they're off trying to figure out where the blackout is coming from," I reason, and place it in my pocket. We follow our noses a few blocks and encounter only one or two cars, crawling by with their headlights on full beam as they try to navigate the darkness. A few people pass us by, huddled up in the December night and probably wishing they were safe in their beds, using their own phones as flashlights to light their way. We walk fast, but it feels like slow progress at first. Ten, then twenty minutes pass and I'm sweating in my winter gear despite the cold. We round a corner, and the eerie sight of Trafalgar Square in the darkness lays before us. The fountains are off and the place is deserted like nothing I've ever seen before.

"This creepy as hell," I say as we hurry through the familiar lions on their plinths.

"Where is everyone? Surely there would be at least a taxi or two on the road?" Jer observes.

"Maybe it's not just a blackout," says Lou. I don't get a chance to ask her what she means because as we reach Parliament street with its clear view down to Westminster, we are greeted by an unusual sight.

"Something tells me we need to hurry," Jer says looking ahead. From where we are, we can make out a harsh light coming from somewhere ahead, almost blinding in its brightness. Everything around us is starting to lighten and I notice that I can actually see my feet in front of me now. At first, I think it's because the power is coming back on, but it seems to be coming from one spot behind the buildings in front of us. "Definitely Ella," Jer confirms as we pick up speed. "I can feel it."

"Time to move," I say and pick up my pace to a jog. Lou keeps pace beside me, the torchlight bouncing up and down with her movement, but before long we don't need it at all. With every step, the street and buildings around us get brighter. I look up at the windows above us and at the street lamps, all still dark. No power yet. So, what is it? We round a corner, and the Houses of Parliament loom like the dark ruins of some forgotten civilisation with Big Ben rising like a blackened skeleton over it. But the green in the centre of Westminster is ablaze with energy. It takes me a moment to work out what I'm seeing.

Four figures stand on the grass with the statues of past ministers watching over them. At the far end I can see a man I've only ever previously seen on television, although he looks bigger and beefier than before. Carlton Munday stands, legs akimbo, his hands held out by his sides as if trying to reason. There's a peculiar black mist swirling over his head some ten feet in the air.

To the left and in the middle, I can see Edward Clarence, which surprises me at first. But he's set himself away from Munday, not opposing him but not against him. I can't quite figure out why he's there or what he's doing, but as my eyes move to the figures closest to me my heart stops. They both have their backs to me but there's no mistaking the

Duke with his wide frame, and next to him, arms outstretched with energy crackling between her finger tips is Ella.

The bright light is coming from above them, evidently being controlled by her as every so often she seems to move her hands and push more energy into the storm that's beginning to rage above their heads.

I call out, but the sound of my voice is drowned out by the hum of electricity coming from the commotion. Where are the police? The people protecting Munday?

I run closer until I'm only ten metres from Ella and can just about hear the Duke bellowing over the thrum of power.

"Give it up, Carlton! You're no match for her," he shouts. Now that I'm closer, I can make out Munday's face, and the sight terrifies me. His eyes are black, like orbs of liquid darkness, and his hands aren't empty as I had thought before but are full of the same kind of black smoke that floats around him. It writhes and wreathes its way around his hands and arms, his face sweating with the strain of whatever it is he seems to be controlling.

"You give up, Jonathan. You'll never stop me or the Magic Circle," he bellows. I stop, stunned. Carlton Munday is an Augur, and a crazy one at that.

"Carlton Munday has been running the Magic Circle this whole time?" Lou says, appearing by my side and I hadn't even noticed. "But the explosion at Downing Street—"

"Was a complete set up to put him in charge," I interrupt, thinking fast.

"Bastard."

"Oh, but I have, Carlton," the Duke continues, oblivious to our presence. "My own son has been one of your most dedicated members these last seven years. He's told me everything, every step of your plan. And that is why I needed to bring you here tonight. This needs to stop. You can't be allowed to oppress Augurs any more—"

"That's rich coming from you!" Munday laughs maniacally, and I don't at all like the sound. His chest seems to be puffing out with the effort of controlling all the blackness. I notice how the far end of the green is shrouded in darkness. Is Munday absorbing the energy that caused the power cut?

"Munday looks like he's going to explode," Jer says on my right.

"If he does it'll put us all out of our misery," Lou quips.

All of the light on the green is coming from Ella, spreading out like an orb over it and fighting against the dark that swirls around the other side. It would look beautiful if it weren't so terrifying.

I can't tell exactly what she's trying to do, but I guess that it's something to do with dampening him. I think she's winning, but it's hard to tell. Every so often the light seems to push the darkness away, but Munday pushes it back with renewed effort. Without warning, he lets out a bellow as the darkness grows and envelopes more of the light. Ella buckles and lands on her knees, temporarily defeated, and I yell out in spite of myself. She doesn't need me distracting her right now. The Duke doesn't even bat an eyelid but keeps his stance. I think I hear him say "get up!", but it's hard to tell.

The only thing that stops me from running over is Jer's firm grip on my arm.

"I've got to do something!" I tell him, trying to wrestle away.

"You'll get yourself killed if you go near that storm, Curtis!"

"But I can't just stand here and watch her get hurt!" I plead. Why isn't the Duke helping? Surely he could use his powers somehow? I almost can't bear to watch as Ella struggles to her feet, bracing herself for another onslaught.

"You've done exactly what I wanted, Jonathan," Munday screams across Parliament Garden Square. His voice, louder than normal, reverberates around us. "You've brought her straight to me, and once I defeat you her powers will be mine!"

"I won't let you do to her what you did to me, Carlton. Besides, she's stronger than anyone you've ever known," the Duke replies. My mind races. Does the Duke not actually have powers anymore? Maybe that's why he needed Ella so much, and now also makes sense of what Edward was saying about the Magic Circle needing her too. It all comes down to Munday.

"We have to do something, now!" I say, unable to bear the sight of Ella's body shaking violently as she puts all that she can into stopping him.

"Hang on," Lou says, "I think I have an idea." She pulls me close to whisper in my ear.

"Now's your chance, wonder-boy," she says, putting her arm over my shoulder, the three of our heads practically touching.

"I need you to distract Munday in the most annoying way possible," she says wryly.

"You're joking. Go over there?" I ask incredulously. My eyes flick over to the cloud of blackness at the far end of the green and I tell myself there's no way I could do anything to stop him.

"Look, you're the only logical option. You'll be no good over here, distracting Ella."

She's right, and I hate that. It's insane, but I don't see any other choice than to go with her plan, steeling myself for whatever the hell might come next. Agnes's words pick the worst time to pop back into my head about her visions. *Half of which end up with you dead.*

With my heart thudding rapidly in my chest, I skirt around just out of sight. I see Lou creep up behind Ella and the Duke as I do. I spot Jer as he goes round to the left where Ed stands, a look of defeat across the young heir's face.

I wonder why he tried to warn us against helping his father if he'd been working for him the entire time. Some kind of intricate trust exercise that the Duke sent him on, perhaps? But then that whole thing with him betraying the Society to Avers doesn't make much sense. I shake it out of my head and try to concentrate on the task at hand. At the edge of my vision I can just about make out police cars gathered around the huge roundabout, but where are the police themselves? The patrol car lights are out, and I figure that whatever Munday is doing involves sapping any energy from around him, including the cars. Like an Augur on steroids.

He's so absorbed with his fight against Ella that he doesn't notice me coming behind him. The switch blade the Duke gave me is in my hand and I flick it out as quietly as I can. I notice how on this side of the struggle the air is thick and quiet, in stark contrast to the loudness on the other side. Will it hurt me, I wonder? Even if it does, it isn't going to stop me. Augurs are mortal just like everyone else, they bleed like everyone else too. Munday is just a few steps from me now, looking much bigger in real life than he does on the telly. He stands at 6'2", although thin but strong. The consuming of so much energy is also beefing him up, which doesn't help me. My hand shakes as I hold the knife and I try to keep my grip on the ivory handle. Before I can put any more thought into it, I drive the blade into the side of his neck and hold it in, my left hand bracing against his shoulder.

I don't know what I expected. A scream? Some kind of electronic explosion? But nothing happens. Nothing.

I stand there for a few moments more, waiting for some recognition that I've done anything at all. Then, very slowly, he turns his head around. The black pools where his eyes should be are dripping, liquid oozing from the sockets.

"And who are you?" he asks, though the voice doesn't sound human. It sounds like a thousand voices in one and it sends a chill up my spine.

"Someone who's decided to stop you!" I yell, because the space around us is so devoid of noise that I feel like I need to shout. Even to my own ears I sound muffled.

He throws his head back and gives a mirthless laugh. The knife slips out of his neck as he does so, and I stumble backwards still holding it in my hand, slick with his blood. Almost as an afterthought, he flicks his blackened hand at me and I find myself being lifted off the ground.

"What is a Normal boy doing meddling with Augur business?" he asks as I rise higher and higher.

"Someone needs to put a stop to this," I say, although my voice sounds choked with the pressure.

"And that someone is a powerless Normal? I admire your courage, boy, but you're a child tampering with things you don't understand."

That pisses me off.

"I've been told that a lot lately," I retort, noticing that the air is being squeezed from my lungs as I hang in midair. He's turned all the way around now, facing me. To my relief I can make out Lou standing beside Ella, helping her somehow as we'd planned. Jer is pulling Edward towards them, urging him to help. Jer was probably the only person fit for that job, his lack of gall and ability to talk to people means he'd be able to convince even someone as stubborn as Ed to help.

The black cloud is shrinking, and the white electricity is pushing it further and further towards us. I try not to let the triumph I feel show and give the game away. I was the perfect choice for a distraction, even though both Jer and Lou tried to convince me otherwise. I feel vindicated seeing that it's working.

Munday's face is the stuff of nightmares. The sweat drips from his forehead and there's nothing left where his eyes were but black holes. His body looks like it's trying to bust open with all the energy he's consuming.

"I promised myself I would protect Normals," he says almost to himself. "I've never killed a Normal before. But I don't think I can keep you alive. You're too much of a nuisance," the words sound stuttered, like he's forcing them through lips that are too big.

"Something wrong?" I ask, outwardly ignoring his death threat but inwardly bricking it.

"NOTHING IS WRONG," he screams, his mouth contorting in a way that should not be possible for a human. "I'm more powerful than ever before. I can feel the energy coursing through everything around me. Even the energy inside you. Just a bit more couldn't hurt, could it?" he licks his lips and even his tongue is black. I want to be sick.

"You don't want me, I've not got much to give, to be honest," I say feebly. I think he's trying to take a step towards me, but his legs are rooted to the ground. He looks down and to my satisfaction I can see that he's being held by the blackness he's trying to control. He lets out an exasperated roar, and without warning he flicks his hand at me again. This time I feel a snap and cry out as my body shudders. He's broken something inside me and the pain is excruciating at first. Then there's a dullness as I notice I can't feel my legs. My back. He's broken my back.

I hear Ella scream somewhere in front of me and the white shield of energy that had been coming out of her expands, consuming not only the cloud above and Munday in it, but me as well. As it touches me I feel the power of whatever Munday had over me release and I fall a few feet to the ground. It knocks the wind out of me but otherwise my body is worryingly numb. I try to lift myself up, but nothing seems to be working.

I lay on the damp grass and look up at the swirl of white above me and then at Munday, who is still facing me with a look of surprise on his misshapen face. The light from Ella's magic is weaving its way around his body, and the blackness seems to be leaving him in waves. Great plumes of darkness come out of his mouth, eyes and nostrils like something from a horror movie, and I look away. From beyond the bubble of light we're in, I can see the fallen shapes of police officers on the ground, which explains something at least. Another sight surprises me; I might be hallucinating, but I think I can see Miss Banks laying amongst the fallen bodies and I wonder if I'm maybe going mad.

I hear a retching noise and turn my head back to see Munday on all fours puking his guts out. It's not a pleasant sight, but it gives me a strange feeling of satisfaction that we've beaten him in some way. I get the surreal feeling like I'm floating in water, my sight blurring at the edges and sounds around me beginning to muffle. I must be passing out, I realise. I try to look down at my body, which is crumpled at an odd angle on the ground, my legs underneath me and my arms spread out. The knife is still in my hand, although barely. I've never understood why in moments of chaos the mind tries to concentrate on one thing, and the little switchblade in my hand is the only thing I can see with clarity. I study the intricate handle, so prettily carved, and the shiny blade, red with Munday's blood, with cold steel gleaming through. It has such pretty designs on it, I think in my state of stupor. There's a letter that looks like an intricately woven 'W' and I feel like I've seen it somewhere before, or something like it.

"Oh my God, Curtis," I hear Ella's voice as if from far away. "Talk to me, can you hear me?"

"Don't leave," I say, slipping out of consciousness.

"I'm not going anywhere," she grasps my hand and I'm relieved that at least I can feel that.

"Did we win?" My voice is faint even to my own ears.

She doesn't answer, and I feel her uncertainty through the silence. I want to see her face properly, but my eyelids don't seem to be obeying. I hear a call for help and further off a faint wailing noise. Sirens. And then I slip away.

CHAPTER 17

I sit on the grass, just in the shade of a large tree, and admire the view. A silvery line in the distance, a river, winds its way through the landscape, cutting through it like a boundary. The clouds over the distant hills loom, and I wonder if it will rain, but for now the winter sun keeps me warm beneath my layers. I close my eyes and breathe deeply, enjoying the sweetness of the air filling my lungs.

It took two weeks for David to repair my spine, fixing it in stages. His mother, Beryl, also a healer, helped whenever it was getting too much for him. I don't know if I'll ever be able to repay him for doing that. I shake my head at the thought of how much I've become reliant upon my Augur friends lately.

Through my recovery, everyone chipped in feeding me, keeping me sane and taking my mind off the events on Parliament Square Gardens. I had nightmares for days afterwards and still feel a bit fragile on the inside.

Lou, Jer and of course Ella have been with me every day since, sometimes all together, sometimes one at a time.

During one of those alone moments, Lou confided in me that we wouldn't have defeated Munday if he hadn't been so distracted by me. I'm not sure if she's been trying to make me feel better, but it's unlike her to be anything but candid.

The combined efforts of Ella, Lou, Jer and even some input from Ed were needed to take him down, although no one has mentioned what the Duke's involvement was. Having had way too much time to think lately, I've surmised that Munday must have sapped his power some years ago. They slagged each other off like old foes, and the Duke's dogged persistence to take him down makes more sense with that explanation, particularly as the Duke appeared to be impotent throughout the whole fight.

The scene that had started in Westminster involved Munday knocking out over two dozen police officers with some kind of impulse and consuming all the magic he could before the ATU could arrive.

I had been surprised to hear that Miss Banks, Steve and the whole motley crew of Anti-Terror Unit members attempted to take him down before the Duke and Ella even arrived. Turns out what I'd seen wasn't a hallucination. When Ella reached the green, Miss Banks was threatening to shoot Munday, the police already long-since out of action. But when Munday knocked them out too, Ella and the Duke stepped in.

I pull the knife out of my pocket, long since cleaned and returned to me. I flick out the blade and study the inscription that I'd noticed as I was lying on the ground. The intricate 'W', I had realised one night during a particularly vivid nightmare, was the same as the one that Federico had drawn for me back when he was in the hospital. The fact that the Duke gave it to me was either accidental or maliciously intentional.

I still haven't figured out what it stands for, but the fact that the person that stabbed Federico has a knife that matches the Duke's has been playing on my mind since then. I've pressed Ella for answers a few times, asking her what happened between in the time that I was kidnapped and then found her on the green, but she's been tight lipped and almost dismissive about it.

After what we've now started calling, 'The Incident', Miss Banks held good on her promise and whisked us away, cleaning us from the records for now. I imagine at some point she'll be back though.

We went to where Mumbe told us to go: a manor house in Hertfordshire belonging to David's mother that is big enough to accommodate all of us. Jer, Lou, David and Mumbe, even Agnes manage to fit in without getting in each other's hair. It feels more like a family than mine has ever been considering everything we've been through together, even if I try to avoid Agnes as much as possible.

Everything was left behind though, and it's taken some difficult telephone conversations with my Mum to explain why I've suddenly disappeared without a real explanation. Especially considering what day it is tomorrow. She also complained that I got a cat without asking her and now she has to feed it, but I feel slightly more comfortable knowing that there's some kind of Augur-cat watching over them for the time being.

Ella approaches me from behind and wraps a blanket around my shoulders before sitting down next to me and tucking her legs underneath her.

She's wearing a blue dress under her winter coat, probably way too cold for this time of year but it matches the colour of her eyes. I like it.

Her blonde hair is loose, spilling down onto her shoulders and framing her pale face.

She gives me a sympathetic smile and puts her hand in mine.

"So, did we win?" I ask again, looking ahead rather than at her now.

She's silent for a while before sighing and leaning her head on my shoulder.

"I think winning is kind of relative. When countries are at war there are always casualties on both sides, but someone always ends up being called the victor." She pulls up a blade of grass with her free hand and twirls it in her fingers. "But to answer your question, I think we did win, in some way at least. There's a lot of work to do after Munday's display, but I'm hoping that it will mean Augurs will be employed properly by the government rather than being pushed out. That's going to take time, gaining people's trust and effectively purging centuries of discrimination. But even Miss Banks wants me to help in the ATU as a start," she laughs, but there's not much humour behind it.

"And Munday?"

"Prison. A special one just for him."

I want to pump my fist in the air at the fact that he's safely behind bars, but there's no doubt that the Magic Circle are probably still in action, and there's a lot more that needs doing to get rid of them. It's my turn to sigh, and I clench her hand a little tighter in mine.

"So, can we pretend to be a regular couple now, at least for a short while?" I ask her. She looks at me searchingly, I suppose wondering if that's even at all possible.

"I'd love that," she eventually replies.

"Good, then I've got something for you," I say relieved, and pull something else out of my pocket. It's a camera lens. A really expensive one that I had to order and have Jer go and collect from the local Post Office. It's heavy, all metal and glass, and I place it in her delicate hand. She looks surprised, then delighted and finally confused.

"But, my camera—" I interrupt her by handing her a package that I've been keeping hidden for a few days. I had to pull some serious strings and get my Mum to post it for me, but not before having her practically break and enter to retrieve it from Ella's bedroom. Mum, normally an absolute saint, decided that because it was 'all for love' it was okay to bend the rules a little.

Ella throws her arms around me, and I smile genuinely for the first time in weeks. She clicks her new lens onto the camera and puts it up to her eye, and instinctively I put my hand up to shield my face as she points it at me.

"Oh, come on, Curtis! I need a picture of my favourite person," she slaps my hand away and focuses. I hear the definitive 'clunk' as the shutter button is pressed and then pull her towards me.

"Merry Christmas," I say, and she gives me a sly grin.

"Christmas is tomorrow, silly."

"I know, but I couldn't wait any longer." I hug her again, wrapping my arms and the blanket around her.

"I have something for you too, but it's not as good as yours, so be warned," she says mysteriously.

"Oh, well when you put it like that it can probably wait until tomorrow," I joke.

"No, no. You started it, so we're swapping presents now, but I need to go and get it," she gets up and heads back towards the house, returning a few moments later with a small box in her hand. She sits back down next to me and hands it over like it's hot. Intrigued, I peel back the plain wrapping to find a shiny new phone underneath.

"Really? You got me a new phone?" I say, shocked.

"Not really. I had your old one replaced for a small fee, but everything should be on there. Phone numbers, messages, the lot," she smiles. It's my turn to hug her. I hadn't missed having a phone much, but it makes it that much easier to stay in touch with Mum at the very least.

I turn it on and watch the screen come to life. Within a few moments, it buzzes with incoming text messages and voicemails that I've missed over the past few weeks, and I feel unusually popular.

"It's probably going to be a lot of old messages from Mum asking where I am," I joke.

"Well, that will keep you busy for a while."

I pocket the phone and take her hand back in mine, happy to stare into the distance for a while and enjoy a moment where our lives aren't being threatened. Today is the first day I've been off my sick bed, and I plan to make the most of being outside even if I freeze in the process. A couple of red kites fly overhead in circles, hunting for food I imagine. A squirrel runs up a nearby tree and everything seems calm for now.

"So, what now?" I ask, eventually breaking the silence.

"Now? You mean apart from figuring out our place in all of this madness and somehow piecing our lives back together?"

"No, I mean right now. What do you want to do right now?"

She frowns, a little crease in between her eyebrows. It's cute.

"Now, we kiss," she replies.

And we do.

***

EPILOGUE

Curtis, this is Matthew Avers. Listen, I don't know why you're not picking up your phone, but I heard about what happened in Westminster. The official statement is that Munday was stopped by a brave group of Augurs and they saved hundreds, if not thousands, of Londoners in the process, but I have a feeling you may know more about it than anyone else.

I've been reading the files you gave me. I count over two hundred case files in there, as well as at least fifty personnel files, but there's one that doesn't make any sense. It indicates that FADE were being funded by a private source, and I think whoever you got this from will have the missing data. The only thing that I've got is a letter with a crest on it giving permission to open the facility, but all the text is blanked out. It makes a reference to more documents and a large symbol, looks a bit like a 'W' printed on the bottom. That's all I've got.

I'm hoping you can help, so give me a call back as soon as you can. Thanks. Bye.

Curtis & Ella will be back in
Broken by Magic

Available to purchase today!

Read on for a bonus chapter…

Ella

I watch him sleep.

Just as I've watched him these past few weeks, like a vigil. Even now that he's nearly completely recovered I still monitor his breathing, the up and down of his chest, the little twitches of muscles and the stutter of his eyelids as he dreams. He looks so young. He *is* so young to have been dragged into my world. My crazy, insane life filled with monsters like Munday, with duplicitous leaders and Augurs that can do everything from heal to hurt, help or hinder.

He murmurs something in his sleep and reaches out, his long fingers splaying on the pillow just next to my face, and my thoughts soften.

I don't know when I realised I was in love with him. Maybe it was that first night I stayed at his house, my body pressed against his as we slept in the single bed he grew up in. Or perhaps it was when he first told me he knew I was an Augur, not wanting the heaviness of the secret to get in the way of us being together. Certainly his consideration for me, what I might feel about him knowing, and his concern, made me recognise the sort of person he really was. Kind. Determined. And just the right amount of fight in him to see it all through.

But really, I muse, as I listen to his breathing, I knew I wanted him from the moment he walked into the restaurant. Awkward and a little self-conscious, but with a spark in his eyes that had me thinking about him long after he'd left after the interview. I'd begged Mr. Gregorio to take him on. I wonder now what would have happened to us if I hadn't been so convincing.

Curtis turns over so that his back is to me, a small movement that he hasn't been able to do for weeks.

Something in my chest pulls when I think about him laying on the grass, staring up at me with vacant eyes, Munday's blood all over his hands. That vision comes to me, unbidden, more often than I like to admit, especially when I try to sleep. That, and the hollow blackness of Munday's eyes, the thick smog of his power trying to consume me, absorb my own.

When I went to the Duke for help, begging him to get Curtis back from the ATU, I didn't understand what he wanted from me.

"Something far bigger than us is about to happen, my dear," he'd said, Mulberry handing him his coat as the Rolls Royce pulled up outside his house. I hadn't grasped what he meant, until we reached the green.

Munday's power had touched me, just for a second, and my whole body had felt infected, burning with poisoned blood. It had been instinct to fight the sucking, pulling feeling that was coming from that black cloud.

I shiver and pull the blankets further over my shoulders, trying to push those thoughts out of my head while I stare at Curtis's back. The faint red lines of healing magic are still there, but they gradually disappear as the days go on.

For the weeks he was being healed by Beryl and David I was only allowed to sit by the bed for fear of undoing any of their work, so I savour curling up next to him on the crisp sheets watching the moonlight through the window play on his dark skin, turning it silver.

There's no chance of me sleeping, my mind too messy, my thoughts like moths around a naked bulb, never settling for more than a second before some other worry or horror comes to mind. Eventually I give up and slide out of bed, pulling on a borrowed robe.

I leave the room as quietly as I can and pad down the thick carpeted corridor, knocking gently when I reach Agnes's room.

"Come in, Ella," she says, softly. I roll my eyes. Of course she knew I was coming.

"You're awake?" I say as I close the door gently behind me.

"I don't sleep much these days," she replies, sitting in a chair by the window with a blanket over her legs. She looks ancient, not like my older sister at all. Not because she's wrinkled or aged, but her eyes are so dark, all the sky-blue that we share muted, hidden by the fact that they're so deep in her skull.

"Visions keeping you up?" I ask, pulling up a stool by her chair and leaning over so that my head rests on her shoulder. When we used to share a room as kids I'd often hear her tossing and turning, the nightmares of whatever future vision she'd seen forcing her awake. When we were really little she used to climb into Mum and Dad's bed. When they were gone, she sometimes used to climb into mine for comfort, even if it was just to listen to me breathing while I slumbered.

From this angle I can see her line of sight out of the window and across the garden to the hills beyond, illuminated by the stars and the pale full moon.

"Mostly, yes. And guilt," she says, putting a cold hand over my warm ones.

"What on Earth could you feel guilty for, Aggie?" I ask, pulling away to study her weary face.

"It's not a sensation I'm all that familiar with, Ella, don't make it worse by trying to deny me it."

I smile at her melodrama.

"Of course, feel as guilty as you like, but at least tell me why you're beating yourself up," I joke. She scowls at the fact that I'm making fun of her, but she answers me anyway.

"I wasn't able to warn you."

"About Curtis getting hurt?" I swallow as the vision of him laying broken fills my mind again.

"I tried to warn him about that. At least he didn't *die*," she retorts unsympathetically. "But about you having to take on Munday. I didn't see what he really was," she shakes her head.

"Pfft, who cares that you didn't warn me? It's all over now, isn't it?" I say giving her arm a gentle pat. Something in the way she stares at me makes me pause. "Isn't it?" I ask, sensing that Agnes as more to confess.

"Not even nearly, from what I can tell."

She doesn't explain, doesn't bother to clarify or elaborate, but it leaves me with a horrible sinking feeling in the pit of my stomach.

We sit in silence for several minutes, watching the moonlight play across the river in the distance, the shine of headlights on a road a few miles away. How many times have we sat like this since Mum and Dad died, together, but worlds apart in our own minds?

"They'd like this place, don't you think?" I say eventually, breaking the quiet.

She smiles wanly. "Yes, I think they would. Beryl is a woman of excellent taste," she says, adjusting the blanket on her knees so that it covers mine as well.

We haven't spoken much about Munday, the Facility or my parents since Curtis filled us in. The fact that the man of my nightmares has a face and a name, and that that face was all over television until not that long ago, isn't lost on me. But every time I think about it I want to scream.

My parents' murderer has a name. If I had known before I faced off with him outside Parliament I would have killed him, I'm sure of it. And if knew where he was now I wouldn't hesitate to hunt him down and end him.

"No you wouldn't," Agnes interrupts my dark thoughts abruptly. I raise an eyebrow. Sometimes I wonder if she's psychic too, but most of the time I think she's just predicting conversations that haven't happened yet.

"I would, Aggie. I'd put an end to the pain and suffering he's caused us."

"You wouldn't, and you won't do anything. Not for me, but for you, and that boy of yours that you're so in love with," she adds with a hint of bitterness.

"Is this one of your riddles?" I ask, trying to wrap my head around what it is she's getting at.

She sighs impatiently.

"Sometimes I wish you were born with the same ability as me, then at least our conversations would be faster," she replies, but I know she's joking. "What I mean is, you are not about to go and avenge Mum and Dad's deaths by hunting down Carlton Munday and killing him. Not only do I think you aren't capable of such brutality, but your lover boy would be heart broken if you ended up in prison."

I blink a few times in surprise. "Is that what you saw?" I ask, knowing that she never usually says things unless she means them.

She wriggles uncomfortably under my gaze. "I've seen too much to tell you, Ella, but please do listen to me when I tell you, you have to let this go."

"How can you say that? After everything we've been through together?" I don't understand how she can be so calm, so *indifferent* about our parent's murderer. He didn't kill them with his own hands, but just having kidnapped me, experimented on me and lured them to his facility… that's enough to make him pay.

"I have no choice but to accept it, Ella. You and I aren't destined to end Munday's life, and I won't hear any more from you on the subject." She uses her 'telling off' voice that she used to reserve for when I was in trouble. A tone that faintly echoes my father's when I'd misbehaved. I hate it when she uses that.

"Enjoy your time here with Curtis. Stay out of London, and out of trouble. For once, just be content and happy." She puts a hand on my cheek and her expression softens. "You deserve it."

I take all the hate and anger for Munday, all the pain and heartbreak for my parents, and compact it. I force it down until it's nothing but a tiny fiery ball of rage. And then I bury it.

Maybe other people can't do that; I feel sorry for them if that's the case, but I've been able to control my emotions fairly well my entire life. I laugh, I cry, but if I need to steel myself and push it away I can. I sometimes wonder if it's one of my abilities.

"Have you seen something you aren't telling me?" I ask her softly.

She studies me, weighing up whether or not to answer as she usually does when I ask her about one of her visions.

"I've seen so many things, half the time I don't know if my abilities are trying to trick me. Telling you any of it will do us no good," she says, once again bearing the burden of what she's seen alone. "But I will say one thing," she adds, her tone hardening, "you have to keep an eye on your boy."

"He has a name, Aggie," I say irritably.

"Either way, he's going to get you into trouble," she warns.

"What kind of trouble?"

"Oh, with him it's anyone's guess. He's got a spark in him Ella. He won't want to stay still for long." She says it like it's a bad thing, and I don't want to tell her it's one of the reasons I love him so much, so I just nod.

A clock chimes midnight somewhere down the hall and it dawns on me what day it is.

"Merry Christmas, Aggie," I say giving her a peck on the cheek.

"You too, little sister," she says, pulling me closer and letting me lean on her again.

We stay like that for a long time, until eventually my eyelids droop and I slink back to my room for a few hours of sleep. I climb back into bed and thread my arms around Curtis, resting my head against his back. I can't tell if he wakes up from the movement, but his hand automatically slides over mine and I allow the warmth of us to wrap me in sleep.

*

"Merry Christmas, Mum!" Curtis says on the phone to his mother from the living room. The rest of us didn't do much in the way of presents this year, but evidence of the little we did do litters the floor all over the comfortable leather couches and the rug, the coffee table strewn with nibbles and empty glasses.

The others have gone for a walk to give Curtis some privacy while he has, possibly, one of the most awkward conversations of the year. I've volunteered to clean up so we can watch movies and play games when they come back. Lucky me.

"Yes, I'm fine. Yes, she loved the camera. Thanks, by the way for your help with that. Yes, I'm eating well," he says, evidently being bombarded with questions.

He disappeared while his parents were on holiday. God knows what they think of me, a girl who appeared in his life one day and vanished him away only a week or two later. I shake my head while he tries to veer away from some choice remarks about why he's been so tardy with his calls.

"Ella's here, actually," he says, quickly, trying to pass the buck and looking at me slightly apologetically, "I'll put you on speakerphone."

I roll my eyes at him and grin. This ought to be fun.

"Merry Christmas, Mrs Mayes!" I chime into the handset of his new phone.

"Oh, love, it's wonderful to finally hear your voice and a Merry Christmas to you. I hope you've all been having a lovely time," her warm, Yorkshire accent comes down the phone. I like her even though I've never met her in person. A woman that would break into my old house just to retrieve my camera is worth her weight in gold.

"It's been amazing so far, thank you so much. How are you enjoying your day?" I ask, while Curtis pretends to wipe the sweat from his brow theatrically.

"The usual, love, the usual. We miss our boy but it sounds like you're keeping him in line. Unfortunately Curtis your Dad would come to the phone but he's already *a bit tipsy*," she whispers and I stifle a laugh. From what Curtis has told me about his family holidays, 'a bit tipsy' means he's already completely drunk.

"It's not the same without him here! The house feels empty!" A gruff voice calls from somewhere in the background. Peter Mayes, no doubt. Curtis scowls.

"No one for him to target with snide remarks, more like," he says to me, almost inaudibly.

"What was that, love?" his Mum asks.

"Nothing, Mum, nothing."

"He's on about long lost family again, love. I think he misses you more than he'll admit," she says as if her husband isn't sitting in the same room as her. "Let us know when you can come by, won't you?"

"Of course, of course. Oh, I think the others are just coming back indoors now so I better crack on. Give my love to dad. Love you lots, bye!" He hangs up just as I managed to squeeze in a few words of farewell and shakes his head, flopping down on the wrapping-paper-covered sofa.

I sit down next to him and run a hand down his arm consolingly.

"That wasn't so bad, now, was it?" I say, allowing my fingers to trail up his neck and into his hair. He closes his eyes and leans into my hand, enjoying the feeling.

"Could have been worse, I suppose," he says, putting a broad hand on my knee and squeezing it gently. "I feel terrible though, for leaving them like that. For lying to them."

That's my fault and I know it is. I was the one who decided to take him to the Duke. I'm the Augur everyone wants a piece of, forcing him to keep my secrets. I try to cover up how much that hurts me.

"You want to visit them maybe, in the new year?" I suggest, hoping that it will help.

"God, no. I mean, Mum, yes, I miss her. But Dad? Forget it. Nothing good would come of that," he shakes his head and pulls me closer to him, so that my face is just inches from his. "Besides, I don't want to leave you for more than five minutes if I can help it," he says, his breath warm on my face. I lean in for a kiss, nothing but the ticking of Beryl's grandfather clock and the birds chirping outside to disturb us.

"I love you," I say, brushing my lips against his.

"I love you too," he replies, just as Jer and Lou burst in the door with David, Mumbe and Beryl not far behind.

"I thought you were going to clean up?" Lou protests.

"Interrupting something?" Jer smirks, dumping his jacket on the side of the sofa.

"I'll put the kettle on!" Beryl says from the hallway.

"Let me give you a hand, Mum," David replies.

"There you all are. When is the panettone coming out then?" Agnes asks, wandering down the stairs in her bathrobe having just woken up from a nap.

The chaos and noise is a stark contrast from the peace of a few minutes before, but we grin at each other, welcoming it.

"Better get on with tidying up then!" I say, untangling myself from the sofa and shoving wrapping paper into a bag.

Everyone has done something to contribute to the day, whether it be helping to prepare food or setting the table, decorating the house or cleaning up. All in a mad cacophony of having eight people under one roof. A very large roof, thanks to Beryl's not insignificant wealth, but it makes for a colourful household all the same.

What's left of the day is taken up with drinking lots of tea, eating far too much panettone, and playing silly games of charades before arguing over what movie to watch. It's possibly the best Christmas I've ever had, I think to myself more than once.

I cast furtive glances in Agnes's direction. Even she smiles and participates, which is a phenomenon itself. Our previous Christmases consisted of the two of us watching TV for most of the day and trying to make something edible. Seeing her crack a joke with Mumbe and play charades on the same team as David makes something in my chest stir. A warmth that I haven't felt in a long time. The both of us are finally starting to belong.

While Jer and Lou try to outvote everyone into watching *Die Hard 2*, while Beryl, David and Mumbe insist on *Elf*, I look up to find Curtis staring at me with a thoughtful expression on his face.

"What is it?" I ask, ignoring the fact that Agnes has just proclaimed we should watch *Gremlins*.

"Are you happy?" he asks, leaning towards me, his mouth brushing my cheek, a flutter of pleasure running through my body.

Agnes said I should be. Said that I deserved to be. And when I'm with him, surrounded by all the people that I love, I believe I can be.

"With you? Always."

***

About the Author

Rebecca Danese is a writer, photographer, artist and illustrator living in London with her husband and two children, along with far too many notebooks and plants.

She has several projects on the go, including further books in the *Divided by Magic* series, and a younger reader adventure series, *The Tree Children*, also available on Amazon.

To find out more about her work visit: www.rebeccadanese.com or follow her on social media:

Facebook: rebecca.danese.creates

Instagram: rebeccadanese_books

Twitter: @thenikongirl88

If you liked this book, please consider leaving a review on Amazon or Goodreads! I will send chocolate. Okay, maybe not, but I'll be very, very grateful!

Printed in Great Britain
by Amazon